For a second, Phyllis thought that someone had rung her doorbell and then run off, the classic prank that neighborhood children used to play before they all became too ironic and postmodern for such innocent high jinks.

Then she saw the dark, huddled shape lying on the front porch.

"Oh, my God!" she cried as she threw open the storm door and rushed out past the giant wreath hung on the wooden door. The storm door bumped the person lying on the porch. Shards of shattered ceramic crunched under Phyllis's feet. The glow from the white icicle lights washed over the crumpled shape, and the multihued lights on the decorations in the yard cast brilliantly colored slashes of illumination over the scene. Phyllis's eyes widened in shock and horror as she gazed down at the body of a woman surrounded by the broken remains of the gingerbread man that had been dressed as Mrs. Claus.

It took only a second for that ghastly sight to soak into her. Then she opened her mouth and screamed . . .

PRAISE FOR THE FRESH-BAKED MYSTERIES

"A delicious whodunit." *—Midwest Book Review*

"Delightful, [with a] realistic small-town vibe [and a] vibrant narrative . . . *A Peach of a Murder* runs the full range of emotions, so be prepared to laugh and cry with this one!"

—Romance Readers Connection

Other Fresh-Baked Mysteries by Livia J. Washburn

The Gingerbread Bump-off

A Fresh-Baked Mystery

LIVIA J. WASHBURN

AN OBSIDIAN MYSTERY

OBSIDIAN

Published by New American Library, a division of Penguin Group (USA) Inc., 375 Hudson Street, New York, New York 10014, USA • Penguin Group (Canada), 90 Eglinton Avenue East, Suite 700, Toronto, Ontario M4P 2Y3, Canada (a division of Pearson Penguin Canada Inc.) • Penguin Books Ltd., 80 Strand, London WC2R 0RL, England • Penguin Ireland, 25 St. Stephen's Green, Dublin 2, Ireland (a division of Penguin Books Ltd.) • Penguin Group (Australia), 250 Camberwell Road, Camberwell, Victoria 3124, Australia (a division of Pearson Australia Group Pty. Ltd.) • Penguin Books India Pvt. Ltd., 11 Community Centre, Panchsheel Park, New Delhi - 110 017, India • Penguin Group (NZ), 67 Apollo Drive, Rosedale, Auckland 0632, New Zealand (a division of Pearson New Zealand Ltd.) • Penguin Books (South Africa) (Pty.) Ltd., 24 Sturdee Avenue, Rosebank, Johannesburg 2196, South Africa

Penguin Books Ltd., Registered Offices:
80 Strand, London WC2R 0RL, England

First published by Obsidian, an imprint of New American Library,
a division of Penguin Group (USA) Inc.

First Printing, November 2011
5 7 9 10 8 6 4

OBSIDIAN and logo are trademarks of Penguin Group (USA) Inc.

LIBRARY OF CONGRESS CATALOGING-IN-PUBLICATION DATA:

Washburn, L. J.
The gingerbread bump-off: a fresh-baked mystery/Livia J. Washburn.
p.   cm.
"An Obsidian mystery."
ISBN 978-0-451-23483-4
1. Newsom, Phyllis (Fictitious character)—Fiction. 2. Retired teachers—Fiction. 3. Women—Crimes against—Fiction. 4. Christmas stories. 5. Baking—Fiction. 6. Weatherford (Tex.)—Fiction. I. Title
PS3573.A787G56   2011
813'.54—dc22   2011026920

Set in New Caledonia • Designed by Elke Sigal

Printed in the United States of America

For Maureen Johnson.
Thanks for suggesting the Candlelight Tour.

The Gingerbread Bump-off

Chapter 1

*P*hyllis Newsom lifted her head and frowned as she heard the unmistakable strains of "Grandma Got Run Over by a Reindeer" drifting through the house.

A baking sheet full of German chocolate cookies ready to go into the oven sat on the kitchen counter in front of her, but she left them sitting there as she walked out to the living room, wiping her hands on a towel as she went.

Sam Fletcher stood in front of the stereo system that rested on a shelf next to the television. His hands were tucked in the hip pockets of his jeans, and his head moved slightly, in time with the music. He was tall and slender, in keeping with his background as a basketball player and coach, and although his rumpled thatch of hair had a lot more white in it now than gray, he still didn't really look his age.

"Sam," Phyllis said, "you know I don't really like that song. It just doesn't seem very . . . *Christmasy* to me."

He looked back over his shoulder at her. "Sorry," he said. "I thought with you out in the kitchen it might not bother you." A smile spread across his rugged face. "I've got 'Jingle Bells' by the singin' dogs, if that'd be better."

She was about to tell him that it wouldn't be, when she realized that he was joking. She wasn't going to give him the satisfaction of seeing that he had almost fooled her, so she just waved a hand casually and said, "Play whatever you want. I really don't care."

With that, she went back to the kitchen. By the time she got there, the music had stopped, as Sam had ejected the CD. A moment later, Nat King Cole started singing about chestnuts roasting on an open fire. Phyllis smiled. That was one of her favorites.

She looked down at the cookies on the baking sheet. The base was a dark chocolate cookie, each with a thumb-sized depression in the middle that Phyllis had filled with a mixture of German chocolate, grated coconut, and crushed pecans. The oven was ready, so she opened the door and slid the baking sheet onto the rack. If these cookies turned out well, she would make another batch. With any luck, this recipe would be her entry in the local newspaper's annual Christmas cookie recipe contest.

The past two years, Carolyn Wilbarger, who also lived in the big house in one of Weatherford's tree-shaded old residential neighborhoods, had won that contest, with Phyllis finishing as runner-up both times. That was fine with Phyllis—she enjoyed just coming up with recipes and sharing them with people—but it might be nice to really give Carolyn a run for her money this year. Not that there was any money at stake, Phyllis reminded herself, only prestige, and she didn't really care all that much about *that*, either. She had a good life here, with a lovely son, daughter-in-law, and grandson, and three good friends who were retired teachers, as she was, to share the house with her.

But that comfortable, well-ordered life was about to be shaken up, and although she knew she ought to be happy about the circumstances, she still wasn't sure how she felt about it.

"Everyone, meet Roy Porter," Eve Turner had said when she brought the silver-haired stranger to the house on Thanksgiving. *"Roy and I are engaged. Do you believe it? We're going to be married!"*

That news had been a bolt out of the blue. None of Eve's housemates had had any idea she was seeing anyone. It shouldn't have been that surprising. Eve had been married several times before and always had her eye out for an eligible bachelor of the proper age. She had even pursued Sam for a while after he moved into the house to rent one of the vacant rooms. But she certainly had been more discreet about her courtship this time.

"We met on the Facebook," Eve had explained. "It turns out we have mutual friends. We started writing on each other's door—"

"Wall, dear," Roy had corrected gently.

"On each other's wall," Eve went on, "and, well, one thing led to another."

With Eve it usually did, given half a chance.

Thanksgiving hadn't necessarily been the best time to break the news of an engagement, but to be fair, when Eve and Roy came in, Eve didn't know that Phyllis had just solved one murder and prevented several more from occurring. That had turned out to be a very busy Thanksgiving, indeed.

Now Christmas was coming up, but before then, a bridal shower on Christmas Eve, to be followed by the wedding itself on New Year's Eve. *An abundance of Eves, including the bride,* Phyllis thought as she stood there in front of the oven for a long moment, thinking about everything that was going on this holiday season.

"Well," she said aloud, "at least nothing else—"

"Don't say it," Sam interrupted sharply from behind her.

She turned her head to look at him. "Don't say what?"

"You were about to say that with all you've got goin' already this year, at least nothin' else can happen," Sam said in a warning tone. "Don't you know that's the surest way to jinx things?"

"Oh, goodness gracious. I'm not superstitious. Anyway, *you* just said it."

"Yeah, but that's all right. I can say things like that without all heck breakin' loose. You're the one who can't."

"That's not fair."

Sam shook his head. "Fair's got nothin' to do with it," he said with a solemn expression on his face. "It's just the way the cosmos is. Some folks seem to attract trouble to start with. You don't want to go makin' the odds even worse."

"Well, that's just silly."

But despite what she said, Phyllis had to wonder whether there might not be something to Sam's idea. There had to be some explanation for why she seemed to keep getting mixed up in murder cases these past few years.

That thought was going through her head when the doorbell rang.

Sam spread his hands. "See? There you go. Trouble at the door."

"Oh, hush," Phyllis said. She took her apron off and thrust it into his hands as she went past him. "Keep an eye on those cookies. Don't let them burn."

"Wait a minute. I don't know anything about bakin' cookies—"

"Take them out if they start to burn," Phyllis told him over her shoulder.

"But . . . they're chocolate. How will I know?" Sam asked as Phyllis went out of the kitchen and up the hall to the living room.

She patted her graying brown hair to make sure it was in place as she went to the front door. It was the middle of the afternoon and she wasn't expecting anyone. Her son, Mike, who was a Parker County deputy sheriff, dropped by unexpectedly sometimes, and so did Mike's wife, Sarah. Carolyn was out somewhere, and so was Eve. Neither of them would have rung the doorbell anyway. This big old house was their home now.

When Phyllis looked out one of the narrow windows that flanked the door, she saw that the visitor wasn't family or one of her housemates. Definitely a friend, though. She opened the door, smiled, and said, "Hello, Georgia. Please, come in. What brings you here?"

December weather in this part of Texas could range anywhere from summerlike heat to snowstorms and wind chills well below zero. Today was on the warm side, but the air still had a pleasant crispness to it that came into the house with Georgia Hallerbee.

Georgia was what people once called "a handsome woman." She was about Phyllis's height, and well shaped despite her age. Her hair was dark brown, and she insisted she didn't color it. Phyllis believed her. Georgia wore a dark blue skirt and a matching blazer over a white blouse. She was an accountant and tax consultant and was also very active in civic affairs.

"How are you, Phyllis?" she asked as Phyllis closed the door behind her.

"I'm fine. How are you?" They had known each other for at least ten years, and while they had never been close friends, Phyllis was always glad to see Georgia.

"Busy, as always," Georgia replied with a smile and a sweet drawl in her voice. She wasn't a native Texan, having grown up somewhere in the Deep South, possibly even the state that bore the same name as she did. Phyllis didn't know about that.

She ushered the visitor into the living room and said, "Have a seat." As Georgia sat down on the sofa, Phyllis stepped over to the stereo to turn off the CD.

"Oh, let it play," Georgia said. "Don't turn it off on my account. I love Christmas music."

"So do I." Phyllis settled for turning down the music to a level that wouldn't interfere with their conversation. She sank into one of the armchairs and went on, "What can I do for you?"

"Maybe I just came by to visit," Georgia said.

Phyllis shook her head. "You said it yourself. You're one of the busiest women I know. You're always up to your elbows in some project or other."

Georgia smiled and tilted her head. "You know me too well," she said. "I've come to ask a favor of you. You may know that I'm in charge of the Jingle Bell Tour this year."

The Christmas Jingle Bell Tour of Homes was an annual tradition in Weatherford, and in many other Texas towns, for that matter. Each holiday season, a dozen or so homes would be selected and beautifully decorated—some might even say extravagantly decorated—both inside and out. Then, on one night a few weeks before Christmas, people could pay a small fee to go on a tour of these houses, with the proceeds going to one of the local civic organizations. There would be caroling, hot cider, and snacks at the homes on the tour, and it was a gala evening for everyone concerned . . . except perhaps for the home-owners, who had to go to the trouble of decorating and then opening their homes to the public.

"I did know that," Phyllis said. "I'm looking forward to it, as always. There are such beautiful decorations every year."

"Yes, there are," Georgia agreed. "And I'm hoping you can give me a hand this year."

"You mean in organizing the tour? I assumed all that was done already—"

"It was. Or at least, it was supposed to be. But this year we have a . . . situation."

Phyllis frowned slightly. "Whenever someone says 'situation' like that, they're usually not talking about anything good."

"I'm afraid you're right," Georgia said with a sigh. "One of the homeowners had to drop out. Doris Treadwell was diagnosed with cancer yesterday."

"Oh, no." Phyllis recognized the name but didn't actually know Doris Treadwell. Still, it was a terrible thing to hear about anyone, especially at this time of year, when everything was supposed to be festive.

Georgia nodded. "She'll be starting chemo right away, and then radiation, of course. And naturally she's not going to feel like participating in the tour."

"Of course not," Phyllis said. An uneasy suspicion stirred in the back of her mind. "But you're not asking *me* to—"

"To take her place, yes," Georgia said, nodding. "We'd like for this lovely old house of yours to be part of the Christmas Jingle Bell Tour of Homes this year."

Phyllis sat back, surprised and unsure of what to say. Georgia was asking her to take on a big responsibility on short notice.

Plus there was the notion of allowing strangers to troop through her house, and with the bridal shower to get ready for . . .

"Excuse me, ladies," Sam said from the door between the living room and the foyer. "I hate to interrupt, Phyllis, but those cookies are startin' to smell a little like they might be gettin' done . . ."

Phyllis got to her feet. "I'm sorry, Georgia, I really need to check on that."

"Of course—go right ahead. I wouldn't want to be to blame for ruining a batch of Phyllis Newsom's cookies."

On her way out of the living room, Phyllis fluttered a hand in Sam's direction and said, "I don't know if you two have met . . . Georgia, this is my friend Sam Fletcher . . . Sam, Georgia Hallerbee."

Sam nodded, smiled, and said, "Pleased to meet you," then followed Phyllis down the hall to the kitchen.

Phyllis picked up a potholder, opened the stove, and leaned down to check the cookies. She reached in and took hold of the baking sheet, pulled it out, and set it on top of the stove.

"They're not burned," she said.

Sam heaved a sigh of relief.

"But they are done," Phyllis went on. "You did the right thing to come and get me." She lowered her voice. "Now tell *me* the right thing to do about what Georgia wants."

"What's that?" Sam asked, equally quietly.

"She wants me to help her with the Jingle Bell Tour."

"You mean that thing where folks go around and look at all the fancy-decorated houses? That doesn't sound so bad."

Phyllis pointed at the floor under their feet. "She wants *this* house to be one of the stops."

Sam's eyes widened a little. "Oh. Well, it's kinda late to be askin' something like that, isn't it?"

"They had an emergency. Someone had to drop out of the tour."

Sam nodded and said, "Yeah, I guess that could happen, all right. What're you gonna tell her?"

"I don't know. It would be a lot of work . . . and we already have this business with Eve's shower and wedding coming up . . ."

"It's gonna be a busy month, all right," Sam agreed.

"On the other hand, it's for a good cause. And I *do* like to decorate for Christmas . . ."

"Yeah, but you'd almost have to go overboard for something like that, wouldn't you?"

"You can have a lot of decorations and still be tasteful."

"I don't know. I've seen some places so lit up with Christmas lights, I wouldn't be surprised if you could see 'em from space. But you know whatever you decide, I'll be glad to give you a hand."

"I know." Phyllis nodded her head as she came to a decision. "I may regret it, but I'm going to do it."

"I'm sure it'll be fine," Sam told her. "You want me to . . . uh . . . sample one of these cookies for you and tell you how it tastes?"

"Keep your hands off of them. They have to cool first. With that topping, you'll burn your mouth if you eat one now."

"I'll try, but they smell mighty good."

He wasn't the only one who thought so. As Phyllis came back into the living room, Georgia Hallerbee said, "My goodness, those cookies smell delicious, Phyllis. Nothing smells much better than cookies right out of the oven."

"I know. They're cooling now. If you can wait a few minutes, you can try one."

"I'd like that, but I really do have to be going soon." Georgia paused. "So have you thought about what I asked you?"

"I have, and . . . I'm going to do it."

A smile lit up Georgia's face. "That's wonderful! Thank you so much, Phyllis. I can't tell you how much it means to me, knowing that you'll step in and do a good job, like you always do at everything."

"I don't know about that. I'm not going to have as much time to prepare as the others. But I'll do the best I can."

"I'm sure the place will be beautiful," Georgia said as she stood up and started for the front door. "Thanks again. I'll be in touch with all the information you need, like which stop you'll be on the tour and when you can expect people to start showing up. And if there's anything I can do to help you get ready, just let me know."

"An extra six or eight hours in the day would be nice."

Georgia laughed. "Don't I know it! I've been wishing for that for a long time now, but it hasn't come true yet."

Phyllis opened the door and followed Georgia out onto the small front porch. Georgia's stylish crossover SUV was parked in the driveway.

She paused and looked down at the pair of large ceramic gingerbread men that stood on the porch, one on each side of the doorway. "These are new, aren't they? They're adorable."

Phyllis nodded. "Yes, Sam and I were out driving around one afternoon, and we stopped at that place between Azle and Springtown that has all the ceramic things. These gingerbread men were cute, and I thought they'd look good up here."

"You were right." Georgia gave Phyllis a look. "You and Sam . . . are the two of you . . . ?"

"Goodness, no. We're just friends," Phyllis said. That wasn't *strictly* true, but she had been raised to believe that it was best to be discreet about some things.

"You know what you should do?" Georgia said, looking down at the gingerbread men again. "You should dress them up for the tour. You could make, I don't know, elves or something out of them."

"Or Mr. and Mrs. Claus," Phyllis said, getting caught up in the spirit of the thing. "I've thought from the start that one of them was male and the other female."

"Well, there you go. You see, I knew you'd be good at this." Georgia lifted a hand in farewell as she started toward her SUV. "I'll be in touch. Enjoy those cookies!"

"We will," Sam said from behind Phyllis. Then he said, "You think they've cooled off enough to eat yet?"

Chapter 2

The cookies were good, all right, but they weren't really attractive. Phyllis knew people judged on looks as much as on taste, so she pondered whether there was anything she could do to tweak the recipe and make them more attractive. Adding flour would make them run less but would also affect the taste. She decided to try cooking the next batch in a mini muffin pan to give them a more uniform shape.

Eve and Roy came in while she and Sam were still sitting at the kitchen table with the plate of cookies between them. Roy drew in a deep breath and said, "My, doesn't that smell good."

Phyllis pushed the plate toward him. "Help yourself," she offered.

"Don't mind if I do." Roy smiled as he reached for the cookies.

"Where have you two been this afternoon?" Phyllis asked.

"Checking out real estate listings." Eve put a hand on Roy's arm. "We're going to have to find a house, you know, and pretty quickly, too, with the wedding coming up in less than a month."

Phyllis nodded and murmured, "Yes, of course."

She didn't like to think about Eve moving out, even though she had known when Eve moved in that it was probably inevitable, given her track record. Eve had always joked that she was between marriages, but it wasn't really a joke.

Mattie Harris's old room was still empty upstairs. Phyllis hadn't been able to bring herself to look for someone else to rent it after Mattie's death. She told herself that it was a good idea to keep the room vacant so it could be used as a guest room if necessary, but that wasn't the real reason. She missed Mattie, and besides, the four of them—Phyllis, Carolyn, Eve, and Sam—got along so well she hadn't wanted to do anything to break up that chemistry.

She couldn't use the guest room excuse to keep Eve's room vacant once Eve moved out. It wasn't that she needed the rent money, because she was well-fixed enough financially, even in the current less-than-stellar economy. She would have to admit that she just didn't want anybody new to move in.

Sam had been new once, she reminded herself. And his arrival in the house had caused a certain amount of disruption—no doubt about that. Carolyn had been adamantly opposed to the idea of a man living there, even a gentlemanly widower like Sam. She had come around, though, and become grudging friends with him.

They might not be as lucky the next time, Phyllis thought now. Bringing in another boarder might turn out to be a disaster. You just never knew about these things.

Which meant that she wanted to resent Roy for taking Eve away and breaking up their old gang . . . but she couldn't quite bring herself to do it when he was standing there looking so pleasant and telling her how delicious the German chocolate cookies were. More important, he made Eve happy. Phyllis could tell that just by looking at her.

"Why don't I put some of the cookies in a plastic bag for you to take back to the motel with you?" Phyllis suggested.

"That'd be great," Roy said. Then he frowned. "But not really fair. Then you won't have as many left here to eat."

Eve laughed. "Oh, goodness, Phyllis doesn't want there to be any left. Carolyn might see them, and then she'd know what recipe Phyllis is going to enter in the cookie contest this year."

"Got a little rivalry going on, eh?" Roy asked with a smile.

Unaccountably, Phyllis felt her face warming a little. "Not really. I don't care who wins."

"Don't believe her," Eve said. "Phyllis isn't as cutthroat about it as Carolyn is, but she likes to win."

"Well, who doesn't?" Phyllis said.

"I think that's fine," Roy told her. "And I'd be glad to help by polishing off another of these cookies and taking some of them with me when I go." He looked at his watch. "Which ought to be soon. I need to go back to the motel and make some calls." He leaned toward Eve and kissed her forehead. "I'll be back to take you to supper, though, like I promised."

"Don't be late," she told him. "I'll miss you."

Phyllis stood up. "Let me get that bag for the cookies . . ."

After Roy was gone, Eve lingered to eat a couple of the cookies herself. Phyllis asked her, "Did you have any luck finding a house?"

"Not really," Eve replied with a shake of her head. "So many of the new houses are those dreadful McMansions that look so much alike. I just can't imagine being comfortable in a place like that, especially after living in a wonderful old house like this. Unfortunately, a lot of the older houses haven't been kept up as well as this one has. Everything we looked at had things wrong with it, things that would have to be repaired or totally redone before we could move in." She sighed. "Roy says that if we don't find anything before the wedding, we'll get an apartment and stay in it while we keep looking. I don't like that idea. I told him we could stay right here just as easily." Eve looked across the table at Phyllis. "I hope that's all right, dear. I didn't mean to speak out of turn . . ."

Phyllis waved off Eve's worried comment. "No, no, that's fine. I don't have any objection." She paused. "Carolyn, on the other hand . . ."

"Hey, she got used to me," Sam pointed out. "And Roy seems to be even more civilized than I am."

"He's very civilized," Eve said solemnly.

"I'm sure it'll be fine," Phyllis said, although deep down she wasn't sure she liked the idea at all. However, she wasn't going to tell her old friend that she and Roy couldn't stay here after they were married. "Maybe it won't come to that. You and Roy could still find something before the wedding."

Eve nodded. "We're going to keep looking."

Sam reached for the last cookie on the plate, then paused and looked at Phyllis and Eve, lifting one of his bushy eyebrows in a quizzical expression.

"Go ahead," Phyllis said, and Eve nodded.

Sam picked up the cookie and took a bite out of it, looking pleased as he did so. Phyllis got up and brushed the crumbs off the plate into the garbage can, then rinsed it and left it in the sink to go in the dishwasher later.

Sam swallowed the last of the cookie and said, "Phyllis got some news today."

"Really? What's that?" Eve asked.

Phyllis sat down at the table again. "I'm going to be taking part in the Jingle Bell Tour this year. One of the participants had to drop out."

"You mean the tour's going to be stopping here?"

"That's right," Phyllis said. "Georgia Hallerbee stopped by and practically begged me to help her out. I couldn't say no, even with everything else we've got going on right now."

"My goodness, that means you're going to have to do a lot of work between now and . . . when is the tour this year, anyway?"

Phyllis winced. That was one question she should have asked Georgia, she supposed.

"Next week sometime," she said. "I don't know the exact day. But there was a story about it in the paper, so we can find out."

Eve reached over and patted Phyllis's hand. "I'll be glad to help as much as I can, but I'm going to be busy myself, you know . . ."

"Of course, looking for a house and getting ready for the wedding," Phyllis said with a nod. "I understand. You just worry about that. Sam and Carolyn and I can take care of everything else."

"Yep," Sam said.

"And of course we'll leave all the decorations up," Phyllis went on. "That way the house will be even more festive for the shower."

"Well, if I can help, just let me know." Eve stood up. "I'm sure everyone will love what you do with it."

After Eve had gone upstairs, Sam said quietly, "She's got a lot on her mind these days. Probably she was more excited about this Jingle Bell Tour business than she sounded like."

"Oh, I know that," Phyllis said. "I understand. I just hope I haven't taken on too much."

"We'll get it all done; don't worry."

She smiled at him. "I don't know what I'd do without you, Sam."

"Well, I don't plan on you havin' to find out anytime soon."

Without really thinking about what she was saying, Phyllis asked, "What do you think of Roy?"

The question appeared to take Sam by surprise. "What do you mean? He seems like a pretty good fella."

Phyllis hesitated, unsure whether to voice any of the thoughts that had nagged at her during the past couple of weeks. After a moment, she decided that she could talk to Sam about this. He would probably understand and not think that she was just being a snoopy old busybody.

"It's just that we don't know much about him. Hardly anything, in fact."

Sam shrugged. "We know he's from Houston and that he's semiretired."

"Semiretired from what?" Phyllis asked. "He's never mentioned what business he's in, has he?"

"Not to me," Sam admitted. "He just said that he was keepin' his hand in, whatever it is. I suppose that's why he had to make those calls. It's obvious he and Eve are plannin' to live up here in Weatherford, though, so I suspect after they're married he'll go ahead and retire the rest of the way."

"That certainly appears to be the case."

"Shoot, I didn't know you were suspicious of him."

Phyllis bristled a little at that. "Well, what do you expect? Eve shows up out of the blue with this man, a man none of us has ever met or even heard of until Thanksgiving Day, and announces that she's going to marry him. Not only that, but it's not one of those 'we'll get married sometime in the future' things. It's already December, and she's planning on getting married before the year is over. But I'm not actually suspicious."

Sam smiled as if he didn't quite believe that. "When you get to be our age, plannin' too far into the future usually isn't a good idea."

"Maybe not, but it just seems to me that they're . . . I don't know . . ." Phyllis lowered her voice even more. "Rushing things."

Sam grinned. "Maybe they *got* to get married."

Phyllis's eyes narrowed as she said, "Only a man would find that funny."

He held up both hands in surrender. "I didn't mean anything by it. And heck, I understand why you'd worry some about Eve. The two of you have been friends for a long time. I worry about her, too, and I've known her for less'n three years. I guess when you get in the habit of askin' questions, it's hard not to wonder about folks."

She knew he was talking about her tendency to dig for the truth in the murders she had solved in the past. She had certainly not set out to become any sort of detective. Circumstances and concern for her friends had forced her into investigating those cases.

"It's nothing like that," she said honestly. "I'm just curious about Roy—that's all. I'd like to know more about him before he marries Eve. After all, if she had any family, I'm sure *they'd* want to know all about him. We're as close to family as she has, at least that she's close to. And don't forget—he may be living here if they can't find a house in time."

"You're right," Sam said, nodding. "You're absolutely right. So what are you gonna do?"

Now that her concerns were out in the open, Phyllis knew it was going to be impossible to ignore them. She said, "I don't have time to do anything. I have to get ready for a shower, a wedding, and the Jingle Bell Tour before that. You're friends with Roy, though, Sam, and you don't have as much on your plate right now."

He sat up straighter and frowned. "You want *me* to play detective? I don't know if that's a good idea, Phyllis. I never minded helpin' you out, but I've told you all along that you're the brains of this operation. I'm just the brawn."

"I just think you should talk to him the next time you get a chance, maybe find out what sort of business he's in. Men talk about business all the time, don't they?"

"I suppose."

"And . . . and you were married, too," Phyllis said, hoping that she wasn't crossing a line. "You could talk about being widowers and maybe find out something about his first wife."

Sam's frown deepened. "Men aren't likely to sit around and talk about things like that. At least, men our age don't. We weren't raised to be all sensitive and open about our feelin's, like fellas are today."

"All right, I'm sorry. Just forget I said anything about it, okay?"

He shook his head. "No, no, it's not a problem. It's just gonna take some figurin' out—that's all. Don't worry, I'll find out what I can. I don't want to insult Roy, though."

"Oh, no," Phyllis said. "That's not what I want at all. I'd rather not know any more than we do now than offend him." She wouldn't be able to stand it if Roy was insulted, and Eve took his side and refused to have anything more to do with her, as she just might.

Sam reached across the table and squeezed Phyllis's hand. "Don't worry. I'll be careful."

"I really am a terrible busybody, aren't I?"

"Not hardly. You're a woman who cares about her friends more than anybody else I know, and nobody can hold that against you."

Phyllis didn't know if he was just trying to make her feel better. If he was, it worked. She turned her fingers in his and squeezed back.

Chapter 3

*P*hyllis had planned on getting the Christmas tree and all the decorations up that weekend, anyway. She knew that some people put their lights up the day after Thanksgiving or even before. She had seen Christmas lights on houses as early as Halloween, which just seemed *wrong* to her. When she was a girl, the decorations had gone up two weeks before Christmas, at the earliest.

The first thing to do, she supposed, was to take inventory of exactly what she had in the way of lights and decorations. Like most people, she and her late husband, Kenny, had accumulated a lot of things over the decades, and she didn't use all of them every year.

This year would be different, though. In order to decorate the house and yard properly for the Jingle Bell Tour, she would need every set of lights, every bit of tinsel, every plastic reindeer, every wooden cutout figure of Santa and his elves and the Grinch and the Whos from Whoville and Snoopy on his doghouse, and . . . and . . .

And every manger scene, she thought as she stood on the porch the next morning, looking at the front yard and trying to figure out what was going to go where. The city had better not come in here and try to tell her she couldn't put up a manger scene, or that any signs she put up had to say HAPPY HOLIDAYS or SEASON'S GREETINGS instead of MERRY CHRISTMAS. She would *not* take kindly to that at all.

"We're going to need some of those lights that wrap around the tree trunks, aren't we?" she asked Sam, who stood beside her.

He nodded. "Probably be a good idea."

"And of course lights along the eaves and then up the ends of the house to the top of the roof and across. I'll see if I can get Mike to do that, so you won't have to clamber around up there."

"I'm perfectly capable of climbin' a ladder and gettin' up on the roof," Sam said. "No need to bother Mike with it."

"I just wouldn't want you falling off and hurting yourself."

Sam shook his head. "I'm not gonna fall off."

"You're going to be stubborn about this, aren't you?"

He smiled. "More than likely."

"Well, we'll see." She turned back to the yard. "Now, what else will we need? I want to pick up anything we have to buy before this weekend, so we'll have all day Saturday and then Sunday afternoon to get ready."

"They have one of those Christmas stores in the mall over in Fort Worth," Sam suggested. "We can go over and just look to see what they have. Maybe get some ideas on how to approach this."

"That's a good idea. First, though, we have to make sure of what we already have. I know you think you can climb up on roofs like Santa himself. How are you at climbing into attics?"

"Pretty good, if I do say so myself."

Unlike newer houses, which usually had a pull-down ladder built in for getting into the attic, this house was old enough that the only way into the attic was through an opening in the wall of the garage, above the door into the house. Phyllis moved her car out so it wouldn't be in the way; then Sam got the ladder and propped it against the wall. He climbed up and disappeared into the attic. A moment later, the light from a bare bulb filled the space as he found the chain attached to the fixture and pulled it.

When Mike was a teenager, he and Kenny had carried sheets of plywood up there and nailed them over the ceiling joists to form a walkway and a good-sized storage area. Some of the Christmas decorations were in the house, in the closet of the room that had been Mattie Harris's, but the things that hadn't been used for several years were up here, packed away in cardboard boxes, each marked with a little Christmas tree that Phyllis had drawn on it with a marker so that she would know what was in it.

She listened to Sam rummaging around up there for a few minutes before her curiosity got the better of her. She was wearing jeans, so, grasping the sides of the metal extension ladder, she climbed until her head was level with the opening and she could look into the attic.

"What have you found?" she asked.

Sam was tall enough and the underside of the roof close enough that he had to stoop a little to keep from hitting his head. He gestured toward three boxes he had stacked between himself and the opening.

"Got those right there, and I've just barely started lookin'. That was a good idea, drawin' a little Christmas tree on 'em.

Keeps me from havin' to open every box." He frowned a little. "You better be careful up there on that ladder, though."

"I'm not going to fall off any more than you are," she told him. "If you'll push those over here closer, I'll start carrying them down."

"That'll speed things up, all right," he agreed. He moved the boxes next to the opening where she could reach them.

She was able to prop each box on her hip and hold it that way while she used her other hand to help her climb down. She was careful because she knew there might be fragile items in all of the boxes. If she dropped one of them, something was bound to break.

Phyllis had the first two boxes stacked on the floor of the garage and was going up again for the third one when the door leading into the house opened. It swung outward, as most of them did in houses from that era, and that made it bump hard against the ladder just as Phyllis's head reached the level of the opening again.

"What the—," Carolyn said as the door hit the ladder and caused it to sway backward a little.

"Oh!" Phyllis cried.

Sam was close to the opening, about to set another box on the plywood floor of the attic. He dropped it instead and lunged forward, stretching out a long arm to grab the ladder while his other hand clamped around one of the bracing boards attached to the rafters. Phyllis clung to the ladder as it settled back into place with a little thump.

"Oh, my God!" Carolyn said as she looked up from the doorway. "Phyllis, I almost knocked you off of there! I didn't mean to!"

"It's all right," Phyllis said as she tried to catch her breath.

"Goodness, I know you didn't mean to, Carolyn. It was just an accident." She looked at Sam, who still wore a worried look as he held on to the ladder. "You can let go now. It's stable enough."

"And you were worried about me fallin' off," he said. He let go of the ladder and straightened up as much as he could.

"The door just bumped it a little. It wasn't going to fall down."

"You don't know that," Carolyn said. "I could have killed you. You might have broken a leg or a hip, at least."

"It's all right," Phyllis said again. "I'm fine. But I'm not so sure about what's in that box you dropped, Sam."

"Whatever it is, if it's broken it'll be a whole heck of a lot easier to replace than you would be." He took the top off the box, looked inside, and grunted. "Looks like a bunch of garland rolled up." He tilted the box so Phyllis could see the plastic greenery. "It appears to be fine."

"Stay where you are," Carolyn said from down below. "I'll go around and come in through the garage door so I can give you a hand. You can pass the boxes down to me, Phyllis, so you won't have to clamber up and down that ladder."

"That's a good idea. We'll make an assembly line of it."

In another twenty minutes, they had all the boxes of Christmas decorations brought down from the attic. Phyllis and Carolyn began carrying them inside while Sam put away the ladder. When he joined them, bringing a couple of the boxes with him, he found them sitting in the living room floor going through the decorations scattered around them.

"Looks like one of those Christmas stores blew up in here," he said with a grin. "You ladies stay where you are and keep doin' what you're doin'. I'll bring the rest of the stuff in."

"Thanks, Sam. For everything," Phyllis added, hoping he knew she meant the way he had leaped to grab that ladder and save her from falling. It had been closer than she'd admitted to Carolyn.

When Carolyn had first heard about Phyllis agreeing to let the house be part of the Jingle Bell Tour, she had been dubious, but she was starting to come around. "I always wanted to go all out on decorating, just one year," she said now.

"I always had to rein Kenny in a little," Phyllis said. "When it came to Christmas, he was just like a big, overgrown kid." A wistful smile crossed her face. "Of course, that always made it good for Mike. I don't know which of them enjoyed Christmas more."

"Those were good times," Carolyn said, "when our children were small and most of our lives were still in front of us."

"Yes . . . but these are good times, too, if we make them that way." Phyllis lifted a beautiful, sparkling treetop angel from a box. "And this is going to be one of the best Christmases ever," she said.

"If no one—" Carolyn stopped herself.

Phyllis looked up from the angel. "What were you going to say?"

"Oh, nothing. Forget about it."

Phyllis knew, though. And given everything that had happened in the past few years, she couldn't blame Carolyn for thinking it.

If no one gets murdered. That was what Carolyn had been about to say.

Going through the decorations and figuring out what was going to go where took most of the day. It was necessary, though, antiques." Roy laughed. "Sort of like the fellas who used them. Like me."

"Don't go remindin' me how old we are. My knees remind me of it all the time."

"We've been using computers for more than twenty years now," Roy went on. "These little handheld calculators the kids have now probably have more capabilities than all of NASA's computers did when we used them to send men to the Moon and back. It's amazing."

"I thought you said you were in the oil and gas business, not NASA."

"Oh, I just meant 'we' in the general sense. I'm from Houston but never had anything to do with space. My company was more concerned with what's under the ground than what's above it."

"Which company's that?"

"You never would have heard of it. It's just a little consulting firm. Nobody outside of the industry has heard of it."

Sam nodded. Roy was being a little evasive now, but his answers weren't really all that suspicious. If somebody not from around here had asked Sam where he used to teach, he might have said, "Oh, just some little town out in the country you never heard of," rather than telling them Poolville. The name wouldn't mean anything to them. This might just be a case of Roy feeling the same way.

"You own the business?" The question was a little blunt, but not out of line. It was something two men who didn't know each other all that well might discuss over power tools.

"No, I was vice president in charge of R and D. Research and development."

Sam nodded even though he knew perfectly well what R and D stood for.

because it was the only way they could determine what else they needed. Phyllis kept a list, and when they were finished she was able to make another list of what they might need.

"It's too late in the day now to go to Fort Worth," she decided. "We'll drive over there to that Christmas store tomorrow, Sam, if that's all right with you."

He nodded. "Sure. I don't have anywhere I have to be. That's one of the perks of bein' retired."

But it wasn't really much of a perk, he thought. After decades of having to get up and go to school nine months out of the year, he still felt the urge. A lot of those years he had worked a summer job, too, pay for schoolteachers being pretty bad in those days, so he'd had responsibilities all year round. It made a fella restless, not having anything to do when he'd always been busy.

Luckily for him, Phyllis was always mixed up in something or other, so he was glad to help her out. Because of that, he didn't mind too much asking Roy Porter to come out to the garage with him when Roy and Eve got back from another fruitless day of looking for a house to buy.

"What for?" Roy asked. "I probably ought to get back to the motel—"

"Oh, no," Eve cut in. "You're going to stay and have supper with us tonight. That's all right, isn't it, Phyllis?"

They were all standing in the kitchen. Phyllis nodded and said, "Of course. You're always welcome, Roy."

"And there's always plenty of food," Sam put in. "Nobody ever goes hungry in this house, which is one reason I really like livin' here."

"And what's the good of being semiretired if you have to check in at the office every day?" Eve asked Roy. "I know you still like to feel needed, dear, but they'll get in touch with you if they have any problems that require your attention."

Roy nodded. "I suppose you're right. What is it you want me to look at, Sam?"

"Actually, I thought I'd put you to work," Sam said as he smiled. "I've got a project goin' that I could use a hand with."

"What sort of project?" Roy asked as they left the kitchen and went into the garage. He looked at the long workbench, the tools, and the boards stacked and leaned here and there. "I've never been much good at woodworking."

"You can handle this just fine. I'm makin' the back for a set of bookshelves, and I need somebody to hold the board while I cut it."

"Oh. Well, I guess I can do that."

Sam had cleared an area and set up a couple of sawhorses, and had the four-by-eight sheet of quarter-inch plywood resting on them. He had already marked the three-by-seven section of the board he was going to cut out. He pointed to the end of the board where he wanted Roy to stand and said, "Once I've started the cut, you hold on to that corner right there. Just hold it up level so it's not droopin', because it'll bind on the saw blade if it does."

"Sure. I understand."

Sam put on a pair of goggles and picked up the circular saw from the bench. He pressed in the safety release with his thumb and triggered the saw, causing it to make a brief high-pitched whine that confirmed he had power to it. Then he rested it on the board, lined up the edge of the blade with the pencil line he had made, and fired up the saw again. He edged it forward and the blade bit into the wood.

Being careful not to veer from the line, Sam moved the saw ahead. Sawdust flew in the air around him. The scent of freshly

cut wood mingled with the smell of oil from the saw. To Sam it smelled almost as good as cookies fresh from the oven. Almost, but definitely not quite.

Roy moved in behind him and supported the cut portion of the board, just as Sam had instructed him. Sam made the cut all the way to the end, so that the one-foot-wide section came loose from the rest of the board. He released the saw's trigger and turned to see that Roy had the piece of wood in his hands, holding it in front of him.

"Where do you want this part?" Roy asked.

"Just lean it against the wall over there," Sam said, pointin with the hand that didn't hold the saw. "I always save the lef over pieces. Never know when you might need 'em for some thing."

"Now you have to cut off a foot from the top?"

"Yep." Sam hefted the saw. "Unless you'd like to do it?"

Roy leaned the board against the wall and shook his hea He chuckled. "No, thanks. I'd probably manage to cut my ar off. I was never good with power tools. Back in my day, thoug I was a demon with the slipstick. You probably don't know wh that is, do you?"

"The heck I don't. You must've been an engineer. Tha what those fellas called a slide rule, wasn't it?"

Roy nodded. "When I started out in the oil and gas bu ness, we all carried them. I even had a holster for mine. Ev more than a pocket protector, a slide-rule holster was a s sign of an engineer."

This was turning out to be easier than Sam thought it wo be. "Math was never my strong suit, but I knew fellas who w real good at it. Haven't seen a slide rule in a long time, thoug

"Oh, no, if any of them are still around now, they'd

"I spent most of my time in front of a computer for the past ten years. I've got to say, it's good to be out and about more."

"I imagine so. Computers have taken over teachin', too. When I started out, my grade book was a real book, and I wrote the grades down with a fountain pen and added them up and figured averages on an addin' machine. Now it's all online, and you get a kid's grade by clickin' on something. In the classrooms they've got 'smart boards' instead of blackboards, and you can hook your computer up to 'em or plug a USB drive into 'em."

"The world doesn't stand still for very long, does it, Sam?"

"No, sir, it sure doesn't. I don't guess we'd really want it to, but sometimes I wouldn't mind if it just slowed down a little."

Roy grinned. "Eve's right. That's the good thing about being retired. You can live life at your own pace, at least part of the time. I intend to slow down and enjoy the time I have left, and Eve's a big part of that."

"She's a fine gal, all right," Sam said. He didn't say anything about how Eve had had her cap set for him for a while after he moved into the house. He didn't figure Roy needed to hear about that.

"I guess we'd better get the other piece of that board cut," Roy said. "You're going to put it on the back of some book-shelves, right?"

"Right." Sam nodded toward the shelves, which were put together, just lacking the back to stabilize them before he could start staining them. He moved around the board sitting on the sawhorses and positioned the saw. Roy caught on fast. This time he didn't need Sam to tell him where to stand or which part of the board to hold.

A moment later, sawdust and the racket of the saw filled the air in the garage again.

Chapter 4

"So, you see, I don't think you have anything to worry about," Sam said later that evening as he and Phyllis sat alone in the living room, talking quietly about the conversation Sam had had with Roy Porter that afternoon. Eve and Carolyn were both upstairs, in their rooms, with the doors closed. Phyllis had checked on that before she motioned for Sam to follow her into the living room, although she felt a little bad about it, almost like she was spying on her friends.

"But he didn't actually tell you the name of the company he worked for?" she asked.

Sam shrugged and shook his head. "No, he didn't. But I don't see anything fishy about that. If he'd told me the name, it wouldn't have meant anything to me. He talked enough about all that engineerin' stuff to convince me that he was tellin' the truth. I mean, how many people this day and age would even know what a slipstick is?"

"A what?" Phyllis asked with a frown.

"Slipstick," Sam repeated. "That's another name for a slide rule."

"Oh, I know what that is, of course. Or was. I don't think I've even seen one for years. They don't make them anymore, do they?"

"You got me," Sam said. "You can probably buy 'em on-line."

Phyllis shook her head. "That doesn't really matter. What's important is . . . you got the feeling that Roy is . . ."

"All right?" Sam finished for her when Phyllis's voice trailed off. "Not an ax murderer who'll chop Eve up and put her in the freezer?"

"Sam! I never said *anything* even *remotely* like that—"

His grin made her stop. "I'm just joshin'," he said. "I know you just want Eve to be happy. I talked to Roy for a good thirty minutes out there, and he seems like a good, solid, decent guy. I think he'll take good care of Eve."

"Did he say anything about his first wife?"

"Not much. He mentioned that she'd been in real estate in Houston."

"Did he tell you her name?"

Sam nodded. "He mentioned it, just in talkin' about her, you know. Julie. That's what he called her."

"Julie Porter," Phyllis repeated.

"Sounds like a nice lady."

"You can't go by somebody's name," Phyllis said, thinking of some of the murderers she had uncovered. Some of them had seemed just as respectable as they could be, but they'd had a fatal flaw that had led them to become killers. Maybe a lot of people had that same flaw, she had thought in her darker moments, but they never committed murder because circumstances never forced them into it.

She went on, "Roy didn't suspect that you were . . ."

"Interrogatin' him?" Sam asked with a twinkle in his eye. "No, I don't think so. We were just two fellas shootin' the breeze while we cut up a board. Nothing suspicious about it." He grew more serious. "I got to admit that I didn't care much for it, though."

"I'm sorry I asked you to do it," Phyllis said, and she meant every word of it.

By the next morning, Phyllis had convinced herself that she'd been crazy to even worry about Roy, and she felt bad about dragooning Sam into digging for information. She thought about apologizing for involving him, then decided it would be better just to let the whole thing go.

Anyway, she had Christmas decorations to buy, and by the time she and Sam headed for Fort Worth in her car, that was all she was thinking about.

The Christmas store took up a big storefront in Ridgmar Mall, on the west side of Fort Worth. Phyllis loved browsing in places like this when she didn't have anything in particular to buy. That wasn't the case today, however.

Today she was on a mission.

She bought strings of multicolored lights. She bought white icicle lights to hang from the eaves. She bought sheets of lights to wrap around tree trunks. She bought lighted lawn ornaments. She couldn't help but wonder just how much electricity all these lights were going to use, even though she bought the more energy-efficient LED lights, and she would have sworn that at one point she heard Sam mutter under his breath, "Visible from space."

There was a lighted manger scene that had to be assembled, and a mechanical Santa that waved, turned from side to side, and said, "Ho, ho, ho," in a booming voice. There were plastic reindeer made to perch on the roof, and they came with their own spotlight to illuminate them. There were bells and white lights that would also work as decorations for Eve's wedding, which would take place in the house on New Year's Eve. There was so much stuff, it took Sam several trips to load all of it in the trunk and backseat of Phyllis's car. By the time he was finished, it was almost noon, so they took the escalator to the mall's upper level and went to the food court to get some lunch.

Since there were fewer than three weeks until Christmas, the mall was crowded, of course. As they sat at one of the tables and ate pizza, Sam watched all the people streaming past them. After a few minutes, he said, "The schools haven't let out for Christmas vacation yet, have they?"

"I don't think so," Phyllis said. "Why do you ask?"

"There are all these little kids, and a lot of 'em look old enough that they ought to be in school."

Phyllis knew what he meant. Even though there weren't as many children in the mall as there would have been if the schools were out for Christmas vacation, a large number of the women shopping had youngsters with them, and not just preschoolers, either. Phyllis saw plenty of kids from the ages of six or eight to fourteen or fifteen.

"I guess they're all homeschooled," she said. "Either that, or their parents just don't make them go all the time."

"That's just crazy," Sam said as he shook his head. "It wasn't that long ago you'd never see a kid more than five years old out anywhere when school was in session. Maybe one every now and then who couldn't go because he was sick. What are people thinkin' when they just can't be bothered to send their kids to school? I swear, parents these days just do whatever's the most convenient for them without ever thinkin' about the kids."

Phyllis reached over and patted his hand where it lay on the table. "I know," she said, "and they get on people's lawns, too."

Sam's eyes narrowed. "You're makin' fun of me."

"Maybe a little."

"After you bought enough Christmas stuff, you could enter a giant lights and display contest. Find the true meanin' of Christmas. Win money, money, money."

"That's right, Charlie Brown."

Sam laughed. "Pardon my French, but I'm damn glad I met you, Phyllis Newsom."

"I'm damn glad you did, too," Phyllis said. "Oh, goodness. There's something I forgot."

"Couldn't have been something in the Christmas store. We bought everything there already."

"No, I'll probably have to go over to the craft store for this. I need to find patterns so I can make Mr. and Mrs. Claus outfits for the gingerbread men."

Sam frowned. "Come again?"

"Those ceramic gingerbread men on the front porch. Georgia Hallerbee suggested that it would be cute if I dressed them up."

Sam thought about it for a moment and then nodded slowly. "I can see that," he said. "Of course, sittin' up on the porch the way they do, folks won't be able to see 'em very well."

"Why not?"

"Because everybody'll be blinded by the glare from all the lights."

Phyllis gave him a mock frown. "There aren't going to be *that* many lights."

"Maybe not, but I reckon the power's gonna drop in the rest of the town when you switch 'em on."

They sparred like that for several more minutes as they finished their pizza, then left the mall and took their soft drinks with them. A large craft store was only a couple of blocks away, so Phyllis went there to look for the patterns she needed while Sam browsed in a nearby used-book store. She knew she wouldn't be able to find patterns made specifically for gingerbread men, but she found patterns for stuffed bears that she thought she could adapt.

She met back up with Sam and went to one more place she had thought of while browsing the pattern books. They stopped at Sam's Club, where she bought industrial-sized bottles of ground cinnamon. Looking around, she also bought a few more decorations.

When they got back to the outskirts of Weatherford in the middle of the afternoon, Phyllis took the old highway into town, rather than fighting the traffic where South Main crossed the interstate.

"Let's just leave everything here in the garage except for the cinnamon," she suggested when they reached the house. "I don't know about you, but I'm tired. I'm not as young as I once was."

"Most days I don't even remember bein' young," Sam said as he climbed out of the car. "I can stack some of the boxes on the workbench. I won't be needin' it for a while."

"What about the shelves you're making?"

"They're ready to stain," Sam explained. "Thanks to Roy givin' me a hand with them yesterday. I don't plan on startin' any other projects until after the New Year."

"Why not?"

"Well . . . I figure with all you've got goin' on, you'll be needin' my help a lot."

"That's nice of you, Sam. I don't want to take you away from what you really like to do, though."

"You won't be," he assured her. "You may not realize it, but you're a lot better lookin' than a circular saw."

"I'm flattered . . . I think."

They unloaded the boxes, stacking them on and below the workbench and putting the mechanical Santa in a corner. Carolyn had heard them drive in, so she came out into the garage to help them.

"Goodness, Phyllis, did you leave anything in the store?" she asked.

"There's not really *that* much stuff," Phyllis said. "Besides, this is probably the only time the house will ever be part of the Jingle Bell Tour, so why not go all out?"

Sam frowned. "So you're sayin' you bought all of this because you'll probably never use it again?"

"No, I . . . well, I guess it did kind of sound like that . . . but what I meant was . . . I don't know. Maybe I just got carried away by the Christmas spirit!"

"There're worse things," Sam said.

That was Thursday. The Christmas Jingle Bell Tour of Homes was scheduled for the next Tuesday evening. That gave Phyllis four days to get ready, leaving Tuesday during the day for any final touches. She took full advantage of the time. On Friday she sketched out a diagram of the yard and house, indicating which decorations she wanted where. She also planned to work on the Mr. and Mrs. Claus outfits for the gingerbread men, but when Carolyn heard about that, she immediately volunteered to make the clothes. Since Carolyn was an excellent seamstress, Phyllis happily turned that part of the project over to her old friend.

Eve had promised that she and Roy would take time off from their house hunting that weekend to help out, and although Mike had to work Saturday, Phyllis's daughter-in-law, Sarah, and grandson, Bobby, would be there to lend a hand as well, and Mike was coming on Sunday afternoon, after church. There would be plenty of willing hands, and Phyllis had a feeling they would all be needed.

In fact, it was almost like a party, with people going in and out of the house, lots of talk and laughter, and plenty of food. Phyllis persuaded Sam to wait until Sunday afternoon to put the lights and decorations on the roof and in the trees, so Mike could be there to help. She explained that Mike really enjoyed doing that sort of thing, which was true enough, but what Phyllis really wanted was for Sam not to be clambering around up there by himself. Sam was smart enough that he probably realized that, too, but he didn't make an issue of it.

The place got even more crowded during the weekend as several of the neighbors saw all the decorating going on and came over to help. For quite a few years, everyone in the neighborhood had gotten together at this time of year for their annual Christmas cookie exchange, but after what had happened a couple of years earlier during that holiday event, the tradition had gone away. In fact, the house next door to Phyllis's where

Agnes Simmons had lived for so many years was still vacant. Between the terrible housing market and the fact that a murder had been committed in this particular house, interested buyers were practically nonexistent.

But it was good to see Lois and Blake Horton again, as well as Vickie and Monte Kimbrough. Both couples had had some very rough patches in their marriages, and Lois had been away for a while in rehab, but at least they were together at the moment and seemed to be reasonably happy. Helen Johannson from the corner of the next block came down to Phyllis's, bringing her young children, Denise and Parker. Oscar Gunderson ambled over, another of the retirees who were common in this neighborhood. He was carrying a pair of live pine trees in nice pots that he set on the porch for the ladies to decorate. Phyllis knew secrets about all these people, she thought as she greeted them, but they were still her friends and she was glad to spend time with them.

The men tended to the outside decorations while the women congregated inside, hanging garlands, placing ornaments on the big artificial tree that was set up in the living room, and decorating the smaller live trees on the porch. They would suddenly think of something they had at home that would work perfectly and would hurry to get it. Phyllis had Sarah and Helen in the kitchen with the kids, making gingerbread men decorations with the cinnamon she bought at Sam's Club. She knew they would make the perfect final touch to the big tree and would make the house smell wonderful. The decorations were coming together beautifully. She moved back and forth, supervising all aspects of the operation.

And that was what it was like, she thought, a military operation with people working in different areas on different jobs but all pulling together in a common effort. She was lucky to have so many friends and so much help. Although there was a part of her that would have liked to do it all herself, she knew she couldn't have managed in the time that was left before the Jingle Bell Tour.

Carolyn found her and showed her the outfits she had made for the gingerbread men. "What do you think of them?"

"I think they're wonderful," Phyllis replied honestly. "They're going to be so cute. Are you finished with them?"

Carolyn nodded. "Yes, I think they're ready to go on the gingerbread men."

"Come on, then. Let's do that right now."

They carried the clothes out onto the porch. Carolyn looked back and forth between the gingerbread men and asked, "Which one is Santa and which one is Mrs. Claus?"

"I don't suppose it really matters, but I think the one on the right would make a good Mrs. Gingerbread Claus. Let's put the Santa suit on the one on the left."

The suit was pretty simple: a red cap with a white, fuzzy ball on the end, a red suit trimmed with white fur, and a fake white beard that tied on under the gingerbread man's chin. What really made the outfit was the small bag of toys the gingerbread Santa had attached to the jacket. When Phyllis and Carolyn had everything in place, they stepped back to study the results.

"It's adorable," Carolyn said.

"It certainly is," Phyllis agreed.

The outfit for Mrs. Claus included a red velvet dress, an apron, a gray wig, and a mobcap. Denise and Parker Johannson came running over while Phyllis and Carolyn were finishing, and Denise clapped and squealed in delight when she saw the dressed-up gingerbread men next to the little trees decorated in red and white balls with red and white ribbon bows on top. Parker, being a boy, was too cool to display his emotions so openly, but he grinned with pleasure and said, "Are we going to put the gingerbread men decorations we made on these trees?"

Phyllis had thought they would just use them on the big tree inside, but she had to admit, it would be cute to have some on the little trees next to Mr. and Mrs. Gingerbread Claus. She smiled and said, "What a wonderful idea, Parker."

"Lookin' mighty good," Sam commented as he came by with his arms full of lights.

"Yes, I can't wait for Georgia to see the gingerbread couple," Phyllis said, "since it was her idea and all."

But that would have to wait, because Phyllis didn't expect Georgia to come by again until the day of the tour. They had traded a couple of e-mails during the week, Phyllis assuring her friend that everything was under control and the house would be ready for visitors on Tuesday evening.

And between now and then there was still a lot of work to do, she told herself, so she had better get back to it.

Chapter 5

"Did you ever think you'd get it all done in time?" Sam asked.

"Of course I did," Phyllis answered without hesitation. "There was never a doubt in my mind; otherwise, I wouldn't have agreed to do it."

But deep down she knew that wasn't quite true. On numerous occasions during the past week, there had been plenty of doubt in her mind, and she had asked herself why she had been so crazy as to tell Georgia Hallerbee that she would take part in the tour. At those moments, Phyllis had done what she always did on such occasions.

She kept working.

And now it was done. Finished. Ready. Although the outside lights weren't switched on yet, Christmas carols already played loudly on the sound system set up in the front yard. In about an hour and a half, the visitors on the Christmas Jingle Bell Tour of Homes would begin to arrive.

They had been lucky when it came to the weather, Phyllis

knew. Sometimes it rained quite a bit during December, but the skies had remained clear while the preparations were going on. And according to all the forecasts she had heard and read, tonight was supposed to be a cool, clear, very pleasant evening, perfect for the Jingle Bell Tour. Of course, if it had been raining the tour organizers simply would have postponed it, but this was better. Phyllis was caught up in the enthusiasm of getting ready, and having to postpone the event itself would have been a letdown.

She walked around the house, double-checking the decorations. She prowled into the kitchen, where plates of cookies sat on the counter. She and Carolyn had already submitted their recipes for the contest, taking the printed-out recipes and plates of samples to the newspaper office to be judged. Everyone who worked there, from the editor to the clerk at the counter, had grinned in anticipation when they saw the two of them coming in, knowing that the cookies Phyllis and Carolyn baked were always good.

So the recipes were no longer a secret. Phyllis had baked several batches of her German chocolate cookies and even experimented on a new nutty cashew butter and chocolate cookie that she thought was pretty good. She might have to use it in a future contest. Carolyn contributed her gingerbread-boy cookies, which Phyllis had to admit were awfully good and not so spicy that they would turn kids off. Each of them had made cookies using recipes from previous contests, as well. Phyllis looked at the plate of lime snowflake cookies and was reminded again of what had happened two Christmases past. She took a deep breath, pushed those thoughts out of her head, and set up a pair of coffeemakers with wonderfully scented coffee. While the cookies were baking earlier, she had made a quick batch of chocolate mint coffee stirrers using plastic spoons, mint chocolate chips, and crushed candy canes. A large pot of winter cranberry cider was staying warm on the stove. Paper cups, plates, and napkins were set up, ready to serve. Satisfied that everything was as it should be, she went back to the living room.

Sam and Carolyn were sitting there. Carolyn said, "Goodness, you're as nervous as a cat, Phyllis. There's no need to be worried. Everything is going to be fine. You've done a spectacular job getting ready for this."

"I had a lot of help," Phyllis said. "I never could have done it without the two of you, and a lot of other people, too."

"It'll be worth all the trouble when you see those folks oohin' and aahin' over all the decorations and all of these cookies," Sam said.

"I hope so."

"When are they supposed to get here?" Carolyn asked.

"About seven thirty, Georgia said. This is the third house on the tour."

"And the best one," Sam declared.

"I don't really care about that. I just want people to be pleased with what they see."

"They will be; don't you worry about that."

Eve came downstairs and joined them in the living room, looking around as she asked, "Is Roy here yet? He said he'd be back by the time the tour started."

"I haven't seen him," Phyllis said. "But it's only six forty-five." The doorbell rang, and she smiled. "That's probably him now."

Eve had just sat down, and although she started to get up, Phyllis gestured for her to stay where she was.

"I'm already on my feet. I'll let him in. Sam, would you go

ahead and turn on the outside lights so I can see how they look?"

"Sure," he said. With his usual long-legged stride, he headed for the kitchen. The power strip and surge protector that controlled all the outside lights was just outside the kitchen door in the garage. One flip of its main switch would turn on the rest of the lights and decorations.

Phyllis went the other way up the hall toward the front door. As she approached it she heard a loud crash from outside that made her heart thump with worry and surprise. Her first thought was that the set of plastic reindeer, along with the attached sleigh, had come loose on the roof and fallen to the ground. She hurried forward, grasped the doorknob, and pulled the door open.

At that moment, Sam hit the switch on the power strip in the garage, turning on the outside lights.

The glare really was a little dazzling, Phyllis had to admit, especially when the lights first came on and her eyes hadn't had the chance to adjust to them. She instinctively lifted a hand and said, "Roy?"

But Roy wasn't standing there. No one was. For a second, Phyllis thought that someone had rung her doorbell and then run off, the classic prank that neighborhood children used to play before they all became too ironic and postmodern for such innocent high jinks.

Then she saw the dark, huddled shape lying on the front porch.

"Oh, my God!" she cried as she threw open the storm door and rushed out past the giant wreath hung on the wooden door. The storm door bumped the person lying on the porch. Shards of shattered ceramic crunched under Phyllis's feet. The glow from the white icicle lights washed over the crumpled shape, and the multihued lights on the decorations in the yard cast brilliantly colored slashes of illumination over the scene. Phyllis's eyes widened in shock and horror as she gazed down at the body of a woman surrounded by the broken remains of the gingerbread man that had been dressed as Mrs. Claus.

It took only a second for that ghastly sight to soak into her. Then she opened her mouth and screamed.

Sam's footsteps pounded up the hall behind her as he ran to see what was wrong. He reached Phyllis a second before Carolyn and Eve did and grasped her shoulders as she stood in the open doorway.

"What is it, Phyllis? Are you all right?"

"Is something wrong with some of the decorations?" Carolyn asked from behind him, unable to see what had provoked Phyllis's reaction.

Phyllis turned and huddled sideways against Sam. She pointed a shaking finger at the woman on the porch.

"Good Lord," Sam muttered.

Carolyn and Eve crowded up where they could see, and both of them uttered shocked exclamations. "Who is that?" Carolyn asked.

Sam turned and eased Phyllis behind him. Carolyn put an arm around her shoulders. "I'll see," Sam said as he carefully stepped out onto the porch.

Phyllis's brain was starting to work again after those first few seconds of stunned disbelief. "Don't move her, Sam," she warned. "If she's still alive, we could hurt her even worse."

"I'm going to call 911," Eve said.

Sam circled the woman, moved onto the top step, and knelt there so he could reach out and rest a couple of fingers on her neck. "She's alive," he said after a couple of seconds. "She's got a pulse."

"Do you know her?" Phyllis asked.

"Yeah," Sam replied, his voice grim. "It's that lady you introduced me to last week . . . Miz Hallerbee."

"Oh, my God," Phyllis said again. "Georgia!"

Georgia Hallerbee didn't stir, though. She lay there motionless, completely unconscious.

Phyllis saw the blood in Georgia's hair and on the porch under her head. It was obvious what had happened here. Someone had picked up that gingerbread man and used it as a weapon to attack Georgia, smashing it over her head with brutal force. Phyllis had *heard* it happen as she was approaching the door.

That meant the attacker had been right here on her front porch, barely a minute ago.

"Sam," she said with urgency in her voice. "I think you should come back over here."

He looked up at her. "I know what you're thinkin'. The fella who did this could still be close by somewhere. I ought to take a look around—"

"No!" she said as he came to his feet. "Anybody who would do a thing like this wouldn't hesitate to hurt you, too. Leave it to the police."

"They'll be here soon," Eve said from inside the house. "An ambulance, too."

That was when they heard sirens wailing, the sounds cutting sharply through the crisp, clear evening air.

The ambulance arrived first, skidding to a stop at the curb a couple of minutes later. Two paramedics got out, not running but moving swiftly, not wasting any time. They trotted up the walk, through the wash of lights. As they came up the steps, Sam moved away from Georgia Hallerbee to give them room.

"What happened?" one of the EMTs asked as he knelt beside Georgia. "Did that thing fall off the roof and hit her?"

Phyllis exchanged a glance with Sam. "We're not really sure," she said. "This is the way we found her."

"That statue wouldn't have been on the roof, Jerry," the other paramedic said. "Look, it's part of a pair. She must have tripped and hit her head on it when she fell."

"That wouldn't have busted it up like that," Jerry replied as he checked Georgia's pulse. "The cops better get here soon. I don't think we should move her until they have a look at the scene."

Phyllis agreed with that in principle, but she also wanted Georgia taken care of. With a head injury like that, her life could easily be at stake.

A vehicle screeched to a halt behind the ambulance with its flashing lights, but it wasn't a Weatherford police cruiser. Instead it was an SUV, and Roy Porter leaped out of it in such a hurry that he left the door open behind him.

"Eve!" he called as he ran across the yard toward the porch, dodging around the Grinch and some Whos. "Oh, Lord, is Eve all right?"

"I'm here, Roy!" she called to him, lifting herself on her toes and leaning over so she could look around the crowd of people. "I'm fine!"

Roy stopped and a look of relief came over his face. It was replaced a second later by a concerned frown. "What happened here?" he asked.

The question wasn't really directed at the paramedics, but one of them answered it anyway. "We don't know yet, sir; we're just checking the lady's vitals."

"I'll go open the garage door, Roy," Sam said. "You can come around into the house that way."

While Sam was doing that, Phyllis and Carolyn stood in the doorway, watching the EMTs work on Georgia. A minute later, Roy came up the hall from the kitchen and hugged Eve.

"I was so worried about you," he said. "When I turned onto the street and saw the flashing lights, then realized the ambulance was here, well, I . . . I thought something might have happened to you."

"I'm fine," she told him, "other than being upset about all this. I'm glad you're here, Roy."

The presence of the ambulance drew attention from the other houses on the street, of course, and some of the neighbors appeared to find out what was wrong. They gathered along the curb and watched as one of the paramedics leaned close to Georgia and examined the injury to her head.

The sound of another siren welled up and stopped as the first police car arrived. The driver's door opened and an officer got out, pausing to say something on his radio before he hurried across the yard.

"What've you got, fellas?" he asked the paramedics.

"Female, approximately sixty, head injury," Jerry replied.

Georgia was a few years older than sixty, Phyllis knew, but that dark hair of hers was deceptive. A shudder went through her as she thought about how blood now clotted thickly in Georgia's hair.

"Something fall on her?"

"I don't think so." Jerry waved a hand toward the gingerbread Santa. "It looks like somebody hit her with a ceramic thing in some sort of Christmas getup."

"It's a gingerbread man," Carolyn said, obviously unable to

contain herself. "And it was dressed like Mrs. Claus. It was part of a pair."

"Okay," the police officer said. "That makes it an assault, maybe attempted murder. I'll call the detectives and the crime-scene team."

He hurried back to his car. While he was calling in, Phyllis asked the EMTs, "How's she doing?"

"Hard to say, ma'am. She's unconscious, and it looks like she's got a fairly severe head injury."

"Shouldn't you be gettin' her to the hospital?" Sam said.

"We're going to; don't worry."

The officer came running back from his car with a digital camera. "Gimme a minute to get some shots," he said, "and then you can take her."

Jerry nodded and told his partner, "Go ahead and get the gurney."

The cop looked up at Phyllis, Sam, and the others and asked, "Did anybody disturb anything when you found her?"

Sam said, "I came outside and got on the top step so I could bend down and check her pulse. I stepped on some of the pieces of the gingerbread man. So did Phyllis. But that's all. Nobody else got close to her."

The officer had been taking pictures while Sam answered, snapping them off as fast as he could from several different angles. By the time he was finished, the paramedic was back from the ambulance with the gurney. The other EMT put a padded collar around Georgia's neck to protect and stabilize it in case there was any spinal injury. Then they carefully and gently moved her onto the gurney, raised it, and wheeled it toward the ambulance.

"Did anybody see what happened?" the officer asked.

Phyllis shook her head. "No, we were all inside." She knew she would be answering a lot of questions once the detectives got here, and she didn't want to have to go over things any more than was necessary.

"Is this your house, ma'am?"

"That's right."

"And your name is . . . ?"

"Phyllis Newsom," she said.

The officer's eyebrows went up, and she knew he had recognized the name. He said, "You're the one who—" Then he stopped and let an awkward silence take the place of what he'd been about to say.

"That's right," Phyllis said. "I am."

Chapter 6

The cop instructed Phyllis and the others to go back in the house and wait for the detective in charge of the case, who would want to speak with them. He stayed outside to make sure the crime scene and all the evidence remained intact.

Phyllis, Sam, Carolyn, Eve, and Roy went into the living room. The curtains were pulled back away from the picture window so that the big, brightly decorated Christmas tree would be visible from outside. The flashing red and blue lights from the emergency vehicles spilled in through the window, over-powering the festive lights from the decorations.

"This is terrible, just terrible," Carolyn said as she sank into an armchair. "Poor Georgia."

"I hope she'll be all right," Eve said. She had settled down on the sofa with Roy. He put his arm around her shoulders and squeezed reassuringly.

Phyllis moved over beside the tree and looked out the window. "I heard it happen," she said without turning around to face the others. "I heard the gingerbread man shatter."

Sam stepped up behind her and rested a big hand on her shoulder. "That doesn't mean you could've done anything to stop it," he told her.

"I should have gotten there sooner. I should have opened the door quicker."

"If you had, you might've seen whoever did it, and then he might've attacked you, too," Sam pointed out.

"We don't know it was a man."

"I loaded those gingerbread men in the pickup when we bought 'em," Sam reminded her. "They were pretty heavy. I guess a woman could've lifted one of 'em, but to raise it up high enough to hit poor Miz Hallerbee in the head with it . . . well, that wouldn't have been easy to do."

A shudder went through Phyllis at the thought of that weight crashing down on Georgia's head. At least the impact must have been quick and stunning. Had Georgia even known what was going on? She must have, Phyllis decided. The attacker would have had to be close behind her in order to lift the gingerbread man and strike her with it. But the assault had taken her by surprise and been carried out quickly, before Georgia could fight back or even cry out.

More police cars arrived, and uniformed officers began moving the crowd back and putting up crime-scene tape. The SUV that carried the forensics and crime-scene team pulled up at the curb, followed by an unmarked car with flashing lights on its grille. A man in a suit got out of it and started giving orders. That would be the detective who'd been put in charge of the case, Phyllis thought.

The crime-scene technicians converged on the porch. The man in the suit walked across the grass toward the driveway, heading for the open garage. He looked up at the picture window and saw Phyllis standing there. He pointed a blunt finger at the garage.

She nodded to him through the glass and said to Sam, "Would you go let the detective in through the kitchen?"

"Sure."

Phyllis hadn't recognized the detective. She knew Chief Ralph Whitmire and Detective Isabel Largo from the previous cases in which she had been involved, but this man was a stranger to her.

He came into the room a minute later with Sam. Short and thick bodied, he had graying red hair and a broad face that looked like a cross between a bulldog's and a cherub's face. He gave Phyllis a polite nod and said, "Mrs. Newsom?"

"You know who I am?"

"Yes, ma'am. My name is Warren Latimer. I'll be in charge of the investigation into the attack on Ms. Hallerbee." He looked around the living room. "Would you mind introducing me to these other folks?"

"Of course. This is Sam Fletcher, Carolyn Wilbarger, Eve Turner, and Roy Porter."

Latimer took a notebook and pen from his pocket and wrote down the names. No matter how many advances were made in police work, some things never changed. Latimer said, "I'll need your addresses."

"Sam, Carolyn, and Eve all live here. They rent rooms from me."

"How about you, sir?" Latimer asked Roy.

"Mrs. Turner and I are engaged," Roy answered rather stiffly. He told Latimer the name of the motel out on the interstate where he was staying and added, "I'm actually from Houston."

"That's fine, just as long as we know where to find you while you're here in Weatherford." Latimer turned back to Phyllis. "The officer outside said you found the body, Mrs. Newsom?"

"Georgia's not dead," Phyllis said.

At least, she hadn't been when the ambulance left with her, and Phyllis hoped that was still the case.

Latimer nodded. "Of course. I meant the victim. Tell me what happened."

Phyllis went through the story with brisk efficiency. Latimer's pen moved quickly as he made notes. Phyllis had been questioned by the police on numerous occasions, so she knew the sort of information they needed.

When Phyllis was finished, Latimer nodded his thanks and turned to the others. "How about the rest of you?" he asked. "Anything to add? Where were you when the incident took place?"

Calling such a brutal attack an "incident" seemed like an understatement to Phyllis.

"I'd gone to the kitchen and reached out through the door into the garage to turn on the outside Christmas lights," Sam said. "The power strip's right by the door where you came in."

"And Eve and I were sitting in here talking," Carolyn added. "We didn't know anything was wrong until Phyllis screamed."

Eve nodded in agreement.

Latimer looked at Roy. "What about you, Mr. Porter?"

"I wasn't here yet," Roy said. "I drove up a few minutes later. The ambulance was already here. In fact, when I saw the flashing lights and saw where it was parked, I . . . I sort of panicked. I thought maybe something had happened to Eve."

"That's right," Eve said. "He was very upset."

Latimer nodded. "Then that's your vehicle parked out there with the driver's door standing open."

Roy looked surprised. "Did I forget to close it? I don't even remember that. I was just so anxious to find out if Eve was all right." He started to get up. "I should go close it—"

Latimer held up a hand to stop him. "That's all right; nobody's going to bother anything with so many officers around. I'll have one of them close the door in a few minutes."

Roy didn't look very happy about that, but he nodded and settled back on the sofa cushions next to Eve.

Latimer turned to Phyllis again. "Were you expecting Ms. Hallerbee this evening?"

"As a matter of fact, I was. She was going to be leading the Jingle Bell Tour, so she would have been here when they came around, but she'd told me in an e-mail that she might stop by beforehand, just to make sure we were ready."

"The Jingle Bell Tour?" Latimer repeated with a puzzled frown.

"Yes, the Christmas Jingle Bell Tour of Homes. This was one of the stops on it." Phyllis put her hand to her mouth. "What's going to happen to that now?"

"I guess it can go on as planned with its other stops," Latimer said, "but they'll have to skip this place. I can't have a bunch of gawkers tromping around." He grunted. "Anyway, a crime scene isn't a very festive spot, is it, no matter how many lights are burning?"

Phyllis didn't say anything. The detective was right about that. Her holiday spirit might return later, but right now, it was completely gone.

"So this Jingle Bell Tour is an annual thing?" Latimer went on.

"That's right." Phyllis found it odd that he hadn't heard of it. Of course, it was possible that he hadn't lived in Weatherford for very long. There were new people coming into town all the time these days. It wasn't the small, rural county seat it had once been.

"And Ms. Hallerbee was connected with it?"

Phyllis nodded. "She was in charge of organizing it this year, and I believe she was going to lead the tour. She's been involved with it in previous years, too."

"You said you'd gotten e-mail from her. When was the last time you actually spoke with her?"

"About a week ago, when she came by to ask me if I'd be willing to have my home be one of the stops on the tour this year."

Latimer frowned again as he looked around at all the elaborate decorations. "You did all this in a week?"

"It was sort of a last-minute deal. One of the other homes had to drop out because the owner is ill."

"I see. You did a bang-up job."

"Thank you," Phyllis said stiffly. "I wish things had worked out so that everyone on the tour could have seen it."

"Yeah, I'm sure Ms. Hallerbee would feel the same way."

Phyllis bristled a little at the tone of the detective's voice, but before she could say anything, Latimer went on, "When you talked to her last week, did she seem upset or worried about anything?"

"Only about the tour. And she wasn't really upset about it, just concerned that all the details would get taken care of."

"How about in her e-mails? Did she say anything about anything being wrong?"

"Not that I recall. I still have them. You're welcome to look at them."

Latimer nodded and said, "I'm sure we'll want to do that. It may not be necessary to bother you about it, though, since I'm sure we'll be getting a search warrant for Ms. Hallerbee's computers and the e-mails will probably be on one of them. Do you know what sort of work she did, besides arranging Christmas tours?"

Phyllis didn't like the way Latimer used the past tense in referring to Georgia, but she didn't correct him again. Instead she said, "She's an accountant and tax consultant."

"We'll need to take a look at her business computers, too, then." Latimer made a note of that. "What about her personal life?" He looked around the room. "Were any of you particularly close to her?"

"Carolyn, Eve, and I have known her for several years," Phyllis said. "I don't think any of us were what you'd call close to her, though."

Carolyn and Eve shook their heads to confirm what Phyllis said.

"I just met the lady last week," Sam said.

"And as far as I know, I never met her," Roy added.

"So you don't know if she was married?" Latimer asked.

Phyllis said, "I'm pretty sure she was divorced. I heard her mention her ex-husband once. But I have no idea how long ago they split up."

"I can find out about that," Latimer said with a confident nod. "Anytime it's a crime of passion, you've got to look at the spouse . . . or the ex-spouse, as the case may be."

He wasn't telling Phyllis anything she didn't already know, but she was curious enough to ask, "What makes you think it was a crime of passion?"

"Somebody picked up a ceramic gingerbread man in a

Christmas outfit and busted it over her head," Latimer said bluntly. "It's kind of hard to plan something like that. Throw in the fact that the attack took place on your front porch, *after* Ms. Hallerbee had rung the doorbell, and it looks to me like the guy was in a hurry and just grabbed whatever was handy."

"Maybe he was trying to rob her," Roy suggested.

"Pretty doubtful under those circumstances. Her purse was still there on the porch where she dropped it. If it was a robbery, he would have grabbed it when he ran off."

Roy nodded. "Yes, I suppose that makes sense."

"It's the work of a lunatic," Carolyn said. "It has to be. I mean . . . he hit her with a dressed-up gingerbread man."

"Maybe," Latimer said. "We'll find out. You can count on that." He closed his notebook and tucked it away. "I think I've got all I need for now. Are you folks all right? Anybody need any medical attention?"

Phyllis and the others all shook their heads.

"I'm afraid our investigators will be out there for a while, maybe most of the night," Latimer went on. "You'll have to come and go through the garage for now, until I let you know it's all right to use the front door again."

"I understand," Phyllis said.

He gave her a speculative look. "Yeah, I figured you would, Mrs. Newsom. Given your history and all."

So he hadn't heard of the Christmas Jingle Bell Tour of Homes, but he did know that she had been involved in several murder investigations in the past. Well, that was his line of work, after all, Phyllis told herself.

When she didn't say anything, Latimer continued. "I'll be in touch if I need to ask any more questions. Mr. Porter, do you have a cell phone number where I can reach you?"

Roy took out his wallet and slid a business card from it. He handed it to Latimer and said, "My number's on there."

"Thanks," Latimer said as he put the card in his pocket. "I'd tell you folks to have a pleasant evening . . . but I suppose it's too late for that."

He gave them a curt nod and walked out through the kitchen and garage.

When the detective was gone, Sam asked, "Should we leave all the Christmas lights on or turn them off?"

"Leave them on," Phyllis said. "That's the way it was when the police got here, and I'm sure they'd prefer that everything be left just the way they found it for now." She looked out the picture window and saw that the crowd of onlookers had dispersed. The neighbors would have found out by now what had happened. They always did when some catastrophe or tragedy occurred, even though the police wouldn't have made any comment. Bad news always found a way to travel, and usually pretty fast . . .

Chapter 7

$\mathcal{B}$ecause of that, Phyllis wasn't the least bit surprised when her phone rang the next morning and her son, Mike, was on the other end.

"Mom," he asked, "are you all right?"

"Of course I am," Phyllis told him.

"I heard that Georgia Hallerbee was attacked on your front porch."

"Do you know how she's doing?" Phyllis asked. "I called the hospital a little while ago, but they wouldn't tell me anything."

"Sorry, I don't have any idea. According to the paper she was in a coma at press time."

Phyllis had seen the same story in the newspaper this morning. It had been pretty skimpy on details, just giving Georgia's name and saying that she had been attacked and was in the hospital in serious condition. The police had held back the details of the attack, as they usually did, and the story hadn't mentioned Phyllis's address, just the street name and which block it was. She was grateful for that. Her name had already been mentioned in connection with various crimes many more times than she would have liked.

"How about you?" Mike went on. "Are you sure you're okay?"

"Yes, of course. The man was gone by the time I opened the door."

"But just barely. He must have run off into the shadows as soon as he attacked Ms. Hallerbee. Too bad all those Christmas lights weren't on when it happened. Somebody might have seen him if they were."

Phyllis had thought about that. The timing of the whole thing had been a matter of seconds. With all the shadows from the trees that grew thickly along both sides of the street, Georgia's assailant would have had time to dash away from the porch before the lights came on, but just barely. She wondered if anybody driving along the street or looking out a window in another house might have caught a glimpse of him. It was possible. She could ask around . . .

No, the police would do that, she reminded herself. They would conduct a canvass of the entire neighborhood, asking if anyone had seen or heard anything unusual the night before. It wasn't her job.

"I'm sure the police will find whoever did this," she said.

"Yeah, and it's not your job to do it," Mike said, unknowingly echoing the very thought that had just gone through her head.

"You know that getting mixed up in those other cases wasn't necessarily something I wanted to do."

"Maybe not, but I've heard rumors that Ralph Whitmire isn't very happy about the way you've solved those murders in the past."

"Chief Whitmire has always been very nice to me," Phyllis pointed out. "He's always seemed grateful when I figured out what happened."

"That's because he's a decent guy. But you can't blame him when a retired schoolteacher catches more killers than his police department does!"

"Oh, now, that can't be true. Sometimes months go by when I don't—"

Phyllis stopped, realizing that she wasn't making a very strong argument by saying that sometimes months went by without her solving a murder.

And in this case, it hadn't even been a month yet since that awful business at the Harvest Festival.

"The detective who came here last night seemed to be a very competent man," she resumed. "His name was Latimer. Warren Latimer, I believe. Do you know him?"

"No, but I've heard of him. I think he used to be on the job down in Austin or San Antonio, somewhere like that. Real hard . . . uh . . . hard-nosed guy."

Phyllis knew that Mike had been about to use a slightly cruder term when he caught himself. She said, "He seemed nice enough. Very businesslike."

"Well, that's good. Maybe he'll catch whoever did this without any problem. I hope so. In the meantime, if there's anything you need me to do, just let me know."

"All right."

They said their good-byes and hung up. Phyllis looked out the window at the front yard. The crime-scene tape was still in place, even though all the police had been gone since sometime after midnight. With all the decorations on the lawn and in the trees, the yellow tape was actually a little hard to see. It was almost like grim tinsel strung here and there.

Carolyn was out doing some Christmas shopping, and Eve and Roy were house hunting again. Sam was in the garage, staining those bookshelves. Phyllis didn't like being left alone in the house with her thoughts. In order to distract herself, she went out into the kitchen and started thinking about the appetizers she would serve at Eve's bridal shower on the day before Christmas. That seemed like an odd time for a shower, but it was Eve's business, not hers, Phyllis told herself. It did seem, though, that they were rushing things a little, and she couldn't help but wonder if that was Eve's idea or Roy's.

Something else was odd, she thought, and that was the way Roy had shown up the night before only minutes after Georgia was attacked. He had been quick to point out to Warren Latimer that he hadn't been there when the incident happened. But he could have parked somewhere down the street, followed Georgia up onto the porch, grabbed the gingerbread man, struck the blow with it, and then run back to his SUV. After that it would have been easy to drive up in a hurry and pretend to be worried about Eve . . .

"And why would he have done that?" Phyllis muttered aloud to herself. As Roy had told Latimer, he had never even met Georgia Hallerbee, and as far as Phyllis knew, that was true. She was letting her imagination run away with itself. She had gotten too much in the habit of questioning people's motives and the things they said. Just because Roy hadn't talked a lot about his background didn't make him an attempted murderer, for goodness' sake!

The kitchen door opened, breaking into Phyllis's haphazard

thoughts, and Sam leaned in to say, "There's a lady out here lookin' for you, Phyllis."

Phyllis didn't know who it could be, but a visitor would be a welcome distraction right now. Putting a smile on her face, she stepped out into the garage as Sam moved back from the door. Both garage doors were raised to let in light and fresh air, and that was necessary because the smell of the stain Sam was putting on the bookshelves was sharp and not very pleasant.

The woman waiting in the garage, next to Phyllis's Lincoln, was middle-aged and heavyset, with short, curly blond hair and glasses. Phyllis recognized her but couldn't recall her name or where she knew the woman from.

"Mrs. Newsom? I'm Claudia Fisk. I was working with poor Georgia on the Jingle Bell Tour."

"Of course." Phyllis reached out to take her hand. "You're always one of the volunteers at the Peach Festival, aren't you?"

Claudia Fisk smiled. "That's right. I guess I have too much time on my hands, so I try to devote it to good works."

"More people should do that. Please, come in. I'm sorry we have to go through the garage."

"Oh, that's fine. I saw all the . . . all the crime-scene tape around the front porch and knew I shouldn't disturb anything up there."

"The police have promised we can use the porch again sometime, but they haven't said when," Phyllis explained as she led Claudia into the kitchen. "We'll go into the living room—"

"We can sit here at the kitchen table and talk, if you'd like," Claudia suggested. "That's always more homey, I guess you'd say."

Phyllis couldn't argue with that. She smiled and said, "There's still some coffee, if you'd like a cup."

"Please."

Phyllis poured for both of them and got out some cookies. She had plenty of all the cookies left over, since there hadn't been any visitors to serve them to the night before. Well, other than the police, she corrected herself, but she hadn't thought to offer them anything. She'd been too upset to remember her manners.

"This is really good," Claudia said as she took another bite of a gingerbread-boy cookie.

Phyllis didn't want to rush her. She was sure Claudia was here because of what had happened to Georgia, or possibly about the Jingle Bell Tour, but she would get around to it in her own manner and her own time.

"I wish I was here just to enjoy the visit," Claudia said after a couple of minutes, "but I'm afraid it's not that pleasant. All of us who worked on the Jingle Bell Tour this year are very upset and worried about Georgia."

"I'm sure you are," Phyllis said with a nod. "So am I."

"I . . . that is, all of us . . . we were hoping you could tell me more about what happened. There weren't very many details in the newspaper story this morning. I'm sort of the . . . uh . . . delegate for the whole group."

Phyllis couldn't blame Georgia's friends and coworkers for being concerned and curious. She said, "Maybe it would be easier if you told me what you already know."

"Just what was in the paper," Claudia said. "And what the police told us last night when the tour got here. By that time we couldn't even get onto the block. There was a police car at both ends. Carl . . . that's Carl Winthrop, another of the volunteers, asked the officer what was going on, and he told us that someone had been hurt in an accident. Then this morning we found out it was Georgia and . . . and . . ." Claudia lowered her voice. "The paper made it sound like it wasn't an accident. Someone attacked her. It must have been here, and all the crime-scene tape confirms it."

Phyllis didn't confirm or deny anything just yet. Instead she asked, "What happened to the rest of the tour?"

"Oh, we went on with it, of course. I'm sorry we had to skip your house. From what I could see outside, it must have been just lovely."

Phyllis sighed and nodded. "I'd like to think so. I guess now we'll never know, though."

"Unless you're part of the tour next year."

Phyllis sipped her coffee. She hadn't thought about that.

"I mean, you already have all the lights and decorations," Claudia went on. "Of course, it's a *lot* of work putting them up and taking them down. Some people actually hire companies to do that, you know. Quite a few of them, in fact, including some of the homes on our tour. I like the ones that the homeowners do themselves, though. It just seems so much more personal that way, you know."

"Yes, it does," Phyllis agreed. "I'll have to give it some thought."

"I understand. After what happened, you might not want to take part. Anyway, can you tell me more about what happened?"

Phyllis suddenly wondered if Claudia was really part of the tour, or if that was just a ruse to ask questions. Some people took an unhealthy interest in the details of a crime, particularly, in Phyllis's experience, a crime committed against a woman.

On the other hand, Claudia certainly seemed sincere, and Phyllis knew she had a history of volunteering at community events like the Peach Festival. Phyllis thought she remembered seeing the woman at the Harvest Festival at Holland Lake Park the previous month, too.

But even if Claudia was telling the truth about why she was here, there was still a problem. Phyllis hesitated a moment, toying with her coffee cup as she did so, then said, "I'm sure the police told everything to the press that they want to reveal about the case. It's really not my place to be talking about any of the details. It might interfere in their investigation in some way."

Claudia frowned. "Well, I really don't see how. Carl and the others and I—we're just friends of Georgia's, and we want to find out what happened to her."

"She was attacked on my front porch a short time before the tour was supposed to start. That's really all I can say."

"You didn't see who did it?"

"I really shouldn't be talking about the case at all," Phyllis said. "I'm sorry—"

"Wait a minute," Claudia said. She was starting to look angry now. "I thought you were supposed to be some sort of a detective. The granny who solved all those murders."

"Look, Claudia, I don't want to upset you—"

"We're Georgia's friends. We just want to find out what happened to her. I thought you were supposed to be her friend, too."

"I was. I mean, I am," Phyllis corrected quickly.

"But you let her be attacked right on your front porch."

Phyllis pushed her empty cup away. She was starting to feel a little irritated herself now. "I didn't *let* anything happen. Don't you think I wish I could have stopped it? There was nothing I could have done."

"You could understand why the people who care about her want to know what happened," Claudia said.

"Maybe you should care more about how she's doing now," Phyllis suggested. "Let the police handle everything else."

Claudia glared across the table at her. "Well, you're not anything like the newspapers make you out to be. I thought you'd have the case solved by now!"

"Sorry," Phyllis said, although she wasn't, really, not at all. She was disappointed, though. Claudia had seemed so nice before she turned unpleasant when she didn't get what she wanted. "I think you should go now."

Claudia sniffed. "Fine," she said as she stood up. "I'll go. But when you start trying to figure out who attacked Georgia, don't expect any of us to help you."

"I won't be doing that," Phyllis told her. "It's up to the police to catch the man."

Claudia pounced on that avidly. "So you're sure it was a man who attacked her!" she said.

Phyllis shook her head. "I didn't say that—"

"Well, that's something, anyway," Claudia said, ignoring what Phyllis was trying to say. She gave Phyllis a curt nod. "Good morning. And thank you for the coffee and cookies."

She didn't sound sincere at all now.

Chapter 8

"Lady left outta here in sort of a hurry," Sam commented when he came in from the garage a few minutes later. "She didn't seem very happy, either."

Phyllis was still sitting at the kitchen table. She said, "She was upset with me because I wouldn't give her all the gory details of what happened to Georgia last night."

Sam frowned. "Well, why would you? Unless she's a cop, that's not any of her business."

"That's what I tried to tell her," Phyllis said. "It wasn't what she wanted to hear, though."

"You reckon she was really who she claimed to be, somebody who worked with Miz Hallerbee on the tour?"

"I think so," Phyllis said. "I seem to remember her helping out with things like that in the past."

Sam pulled back a chair and sat down at the table. "Well, I wouldn't worry about it too much. Some folks are always gonna get their nose out of joint about something. If it wasn't this, it would be something else."

"Yes, I know, but she seemed almost angry that I hadn't figured out who attacked Georgia. She *expected* me to have solved the case already."

Sam smiled across the table at her. "Well, you do have a certain reputation around here . . ."

"What if I don't want to be known as somebody who catches killers?"

"It's too late for that, I'd say," Sam replied with a shrug. "But there are plenty worse things to be known for."

Phyllis sighed. "Yes, I suppose." She hesitated, then said, "I realize that after what I was just complaining about, I shouldn't even be thinking about this, but . . . have you considered the fact that Roy wasn't here yesterday evening when Georgia was attacked?"

Sam frowned. "Neither were a whole bunch of other people," he pointed out. "Namely, everybody else in Weatherford except you, me, Carolyn, and Eve. Since we were the only ones in the house, I reckon everybody else in town is technically a suspect."

Phyllis felt a flash of irritation, even though she knew he was right. She said, "But Roy was close by. He had to be, to show up when he did." Quickly, she explained the theory that had sprung unbidden into her mind about Roy parking down the street and running back to his SUV after breaking the gingerbread man over Georgia's head.

Sam listened intently and nodded when she was finished. "Yeah, I suppose it could have happened that way," he admitted. "But why would Roy do such a thing? He wouldn't have any reason to hurt that poor woman."

"No reason that we know of," Phyllis said. "But we don't really know all that much about him, remember?"

"I don't believe it. Roy just doesn't seem like the type, and anyway, I'm not sure he's strong enough to have hefted that gingerbread man like that. It'd be a strain for me to lift it that high, and I'm in pretty good shape for my age, if I do say so myself."

Phyllis knew that was true. Sam ran and worked out several times a week, and he did enough physical work around the place to help keep him in shape, too. Roy, on the other hand, if he hadn't been lying about his job, had spent most of his time sitting in front of a computer for the past twenty years. That didn't do much to build strength.

"You're right," she said. "But sometimes in the heat of the moment, people can do things you wouldn't think they were capable of. Like Detective Latimer said, this was a crime of passion."

"So what do we do? Try to find out more about Roy?"

Phyllis thought about it for a moment before shaking her head. "No, we'll let the police handle it. Who knows, they might find out who did it and make an arrest at any time, and then we'll know that Roy couldn't have had anything to do with it."

"Because Lord knows the police never arrest the wrong fella," Sam said in a dry drawl that made his point. Arrests had been made in several of the cases in which Phyllis had been involved, and each time the suspect had turned out to be innocent. Phyllis had been convinced of their innocence, too, which had played a large part in prompting her to launch her own investigations.

"Let's just wait and see," she said.

And hope for the best, she added to herself.

The actual Jingle Bell Tour might be over, but there were still two weeks until Christmas, so Phyllis planned to leave all the lights and decorations up and turn them on at night. A lot of families, especially those with young children, liked to drive around at this time of year and look at all the lights. They would have plenty to look at when they drove down this street, Phyllis thought. Personally, she had always considered such elaborate displays to be a little gaudy, but it would be a shame to let so much time and effort—not to mention money—go to waste.

That afternoon she happened to notice an unmarked police car parked at the curb across the street. It was empty, so it came as no surprise to her when she saw Warren Latimer emerge from the Kimbrough house a short time later. From there he went next door, stepping inside when someone answered the bell. Phyllis knew Latimer was going through the neighborhood questioning everyone, just as she had expected him to do.

An hour later she was in the kitchen leafing through cookbooks and thinking about appetizers she could serve at Eve's shower. There was also the wedding reception itself to consider. The prospect of baking a wedding cake loomed large in Phyllis's mind. Eve hadn't decided yet whether to have one made professionally or entrust the job to Phyllis and Carolyn. With the wedding only three weeks away, she was going to have to make up her mind soon.

Phyllis got to her feet when the doorbell rang. Carolyn had come back from her shopping but was upstairs in her room. Sam was out in the garage putting the finishing touches on that staining job. Phyllis was the closest one to the door.

When she opened it, she found Detective Latimer standing there, rolling up crime-scene tape around his left hand. Phyllis opened the storm door and said, "Hello, Detective. I take it this means I can have my front porch back?"

"Yeah, we're through with it," he said with a nod. "We have

photos of everything, and the forensics team has gone over it and collected all the evidence there is to find. I just wanted to let you know."

"Would you like to come in and have a cup of coffee?"

"I don't know; I've got things to do . . ."

Phyllis smiled. "There are plenty of cookies, too."

Latimer laughed. "You talked me into it." Awkwardly, he stuffed the balled-up crime-scene tape in his pocket.

When he smiled, he looked less like a bulldog and more like a cherub, Phyllis noticed.

Latimer sat down on the sofa in the living room while Phyllis brought a cup of coffee and a plate of assorted cookies from the kitchen. She placed the cup and plate on the table in front of the sofa and took a couple of the cookies for herself. As she sat down in one of the armchairs, she said, "I saw you canvassing the neighborhood a while ago."

"You don't miss much, do you?" Latimer asked. He picked up the coffee and took a sip. "This is really good."

"Thank you."

"But you can't ply me with coffee and cookies and find out how the investigation is going," he said.

Phyllis thought about whether to be angry at his comment and decided to smile instead. "Is that what you think I'm doing?"

He picked up one of the lime snowflake cookies. "I've heard about you. Isabel Largo says you like to get involved."

"Sometimes I haven't had any choice."

"People always have choices," Latimer said. "Somebody chose to bust that dressed-up gingerbread man over Ms. Hallerbee's head."

"You're a plainspoken man, aren't you?"

The detective's heavy shoulders rose and fell in a shrug. "I've just never seen any point in beating around the bush. If you want to ask me something, Mrs. Newsom, just ask it. Maybe I'll answer, and maybe I won't."

"What I really want to know is how Georgia is doing. Has she regained consciousness?"

Latimer looked at her for a couple of seconds, then obviously decided to answer. "No, she's still in a coma. I wish she wasn't. If she came to, she might be able to tell us who attacked her."

"Do you think she actually saw him? I thought he came up from behind her."

Latimer swallowed the bite of cookie he'd been chewing. "He did, but think about where she would have been standing when she rang your doorbell. The gingerbread men decorations were on both sides of her, not more than a couple of feet away. Nobody could have come close enough to reach down beside her and pick up the one dressed like Mrs. Claus without her being aware of it."

"And when that happened, the natural thing would be for her to turn and look," Phyllis said. She was picturing the scene in her mind, not because she actually wanted to but because she couldn't help herself. "The porch light wasn't on, and neither were the Christmas lights. But the curtains were open on the narrow windows beside the door, so some light from inside would fall onto the porch from them. Georgia might have had time to see whoever picked up the gingerbread man."

Latimer nodded. "That's my thinking. And that's why there's an officer in the ICU with her around the clock. If she wakes up, I want somebody there to question her as soon as possible."

"And to keep the attacker from trying again to kill her."

"That, too," Latimer agreed. "He has to know that as long as she's alive, she represents a threat to him."

"Why are you telling me all this?" Phyllis asked. "I was under the impression that Chief Whitmire really doesn't want me mixed up in this case."

"The chief hasn't given me any orders about you, if that's what you're thinking. And I believe in being reasonable about things. I haven't told you anything you didn't already know, except that Ms. Hallerbee is still unconscious. I mean, good grief, you were right on the other side of the door when it happened, and you saw the scene when it was fresh. I've heard enough about you to know that you'd already figured out everything we talked about."

Phyllis had seen the immediate aftermath of the attack, all right. It was imprinted on her brain with more clarity than she would have liked. Georgia had been lying at an angle across the porch, her body twisted some but generally on her right side, and that was the side of her head that had the most blood on it, too.

"She turned toward him and probably opened her mouth to say something or to cry out, but he hit her before she could make a sound," Phyllis mused, watching the scene play out in her head like something from a movie. "The impact was enough to make her turn back the other way and fall. The blow was a glancing one, though. If it came straight down on top of her head, she would have crumpled without turning. Which means that the attacker wasn't tall enough, or strong enough, to get the gingerbread man all the way over Georgia's head."

Latimer nodded. "That's the way I see it, too. We're looking for somebody as tall as Ms. Hallerbee or probably a little taller, but not somebody who would tower over her."

"Georgia is fairly tall," Phyllis pointed out. "But a man who was six feet tall would be big enough to strike her that way."

"Doesn't rule out very many people, does it?" Latimer asked. He took another drink of his coffee.

"No, but it helps. You can eliminate men who are shorter than, say, five-eight."

"And women shorter than that."

Phyllis frowned. "Do you really think a woman would be strong enough to lift that gingerbread man? I've been going under the assumption that the attacker had to be a man."

"That's more likely, sure, but there are plenty of women who are pretty strong. Stronger than some guys."

Phyllis couldn't deny that. It still seemed far-fetched to her, though, that a woman would carry out such a vicious attack.

But as she had seen demonstrated on numerous occasions, you never actually knew what people were capable of until they were pushed into a corner . . .

"These are really good cookies," Latimer went on.

"Take some of them with you if you'd like," Phyllis offered out of habit.

"Thanks. I'll do that."

"Would you let me know if you find out anything else, Detective?"

Latimer shook his head. "No. Sorry. If there are any new developments, you'll hear about them when we announce them to the press."

For a second, Phyllis thought about taking back the cookie offer. But instead she said, "Will you at least notify me if there's any change in Georgia's condition?"

"I can't do that, either. You're not a family member. There

are privacy laws, you know. I shouldn't have told you as much as I did before."

"Fine."

"Can I still have the cookies?"

She couldn't help but laugh. He must have read her mind. "Of course," she told him.

"Thanks again," Latimer said as he got to his feet with a couple of cookies in his hand. "You're not going anywhere for the holidays, are you? Just in case we need to get in touch with you again, I mean."

"No, I'll be right here," Phyllis said. "We all will."

"That's good." Latimer gave her a polite nod and went to the front door. "I'll see myself out."

The door closed behind him. Phyllis sighed and shook her head.

What was the world coming to when you couldn't get confidential information out of a police detective by bribing him with lime snowflake cookies?

Chapter 9

Over the next few nights, Phyllis's prediction turned out to be true. Traffic picked up considerably on the street, and most of the cars slowed down to a crawl as they passed in front of the house. Sometimes more than a dozen vehicles would be lined up as people took advantage of the opportunity to see the magnificent display of lights and decorations.

At least, that was how Phyllis preferred to think of it. Carolyn, as usual, was more cynical about the situation, insisting that at least some of the onlookers were there to gawk in morbid fascination at the house where a woman had been attacked.

One afternoon when Eve came in after being out with Roy all day, Phyllis could tell immediately that her old friend was upset, even angry. Since it was unusual to see Eve ever get mad about anything, when Phyllis met her at the bottom of the stairs and saw the tight lines in which Eve's face was set, she put a hand on Eve's arm and said, "Oh, dear. What is it?"

Eve had taken off her coat when she came inside. The weather had turned chilly and blustery, which wasn't at all unusual for December. Phyllis hoped it was the cold wind that had put so much color in Eve's cheeks, but she was afraid that wasn't the case.

"It's nothing," Eve said. "I'm fine."

"I can tell that you're not. Would you like to talk about it?"

Eve opened her mouth, and Phyllis could tell that she was about to repeat her claim that everything was fine. But then Eve changed her mind, closed her mouth, and sighed.

"That man is just so *infuriating* sometimes," she said.

"You're talking about Roy?"

"Well, I'm certainly not talking about Sam. You don't know how lucky you are to have had somebody reasonable like Sam fall for you, instead of a . . . a pigheaded old codger like Roy!"

Phyllis didn't know whether she was more shocked to hear Eve describe her fiancé as a pigheaded old codger or to hear her characterize the friendship she shared with Sam in that manner. After a moment she said, "I don't know that I'd go so far as to say that Sam fell for me—"

"Oh, please. I've seen the two of you smooching when you think that nobody's around. Lord knows what *else* goes on. But you shouldn't think it's some sort of big secret that you have a boyfriend."

Phyllis didn't know whether to be angry, scandalized, or amused, but she was leaning toward angry. Keeping her voice cool and calm, she said, "You're starting to sound like those eighth graders I used to teach history to, Eve."

Eve started to say something, then stopped herself again. "You're right," she told Phyllis. "I'm just upset. It's none of my business whether you and Sam are friends, or just how friendly you are. Roy's just got me so . . . so flustered."

"No one's in the living room right now," Phyllis said. "Why don't we go talk about it?"

Eve considered the suggestion for a moment before nodding. "Maybe that's exactly what I need," she said.

She draped her coat over one of the newel posts at the bottom of the stairs and went into the living room with Phyllis. They both sat on the sofa. Eve started to say something, stopped, then started again.

"You know Roy and I have been looking for a house."

Phyllis nodded. "Of course."

"And we haven't found anything."

"I know."

"We can afford whatever we want, you understand . . . well, within reason, anyway . . . so that's not the issue. We're just having trouble finding something we both like. Or maybe I should say, something that Roy likes. Some of the houses we've looked at would probably work out all right, but he always finds enough wrong with them that he says it wouldn't be a good idea to buy them."

"It sounds like he's just trying to find the best possible place for the two of you to be happy," Phyllis said. She was going to opt for giving Roy the benefit of the doubt here. When a couple was fighting, the worst thing you could do was agree with one of them that the other was totally wrong, morally deficient, and an absolute jerk. That sort of thing *always* came back to haunt a friendship.

"That's what he tells me, but I don't know . . . I just don't know." Eve looked at Phyllis with pain in her eyes and said, "I'm starting to wonder if he really wants to marry me after all. Maybe this is just his way of getting out of it."

Phyllis shook her head. "I don't believe that for a second. I've seen the way Roy looks at you. He's devoted to you."

"I'd like to think so, but I'm not sure anymore."

"Anyway, this doesn't have to be an issue. We've talked about this. If you don't find just the right house before the wedding, the two of you can stay here after you get back from your honeymoon. It's obvious that we have plenty of room here, and anyway, Sam would probably enjoy having another man around for a while, after being stuck in this henhouse for the past three years."

"That's another thing," Eve said. "Roy doesn't want to stay here. He's stuck on the idea of us getting an apartment if we don't find a house in time. I've lived in apartments, Phyllis. I don't like them very much. They never really feel like home. I like being in a *house*. I suppose we could rent one, but it would still feel like someone else's place."

Phyllis patted her arm. "Maybe if I talked to Roy about the two of you staying here—"

Eve shook her head and said, "That wouldn't do any good. He'd be nice about it, but he's awfully stubborn. Mule headed, in fact."

"Well, then, what about Sam?" Phyllis knew that Sam might not appreciate being volunteered for the job of talking some sense into Roy Porter's head, but he would understand.

"I don't know . . ."

"You should let him give it a try, anyway. I'm sure he wouldn't mind."

"You think so?"

"Didn't I just say I was sure of it?" Phyllis squeezed Eve's arm. "You've just got a lot on your mind right now. There's too much for any sane person to keep up with, what with all these shower and wedding preparations."

"You're doing most of it," Eve pointed out. "You and Carolyn. I don't know what I'd do without the two of you."

"You won't ever have to find out. Just leave Roy to Sam and me. We'll make him understand how important it is that you be around your friends."

"Thank you." Impulsively, Eve put her arms around Phyllis and gave her a hug. "I just hope you're right."

"I know I am."

After Eve had gone upstairs, though, Phyllis sat there and thought that she wasn't nearly as confident as she had sounded. She didn't have any right to interfere in what went on between Eve and Roy. If they were going to be married, they needed to be working out their own problems.

On the other hand, Eve was her friend and had been for years, and she told herself that she had every right to do what she could to help Eve be happy. Phyllis didn't know how long Roy had been a widower. Maybe he had forgotten how important it was to be able to compromise in a marriage. Goodness knows she and Kenny hadn't agreed on everything, but they had been able to work things out so that neither of them ever had to draw a line in the sand or issue ultimatums. That was no way for a marriage to be.

Besides, Phyllis found something vaguely troubling about this whole situation. She had seen enough to know that men with abusive personalities tried to isolate their wives and keep them away from their friends. She was sure that wasn't what Roy was trying to do here by insisting that he and Eve live in an apartment instead of staying here, but it was still worrisome.

Of course, if the two of them had bought a house and moved into it after the wedding, she never would have thought anything about it, Phyllis reminded herself. Maybe she was creating problems where none really existed.

Those thoughts were going through her mind when Sam

spoke up from the door into the hall. "You look like you're a million miles away, Phyllis," he said as he lounged there with a shoulder propped against the doorjamb. He straightened abruptly as a thought obviously occurred to him. "Son of a gun," he said. "You've solved the case. You know who busted that gingerbread man over Miz Hallerbee's head."

"What?" Phyllis blinked and shook her head. "Oh. No. I don't have any idea. That's not what I was thinking about at all."

"Sorry. It's just that when you get that faraway look on your face, you're usually thinkin' about the solution to some crime."

"Not this time," Phyllis said as she got to her feet without offering any explanation about what she had been pondering. She would talk to Sam about Eve's dilemma with Roy later. "Maybe you don't know me as well as you think you do, Sam Fletcher."

Boyfriend, indeed!

The usual parade of cars crept by in the street that night. Phyllis ignored them for the most part. She was glad that people seemed to be enjoying the lights and decorations, but that was as far as it went.

But it was hard to ignore the car that pulled into her driveway and parked while she was looking out the picture window at the long line of headlights. This was a new wrinkle. Maybe whoever was inside wanted to get a close-up look at the decorations.

The man who got out of the car and walked toward the front porch didn't seem to care about the decorations, though. Distractedly, he stepped around the ones that were in his way and came up the steps to the porch. Phyllis was already on her way to the door when the bell rang.

Her breath caught in her throat as she approached the door. She couldn't help but remember in vivid detail what had happened several nights earlier. Even though she knew it was crazy, she halfway expected to hear another crash from outside and jerk the door open to find a body crumpled on her porch.

Of course, there was no crash, and when she opened the door, she found a tall, well-built man in his late forties standing there. He had close-cropped, graying brown hair and a slightly angular jaw. He wore a business suit, but the tie around his neck was loosened and he looked tired and upset about something. Phyllis also thought he looked vaguely familiar, but she couldn't place him.

"Yes, can I help you?" she asked through the storm door without opening it. The latch was fastened, so he couldn't open it without going to some effort.

"Mrs. Newsom? Do you remember me? I'm Carl Winthrop."

The name came back to her right away. Claudia Fisk had mentioned it during her ill-fated visit a few days earlier. Carl Winthrop was one of the volunteer organizers of the Jingle Bell Tour, as well. And now that she had seen him, Phyllis knew him for another reason. One of his daughters had been in Phyllis's history class, about ten years earlier. The girl's name was . . . Donna—that was it. Donna Winthrop.

"Of course," Phyllis said as she reached down and unfastened the latch so she could open the storm door. "Won't you come in, Mr. Winthrop? How are you?"

"All right, I guess," he said, still clearly distracted as he stepped into the foyer. "I hate to bother you, especially this late and at this time of year . . ."

"It's no bother," Phyllis assured him. She gestured toward

the throng of cars in the street. "Things won't get peaceful around here until much later in the evening."

"Yeah, people like to look at lights," he agreed. "I used to take my kids, when they were little."

"How's Donna these days?"

"You remember her?"

"Of course. I remember all my students."

That wasn't actually true. Phyllis recalled a lot of her students, particularly the very good ones and the very bad ones—Donna Winthrop had been a good one—but she did not remember all of them by any means. But remembering every student was an illusion teachers liked to maintain.

"She's doing fine," Winthrop said. "She's married now, lives in Grapevine. Got a couple of kids of her own." He smiled. "I get to play grandpa every now and then."

"It's wonderful, isn't it?"

"Sure is." The smile went away and he grew solemn again. "But that's not why I stopped by here tonight. It's about Georgia Hallerbee."

"Oh, dear." Phyllis felt the floor seeming to sink under her feet. "You don't have bad news, do you? She's not . . ."

Winthrop shook his head. "No, no, she's still in a coma, as far as I know. That's terrible enough."

"Yes, of course. My goodness, where are my manners?" Phyllis gestured toward the living room. "Let's go and sit down. Would you like something to drink?"

She didn't offer the cookies this time. Carl Winthrop looked too upset for that.

"No, thanks," he said as he followed her into the living room. He took a seat in one of the armchairs while she perched on the edge of the sofa. He sat forward and clasped his hands together between his knees. "I was just thinking about her and wondering . . . did you get a chance to talk to her at all that night?"

"You mean the night she was attacked?"

Winthrop nodded. "Yeah. All the stories in the newspaper have been pretty vague. Was she still conscious when you found her? Did she say anything?"

Phyllis suddenly felt nervous. She didn't know Carl Winthrop well at all, and he certainly looked big and strong enough to have lifted one of those gingerbread men high enough to hit Georgia with it. Sam, Carolyn, and Eve were all upstairs right now, as far as she knew, and she found herself wishing that weren't the case.

Winthrop was staring at her, waiting for an answer. She said, "I really don't think the police would want me to be talking about that, Mr. Winthrop. The detective in charge of the case made it clear—"

"I don't want to get you in trouble," Winthrop broke in. "I just . . . I just hoped that maybe Georgia was able to tell you why she was so upset. I thought that might help the cops catch whoever did this awful thing."

"Georgia was upset?" Phyllis repeated. This was the first she had heard about that.

Winthrop nodded. "Yeah. The tour committee got together late that afternoon to go over the route and the plan for that evening, and I could tell then that something was bothering her. I thought it was something about the tour, but she insisted everything was fine. I didn't really believe her, though. And then she made some comment about stopping by here to see you before the tour started—"

"She told you she was coming to see me?"

"Yeah, but she wouldn't say why. She just said she needed to talk something over with you. She thought maybe you could help her because you had more experience in that area than anybody else she knew."

"Something about school, maybe?"

Winthrop shook his head. "No, not school. Detective work. She said she was curious about something, and she thought you could figure it out because you'd solved all those murders."

Phyllis sat back, a little stunned. Her brain considered the implications of what Carl Winthrop had just told her, and one of them stood out just as bright and obvious as any of those decorations out on her lawn.

Someone had followed Georgia here and attacked her specifically to keep her from revealing something to Phyllis.

In other words, if not for her reputation as a detective, it was possible Georgia might not have been attacked, might not be lying in the hospital right now, desperately clinging to life.

Chapter 10

"Mrs. Newsom? Mrs. Newsom, are you all right? You look . . . you look like you got sick all of a sudden."

Phyllis gradually became aware that Winthrop was still talking to her. She made out his words over the sudden pounding of her pulse inside her head. He went on. "I didn't mean to upset you—"

She lifted a hand to stop him. "No, it's fine. I'm all right. I'm just surprised that Georgia would say such a thing."

Winthrop smiled. "You shouldn't be. You're something of a celebrity around here."

Phyllis let that go by. She didn't bother explaining that that sort of celebrity—or notoriety was more like it, she sometimes thought—was something she hadn't sought and didn't want.

"Georgia didn't give you any details about what was bothering her?"

Winthrop settled back a little in the chair and shook his head. "Nope. Like I said, at first she even denied that anything was wrong. I wish she had just confided in me. I might not have been able to help her, but that way she wouldn't have been here later on. Wouldn't have been in the wrong place at the wrong time."

That wasn't the case at all, Phyllis thought. There was nothing accidental about the attack on Georgia. Picking up the gingerbread man and striking her with it might have been a spur-of-the-moment thing, but the assailant had followed her here to shut her up, one way or another. Phyllis was sure of that.

"Well, I'm afraid I can't be of any help at all," she said. "Georgia was unconscious when I opened the door. She didn't say anything to me."

She hoped she wasn't doing the wrong thing by revealing that to Carl Winthrop. It hadn't escaped her mind that he could have an ulterior motive for angling to find out what Georgia might have told her. If *he* was the assailant, he might be trying to make sure his attack had served its purpose and prevented Georgia from telling anyone what was bothering her. Phyllis had no reason to believe that about Winthrop, and in truth, her hunch was that he *wasn't* the attacker, but it couldn't be ruled out.

And she was all alone with him down here, she reminded herself.

He shook his head. "I'm sorry to hear that. I was hoping there was *something* we could tell the cops, something that would help flush out the son of a—" He clasped his hands on his knees and heaved a sigh. "Sorry. I didn't mean to get upset. I'm just so worried about Georgia, and so mad that somebody would do such a terrible thing."

"I understand the feeling completely, Mr. Winthrop."

"Please, call me Carl."

"You must know Georgia fairly well, since you worked on the Jingle Bell Tour with her."

Winthrop smiled again. "Yeah, we're on several of the same committees and boards. And she helped out with my campaign when I ran for city council a couple of years ago."

That was another reason Carl Winthrop's name was familiar, Phyllis realized. She had seen it on election campaign signs, plastered all over the city. She hadn't even thought about that until he'd reminded her of it just now. Winthrop had lost that election by a considerable margin, she recalled.

"Georgia was very civic-minded, all right," she said.

"Is," Winthrop said. "She *is* very civic-minded."

Phyllis realized she had just committed the same mistake that had annoyed her when Detective Latimer did it, by referring to Georgia in the past tense. But Latimer had done it the night of the attack, as if it were a foregone conclusion that Georgia was going to die. Now, after several days had passed without her coming out of her coma, the possibility that she might recover was getting more and more remote.

But it couldn't be ruled out, Phyllis thought. Miracles happened every day.

"Of course she is," Phyllis said. "I'm sorry."

Winthrop waved a hand. "It's easy to get discouraged. I'm not going to give up as long as there's any hope, though."

"Certainly not."

The visitor pushed himself to his feet. "Well, I appreciate the time you've given me, Mrs. Newsom. I'm sorry to have bothered you."

"It's no bother at all," Phyllis assured him.

They went to the front door. Winthrop took a card from his pocket and held it out to her.

"If you hear anything about Georgia, I'd appreciate it if you'd give me a call."

"Of course," Phyllis said as she took the card. "And if you could do the same . . . ?"

He nodded. "Sure. Well, good night, now."

"You may have trouble getting back out into the street with all that traffic," she warned him as he stepped out onto the porch.

"Tell me about it," he said with a smile. "But maybe somebody will take pity on me and let me out. I mean, nobody's in a hurry. They're all going slow to look at those lights." He glanced around and nodded. "This would have made a great stop on the tour, all right. Maybe next year."

"Maybe," Phyllis said.

She waited at the door and watched until Carl Winthrop succeeded in backing out into the street and joining the slow procession of cars in front of the house. She glanced down at the card he had given her.

Carl Winthrop—Financial Consultant—Annuities—IRA Accounts. The card also had an address, office and cell phone numbers, and an e-mail address on it. It wasn't really a surprise that Winthrop and Georgia had been friends, since they not only volunteered on a lot of the same projects but also were in roughly the same line of work, although Georgia specialized in accounting and tax consulting. It was all a sea of numbers where Phyllis was concerned. Math had never been her strong suit.

She knew people, though—teaching history for so many years had been as much an education for her as it was for her students—and she suddenly found herself wondering if there was anything between Georgia and Winthrop other than being friends and colleagues. It was true that Georgia was fourteen or fifteen years older than he was—that is, if Phyllis's estimate of Winthrop's age was accurate—but she looked considerably younger than she really was and was still in good shape. Winthrop might not have known how old she was and might not have cared if he did. Age was mostly a state of mind anyway, Phyllis had always believed.

She tried to recall if he had been wearing a wedding ring. She didn't think so. Of course, that wasn't conclusive evidence that he was single. Plenty of married men didn't wear rings, although most men from her generation did. Sam still wore his ring, even though he had been a widower for several years.

Phyllis closed the door and started back toward the living room. As she did so, Sam came down the stairs. "Did I hear the doorbell a little while ago?" he asked.

"Yes, one of Georgia's friends from the tour committee stopped by," Phyllis said.

Sam frowned. "Not that Fisk lady again, I hope."

"No, not her," Phyllis replied with a shake of her head. "I don't expect to see her visiting again anytime soon. This was a man named Carl Winthrop."

"What did he want?"

Phyllis hesitated. Ever since Sam had moved in, he had been an excellent sounding board for her theories, and she was upset enough about the one stuck in her head now that she thought it might be a good idea to talk about it.

"Are you busy right now?" she asked instead of answering his question.

He shook his head. "Nope. I was just upstairs watchin' *Rudolph the Red-Nosed Reindeer*. That Yukon Cornelius always cracks me up, even though I've seen it thirty or forty times."

"Come out to the kitchen with me."

The two of them went down the hall to the kitchen. Phyllis didn't want the distraction of all those headlights going past on the street.

She poured cups of herbal tea for both of them. She knew Sam didn't care that much for it, but he never complained. When they were seated on opposite sides of the table, Phyllis said quietly, "Mr. Winthrop wanted to know if Georgia was still conscious when I found her. He asked if she said anything to me."

Sam's bushy eyebrows lowered, making his forehead crease in a frown. "That's sort of suspicious, isn't it?"

"That was my first thought, too, but he explained that earlier that afternoon, Georgia mentioned she was coming by here to talk to me before the tour started. Something was bothering her, according to Mr. Winthrop, and she wanted to ask me about it because she knew that I had some experience as a detective."

Sam's frown deepened. "That makes it sound like whoever attacked her did it to keep her from talkin' to you."

"That's exactly what I thought."

"I guess I've learned a little about figurin' things out from bein' around you."

Phyllis sipped her tea. "What in the world could Georgia have been worried about? Why would she want to talk to me about it?"

"Maybe she was afraid that somebody she knew was up to no good," Sam suggested. "Maybe whoever it was, was mixed up in some sort of crime."

"In that case, wouldn't she have just gone to the police and reported it?"

Sam turned sideways in his chair so he could stretch out his long legs and cross them at the ankle. He shrugged and said, "Maybe, maybe not. Maybe it was a friend of hers, or a relative, and she didn't want to get 'em in trouble. She might've thought that you could tell her a way to get 'em to stop whatever it was they were doin'. Or maybe she wasn't even sure that anything was wrong and just wanted to see what you thought about it. There's no tellin'."

"Everything you say makes sense," Phyllis mused. "Those things are certainly possible. But if she'd let on to the person that she suspected them, then he—or she—could have followed her and attacked her before she could say anything to me about it."

"Which brings up another question," Sam said. "How'd this mystery person know that Miz Hallerbee intended to talk to you about whatever it is they were doin'?"

"She told Carl Winthrop that those were her intentions, straight out."

"Which brings us right back to this Winthrop fella."

"But we don't know who else she might have told, or who else could have overheard her talking to him," Phyllis pointed out. "All these things are starting to go around and around in my head."

"Well, there's one surefire way to stop that from happenin'," Sam said from the other side of the table.

"How? Tell myself to just not think about it?"

"Nope," he said. "Find out the truth."

Chapter 11

*S*am claimed that he wasn't trying to prod her into carrying out her own investigation into the attack on Georgia Hallerbee, but it sure sounded like it to Phyllis. By the next morning, after thinking it over, she was more sure of that than ever.

The problem was that he was right. The one guaranteed way to stop all the theories and suspicions from crowding into her brain was to sort out the truth from all the false trails. Mike had warned her that Chief of Police Ralph Whitmire didn't want her interfering with any active investigations, and although Warren Latimer hadn't come right out and said it, his attitude was that she ought to keep her hands off the case, too.

It might be possible for her to nudge things in the right direction, though . . . if she could figure out what direction that was.

She had an idea where to start, but first she needed to talk to Sam again, about the other matter that was weighing on her mind.

She found him in his room, sitting in his recliner and reading a Western. Phyllis tapped on the partially open door, smiled at him, and asked, "May I come in?"

"Sure," he said as he sat up in the recliner. He slipped a bookmark into the paperback and tossed it onto the dresser. "What's on your mind? Still thinkin' about what happened to Miz Hallerbee and what might've been behind it?"

"Of course. And I believe you're right about trying to figure out who's to blame for it. But I came to talk to you about something else."

He waved a hand at the neatly made bed. "Sit down and shoot," he invited.

Phyllis sat. "Eve talked to me yesterday afternoon."

"She's not still upset with Roy, is she?" Sam asked with a slight frown.

"No, I wouldn't say so."

Sam looked at her intently for a moment and then said, "But you're a mite suspicious of him, aren't you?"

"They had another disagreement—based on what Eve said, I wouldn't go so far as to call it an argument—about where they should live if they don't find a suitable house by the time they're married. Roy still insists that they should get an apartment. He doesn't want to live here."

"Well, I suppose I can understand that," Sam said. "They're gonna be newlyweds, after all. Roy just wants 'em to have some privacy."

"Technically they'll be newlyweds. But you know good and well, Sam, it's not the same at their age as it would be if they were in their twenties."

Sam shrugged, obviously not willing to dispute that point.

"There's no good reason I can think of why Roy would be so adamant about not staying here," Phyllis went on.

"Unless he just doesn't want to."

"But Eve does. I don't like the way he's trying to control her."

"Isn't she tryin' to control him just as much?"

Phyllis felt a flash of irritation that faded just as quickly as it came. Her first impulse was to argue with Sam that it wasn't the same thing at all, but when she stopped to think about it, she realized that it was. Logically speaking, Roy had just as much right to his opinion as Eve did to hers.

But Eve was her friend and had been for years, so Phyllis didn't see anything wrong with taking her side.

"I suppose you're right," she said to Sam, even though she hated to admit it. "But I still think they should be able to work this out. I was hoping you could talk to Roy again and find out why he's so opposed to the idea. Maybe you can make him see that it wouldn't be such a bad idea."

Sam nodded. "I sort of figured that was where you were goin' with this. You know I'm not real comfortable with the idea of gettin' mixed up in this."

"I know, and I'm sorry," Phyllis said. "But Eve's happiness may be at stake. Men who . . . who isolate their wives from their friends sometimes don't treat them very well in other ways, too."

Sam looked dubious. "Roy doesn't seem like that sort of fella at all." He sighed. "You could be right, though. And Eve's my friend, too, so I want what's best for her. I'll talk to Roy, soon as I get a chance. It's kind of hard to catch him when Eve's not around, though."

"I'll think about that," Phyllis said. "Maybe I can arrange something to make it easier."

"All right. Let me know."

Sam's recliner was close enough that Phyllis could reach over and rest a hand on his knee for a moment. "Thank you. I appreciate you putting up with my wild ideas."

"Your ideas usually don't turn out to be so wild," he pointed out. "Whenever you've been suspicious of somebody in the past, there was a good reason for it."

"You don't know how much I hope that's not the case this time," Phyllis said.

That afternoon, Phyllis ventured into the traffic on South Main, which was even heavier than usual because this was the Christmas season and people were out shopping. She avoided the worst of it, though, because she turned off before the street reached the interstate and pulled into the parking lot of a small shopping center on one of the side roads.

This was where Georgia Hallerbee had her office, between a steakhouse at one end of the center and a real estate title company at the other. The OPEN sign was up on the door, Phyllis noted as she parked the Lincoln.

A woman in her thirties, with dark hair pulled back into a bun, and glasses, sat at the desk in the front part of the office, typing on a computer keyboard. Behind her were a hallway and a window that looked into another office. The light was on in there but the desk was empty because that was where Georgia worked.

The woman paused in her typing and looked up at Phyllis with a professional smile. "I'm sorry," she said, "but unless you're here to pick up some documents we've already prepared, we won't be able to help you right now. We're not accepting any new clients at the moment."

Phyllis had never been here before because Georgia had never prepared her taxes. She had driven by and seen the office often enough to know where it was, though.

"I'm not a client, old or new," she said.

"If you're selling something, I'm afraid I can't help you with that, either," the woman broke in before Phyllis could go on. "The owner's not here now, and I'm not sure when she'll be back in the office . . ."

An emotional little catch in her voice stopped her right there. Phyllis said, "It's all right. I know what happened to Georgia. My name is Phyllis Newsom. She was at my house when she . . . when she was attacked."

The woman's eyes widened. "Oh, my God," she said. "I've heard of you."

It seemed that everyone had, like it or not, Phyllis thought.

"My name is Laura Kearns," the woman went on as she got to her feet. "I'm the office manager and Georgia's assistant. I've heard a lot about you, Mrs. Newsom. I helped Georgia put together the itinerary for the Jingle Bell Tour."

Laura Kearns shook hands with Phyllis, who said, "I wish we were meeting under more pleasant circumstances, Mrs. Kearns." She had seen the wedding band on Laura's left hand.

"I do, too. Please, have a seat. What can I do for you?"

There were a couple of wood and leather wing chairs in front of the desk for clients. Phyllis sat down in one of them and started off with the question she always asked these days when she met one of Georgia's acquaintances.

"Have you heard anything today about how she's doing?"

Laura looked regretful and shook her head. "No, the hospital won't release any information to anybody who's not a family member."

"I didn't think Georgia had any family around here."

"She doesn't," Laura said. "But she has a sister who lives in Waco who came up here to be with her. I guess she's the only one the people at the hospital will tell anything . . . other than the police, of course."

"I suppose Detective Latimer has been here?"

"You know him?" Laura asked, then said quickly, "Of course you would. He's investigating what happened, so I'm sure he's talked to you several times."

"That's right," Phyllis said with a nod. "He told me they were going to search the files on Georgia's computers. Have they already done that?"

The confident way she asked the question made it sound like she was privy to all the detective's plans. Laura must have taken it that way, because she nodded and said without hesitation, "Yes, they copied all the files from Georgia's desktop and mine, too, and they took her laptop with them. It was all right that I let them do that, wasn't it? Detective Latimer had a search warrant that covered everything in the office, he said."

"He didn't show it to you?"

"He did," Laura said, "but I couldn't really make sense of it. It had too much legal talk in it."

Phyllis thought it was a little odd that Laura could make sense of the Internal Revenue Service's labyrinthine forms, documents, and instructions but a police search warrant threw her for a loop. Of course, it all depended on what you were used to, she supposed. Laura handled IRS paperwork all the time, but that was probably the first search warrant she had ever seen.

"You were right to let them look at whatever they wanted to look at," Phyllis said. "They're trying to find out who did that terrible thing to Georgia, and we want to help them as much as we can."

Laura nodded. "That's right. I hope they catch whoever it was soon."

"So do I."

"So what can I do for you?" Laura asked. "Or did you just stop by to talk about Georgia?"

"Actually, that's true. I'd like to know if anything was bothering her in the last few days before she was attacked."

"Isn't that the sort of thing the police usually ask? In fact, Detective Latimer asked me that same question."

"Oh, it's standard for the police to do that," Phyllis said easily. "But I was told specifically by someone who knows Georgia that she was upset about something and wanted to talk to me about it. I'd like to know what that was."

"I'm sorry, all I can tell you is the same thing I told the police. Georgia seemed fine to me. She was really busy, of course, what with getting ready for the Jingle Bell Tour, but I was giving her a hand with it and there were several other volunteers, too, so everything seemed to be pretty much under control."

"There were no problems with her work here?"

Laura smiled. "No, things won't really pick up until after the first of the year, when tax season kicks in. December is busier than some of the other months because we're helping some of our clients put together end-of-the-year statements and things like that, and there are always some early birds who want their taxes filed as soon as possible after the first of January, so we were already working on those returns." She shrugged. "But really, this isn't a bad time of year for us."

"No angry clients? No disputes about anything?"

Laura thought about it and shook her head. "No, everything was fine, at least as far as I know."

Working as closely with Georgia as Laura did, it was likely she would have been aware of any problems with the business bad enough for Georgia to seek Phyllis's advice about them. The possibility couldn't be ruled out, but Phyllis thought the odds were clearly against it.

Which meant that the trouble was probably in some other area of Georgia's life. The main thing on Georgia's plate these days had been the Jingle Bell Tour.

"You said you helped with the itinerary for the Jingle Bell Tour?"

"That's right. I went on the tour, too, so I knew something was wrong when we got to your block and the police wouldn't let us go to your house. But I never dreamed that . . . that . . ."

Again emotion overcame Laura, and she had to stop.

Phyllis nodded. "I know. It's unbelievable that anybody could do such a thing to someone as nice as Georgia. I suppose the two of you must have gotten along well."

"Of course. I wouldn't say she was like a mother to me, but an aunt, maybe."

"You wouldn't happen to still have a list of all the tour stops, would you?" All the participants had been listed in the newspaper, along with their addresses, but if Laura had a list handy, that would be easier than trying to find the information, Phyllis thought.

Laura adjusted her keyboard a little. "Oh, sure, I've got it here on the computer. Wouldn't take but a minute to print it out if you'd like a copy."

"Thanks, I would."

If the motive for the attack on Georgia was connected with

the tour, that meant Phyllis would have to talk to the people who had been involved with it. The list that started coming out of the printer on Laura's desk after a few mouse clicks and keystrokes would be very helpful.

"There you go," Laura said as she handed Phyllis the single sheet of paper that contained a dozen names and addresses, including her own. "Is there anything else I can do for you?"

"No, that's all," Phyllis said as she stood up. "Thank you for the list, and for talking to me."

"I was glad to."

Phyllis turned toward the door but stopped herself and swung back around.

"I'll bet you know Carl Winthrop, don't you?" she asked.

Laura smiled. "Carl? He comes by here a lot. He and Georgia actually have quite a few clients in common. And they're friends."

"Good friends?"

Laura's face reddened slightly. "Really, I . . . I can't gossip about Georgia. She's my boss, after all, and my friend, too."

"Of course. I didn't mean for it to sound like that. I know Carl was involved with the Jingle Bell Tour, too."

"Oh, yes, he was with us that night."

Claudia Fisk had said the same thing, Phyllis recalled. That was important, because if Winthrop was accompanying the people in the tour, he couldn't have attacked Georgia. The possibility that he might have slipped away from the others, smashed that gingerbread man over Georgia's head, and then rejoined the tour seemed awfully far-fetched to Phyllis, but she didn't think it would hurt to confirm Winthrop's alibi.

"He stayed with the tour the entire night?"

"That's right. In fact, he sort of took over when it was time to get started and Georgia hadn't shown up. She was supposed to be the leader, you know."

Phyllis nodded. "Yes, I know." What Laura had just said eliminated Carl Winthrop as a suspect. He had dozens of witnesses to provide him with an alibi.

"Thanks again," Phyllis went on as she put a hand on the door. "You'll let me know if you hear anything about Georgia's condition?"

"Sure, but I don't expect that to happen."

Neither did Phyllis, but she was going to line up as many potential sources of information as she could, anyway.

When she got in her car, she glanced over the list Laura Kearns had given her. A couple of the names were familiar, but most of them Phyllis recognized only because she had seen them in the newspaper in stories about the tour. Having lived in Weatherford for so long, she knew where all the streets were except for a few. Those would be in newer areas of town, she supposed. She could look them up on the Internet and find out where they were.

Yes, these were just names and addresses, Phyllis thought. Just ink on paper.

But somewhere among them might lie the reason why someone had tried to kill Georgia Hallerbee.

All Phyllis had to do was find it.

Chapter 12

It was too late in the day for her to start now. She needed to think about what she was going to do and work out a plan of action. Also, she intended to ponder the whole situation a little more and ask herself if she really wanted to go through with investigating another crime. So far the police hadn't arrested anyone she just *knew* had to be innocent, and they seemed to be carrying out their investigation diligently. It would be perfectly all right for her just to wait and see what happened.

But things got to the point where it was just foolish to deny what was going on. History had taught her that. The need to find the truth was strong in her, and if that made her a busybody, a troublemaker, or whatever anybody wanted to call her, then so be it. If she could help bring Georgia's attacker to justice, she was going to do everything in her power to make that happen.

But not today. Today she still had other problems to tend to.

When she got back to the house, she saw Roy's SUV parked at the curb in front. Maybe today he and Eve had found a house they liked enough to buy, Phyllis thought. Maybe the problem had solved itself.

When she went into the house, though, some instinct told her that wasn't the case. The kitchen was empty. She went up the hall to the living room and found Eve, Roy, and Carolyn sitting there in awkward silence.

"Hello, everyone," Phyllis said with a smile as she took off her jacket. "Eve, how are you?"

"Fine," Eve replied, but there was no trace of her normal spirit in her voice.

"Roy, you're staying for supper, aren't you?" Phyllis asked. She wanted to try to maneuver things so that Sam could get some time to talk with Roy in private.

"No, as a matter of fact, I'm not," Roy said, and Phyllis was about to open her mouth again in an attempt to persuade him to change his mind when he went on, "Sam and I are going out for dinner this evening."

"Oh," Phyllis said. The news took her by surprise, but at the same time she was glad to hear it. That meant she wouldn't have to orchestrate the thing herself. "Well, I hope you have a good time."

"I think he wants to talk about throwing a bachelor party for me. He's agreed to be my best man, so he may consider that his duty." Roy shook his head. "But I hope not. I'm too old for such foolishness."

There had been a time when Eve would have argued with such a sentiment, on general principles if for no other reason, but not today, Phyllis noted. In fact, Eve didn't say anything.

To forestall at least for a moment the silence that was threatening to settle over the room again, Phyllis said, "Just let me go hang up my jacket. I'll be right back."

Sam was starting down the stairs as she started up. They met in the middle, and each paused.

"Took matters into my own hands and invited Roy to have dinner with me," Sam said in a quiet voice that wouldn't reach the living room. "I hope that's all right."

"It's more than all right," Phyllis told him. "It's just fine. Thank you."

Sam nodded. He didn't look particularly enthusiastic, but obviously he was going to go through with what they had talked about. Phyllis felt a surge of gratitude toward him and leaned closer to give him a quick kiss on the cheek. Sam smiled.

"I'll see you later," he said.

"Good luck," she told him.

Considering the tense atmosphere in the house, he was liable to need it.

"We'll take my pickup," Sam said as he and Roy left the house, "seein' as how I know these parts better than you do."

"That's fine with me," Roy said. "What did you have in mind?"

"How's Mexican food sound to you?"

That brought a smile to Roy's face, replacing the rather glum expression he'd been wearing. "I love Mexican food."

"I got just the place for you, then."

Sam drove to a restaurant on the Fort Worth Highway, an unpretentious establishment. "It's not fancy," he told Roy, "but the food's mighty good."

Mariachi music played softly as they went inside and were seated. The hostess took their drink orders as well. Sam ordered iced tea. Roy said, "Since I'm not driving, I think I'll have a margarita." After the woman smiled, nodded, and moved away from the table, Roy added, "After the day I've had, I need it."

Roy had just given him a good opening, Sam realized. He said, "I wouldn't think lookin' for a house with a gal like Eve would be that rough."

Roy grunted. "I never dreamed it would be, either. I didn't think we'd have any trouble finding something we both liked. It hasn't worked out that way, though. Neither of us cares for the sort of house they build these days, but all the older ones have problems, too, usually with the upkeep or the original design. For example, I've been surprised at how many houses there still are that have just one bathroom."

"I remember when folks were lucky if the one bathroom they had was inside," Sam said with a smile.

"Believe me, I do, too. But you get used to things being a certain way . . ." Roy shrugged. "Maybe it's just been too long since I lived in an actual house. I've lived in condos, town houses, and apartments ever since . . . ever since my wife passed away."

"Did the two of you have a house?"

Roy nodded. "Yes, a fine house. But when she wasn't there anymore . . . I couldn't bring myself to stay there, either."

"I understand," Sam said, thinking about the house in Poolville he had shared with his wife. When someone suffered a great loss in life, it was a fine line to walk, choosing between staying someplace familiar and getting away from all the painful memories.

And painful memories, Sam had learned, were everywhere. To this day, if he closed his eyes and cast his mind back, he could see every detail of the house he had shared with Vicky for all those years. He knew where the light switches were. He could have reached up to the bookshelves and taken down a particular book. He could have run his fingers over a place on the wall in the living room where the plaster was a little rougher and known that was where the doorknob on the front door had knocked a hole in the sheetrock and he'd had to repair it. Maybe some of the memories really had faded and he just didn't realize it, but most of the time it seemed as though they were still as sharp as a razor-edged knife in his brain . . . or in his heart.

Instead of dwelling on that, he forced himself to say, "There's still time before the wedding. Maybe you'll find a house that suits both of you."

"I hope so, but I'm starting to doubt it. I'm starting to think that it's going to be a long, drawn-out process."

Their server arrived then with their drinks. They'd been talking and hadn't really studied their menus, so Sam asked her to give them a few more minutes. She smiled and went to check on another table.

"What do you recommend?" Roy asked.

Going along with what Eve wanted so things would settle down, Sam thought, but he couldn't very well say that. Instead, he said, "The fajitas are mighty good here, but you can't go wrong with the chimichanga, either."

They decided on their orders and closed the menus to wait for the server to come back. Roy sipped his margarita, then took a healthy slug of it. "Ah," he said in satisfaction as he put the frosty glass back on the table. "That helps."

"You know," Sam said, picking back up on what they'd been talking about, "Phyllis offered to let you and Eve stay on there at the house when you get back from your honeymoon, until you can find the right house."

"I know." Roy frowned. "It doesn't really seem like a good solution, though, does it? I mean, two people who are freshly married don't need a lot of company around, do they?"

"Well, you *are* goin' on a honeymoon," Sam said, and he waggled his eyebrows like Groucho Marx.

Roy laughed. "You're right about that, of course. But I was talking more about the fact that when two people live together, they really have to get to know one another. That takes time and privacy." He paused. "Although I must admit, it already seems like I've known Eve for years, instead of just a few months."

"See? There you go."

"And I know it would make her happy . . ."

Sam nodded. "It sure would." This was turning out to be easier than he'd thought it would be. Roy was making all of his arguments for him and talking himself into going along with Eve.

"I still think it would be better if we got an apartment, so we could be alone . . . but I guess it wouldn't hurt anything to at least consider the idea of staying there with you folks for a little while."

"I'm pretty sure you'd like it there," Sam said. "I do."

Roy smiled. "Yes, but you and Phyllis—you've got a little thing going on. Right?"

"Phyllis and I are friends," Sam said as he tried not to frown. He had brought Roy out this evening so they could talk about Roy's personal life, not his.

Roy held up a hand. "Oh, I'm not making any judgments, my friend. I'm sure it's a fine arrangement for all concerned. Takes all the pressure off, and when you get to be our age, you don't really need any more pressure, do you? Bad for the old ticker."

"My ticker's fine," Sam said.

"I'm sure it is. A little cardio's good for it, if you know what I mean."

Sam was starting to feel a little exasperated, even irritated. His impulse was to defend Phyllis's honor, but on the other hand, it didn't really need defending, no matter what Roy thought.

He was saved from having to figure out a way to change the subject by the arrival of their food. "My God, that's huge," Roy said as he gazed down at his plate. "Look at the size of that chimichanga."

They were busy eating for a while. The food was as good as it had been the last time Sam was there. When they started talking again, it was about something completely different.

"Have you heard any more about the attack on that poor woman the night of the Christmas light tour?" Roy asked.

"Nope," Sam said. "As far as I know, the police are still lookin' into it." He didn't mention that Phyllis was starting her own investigation.

"Yes, they are, and I have good reason to know it." Roy paused. "I'd appreciate it if you didn't say anything to Eve about this, Sam, because I don't want to worry her with everything else that's going on . . . but that detective, Latimer, questioned me."

Sam's eyebrows rose. "He did?" Phyllis had mentioned the idea that Roy could have parked down the street, attacked Georgia Hallerbee, then run back to his vehicle and pretended to have just arrived in the neighborhood.

"That's right," Roy said. "He called me and came out to the motel one evening to talk to me. But it was actually more of an interrogation."

"Why would he do that?"

Roy shrugged. "I suppose he had to consider me a suspect. After all, I wasn't there when the assault on that woman took place, but I arrived just a couple of minutes later. To Latimer, that put me in proximity to the scene, as he phrased it."

So Latimer has the same idea as Phyllis, Sam mused. He didn't know if that would please her or not.

"Well, that's just crazy," he said. "You didn't even know Georgia Hallerbee."

"That's true," Roy said with a nod. "But Latimer still wanted to know if I could prove my story." He took a drink from the margarita. "As it happens, I was lucky. I had proof."

"What's that?" Sam asked, giving in to his natural curiosity.

"I'd stopped at a gas station on Main Street to fill up just before I came to Phyllis's house. Since I paid at the pump with a credit card, the receipt had the time printed on it. It was two minutes before the time Mrs. Hallerbee was attacked. I couldn't have gotten from the station where I was to Phyllis's house in that time, and Latimer realized that. I could tell he crossed me off his list of suspects as soon as he saw the receipt. And I'll tell you, that was a weight off my shoulders." Roy frowned. "Nobody likes to be thought of as a suspect in a crime."

"No, I reckon not," Sam agreed.

Roy waved a hand. "Oh, I'm sure he would have cleared me sooner or later. After all, I didn't know the woman, never had any contact with her, and wouldn't have had any reason to wish her harm. Still, it's nice to get it over and done with."

"I'm sure."

When they had finished up their meals, Roy leaned back in his chair and chuckled. "You know," he said, "I was afraid you were going to talk about having a bachelor party for me."

Sam frowned. "You want one?"

"Good Lord, no! I don't really know any fellows up here except you, Sam, and I don't think the two of us sitting around and getting drunk and ogling a stripper would be much of a party, do you?"

"I wouldn't even know how to go about hirin' a stripper," Sam said.

"Frivolity like that is for younger men."

"Yep."

"Now, *this* has been a pleasant evening. Good food, a drink, pleasant companionship. When you're our age, that beats debauchery anytime."

"Well . . . we don't either one of us exactly have one foot in the grave just yet," Sam pointed out.

"Oh, no, I didn't mean to imply that. But it doesn't hurt to slow down a little, just take it easy and enjoy the time we have left." Roy picked up his glass and drained the last of the drink. "Because you never know. You just never know."

Sam couldn't argue with that, even though a part of him wanted to. Roy was right. Sam had said basically the same thing to Phyllis a couple of Christmases earlier, when he told her that a person only got so many opportunities in life.

He hoped he hadn't already let too many of them go by.

Chapter 13

*E*ve had already gone up to her room by the time Sam and Roy got back. She had picked at her supper and was very quiet. Phyllis and Carolyn didn't push her into telling them what had happened that day, but it was obvious that she and Roy hadn't found a house they liked and had clashed once again on what they ought to do after the wedding if they still didn't have a place of their own.

Phyllis and Carolyn were in the living room, the steady stream of cars going by in the street outside, with people looking at the lights and decorations, as usual, when Sam's pickup dropped out of the line and pulled into the driveway. The two men came in through the garage, and as they reached the living room, Phyllis saw the smile on Roy's face. He was in a good mood, at least, whatever that meant.

"Did the two of you have a good dinner?" Phyllis asked.

Sam grinned and patted his stomach. "Mexican food," he said with obvious satisfaction.

"Where's Eve?" Roy asked. "She can't have turned in already. It's much too early for that."

"She's up in her room, I believe," Phyllis said.

Roy pointed upstairs with a thumb. "All right if I go up and talk to her? We'll leave the door open," he added with a smile.

"Of course," Phyllis told him. She shot a quizzical glance at Sam, who held up a finger where Roy couldn't see it, indicating that she should wait a minute.

Roy went upstairs, and Sam came over to sit down on the sofa beside Phyllis. Carolyn leaned over from the armchair where she sat and asked quietly, "Is he drunk?"

Sam shook his head. "I don't see how he could be. He just had one margarita. But I think he is feelin' it a little. Mostly, though, he's just in a good mood because he's decided to give livin' here after the wedding a chance if they don't find a house by then."

"Oh, Sam, that's wonderful," Phyllis said as she squeezed his arm. "How did you talk him into it?"

"That's the funny thing. I didn't really have to talk him into it. We were just talkin' about it, and he sort of persuaded himself. I guess he finally realized that he was more worried about makin' Eve happy than anything else."

"Well, you can be modest if you want, but I give you most of the credit for this."

Sam shook his head. "I wouldn't go handin' out credit just yet. He didn't promise for sure that he'd be willin' to live here. He just said he'd consider it. The way he was talkin' about it, though, I think he's gonna agree to it when the time comes."

"I think so, too," Phyllis agreed. "Otherwise he wouldn't have gone up to talk to Eve about it."

"Now, here's somethin' that's interesting," Sam went on. "That police detective went out to his hotel to talk to him about what happened to Miz Hallerbee."

"You mean Warren Latimer?" Phyllis asked.

"Yep. And accordin' to Roy, it was more like an interrogation than just a simple talkin'-to."

Carolyn said, "How could Roy be a suspect? He didn't even know Georgia."

"At least not that we're aware of," Phyllis pointed out. "But he wasn't here when the attack took place. He showed up a couple of minutes later, remember?"

Sam shook his head. "That's true, but accordin' to what Roy told me, he's got an alibi. He was buyin' gas over on Main Street just a couple of minutes before Miz Hallerbee was hurt. The time's printed on his credit card receipt. He couldn't have gotten over here that fast."

"Main's just a few blocks away," Phyllis said with a frown. "Are you sure he couldn't have covered the distance in that amount of time?"

"Quick enough to park down the street and sneak up behind Miz Hallerbee like that? Maybe . . . if he hit every light when it was green, ran every stop sign, and drove eighty miles an hour between here and there. But even if all that was true, I'm not sure he could've made it that fast."

"Well, then, it sounds like he's been cleared as a suspect," Phyllis said.

"Detective Latimer seemed to think so."

Carolyn said, "Good grief, Phyllis, you sound almost like you're disappointed. Think what a horrible thing it would have been for Eve if her fiancé turned out to be a murderer."

"Georgia's not dead," Phyllis said.

"Well, a would-be murderer, then."

"And I'm not disappointed at all. In fact, I'm glad. The fewer suspects, the better. That makes it easier to find the real culprit."

"Land's sake," Carolyn said, staring at Phyllis. "You're investigating again, aren't you? I thought you sent Sam to have dinner with Roy so he could talk some sense into him about this house business, not pump him for information about a crime!"

"I didn't . . . I'm not . . ."

Sam said, "Roy brought it up himself. I wasn't tryin' to question him."

"And I'm not trying to interfere in Eve's life," Phyllis said. "I just want to help."

"I can't blame you for that," Carolyn said. "We all just want Eve to be happy."

The sound of footsteps on the stairs made them all be quiet. Roy came along the hall and looked into the living room, smiling as he nodded at the three of them.

"I guess I'll be going," he said. "Thanks for dinner, Sam. It was a fine evening."

"You're welcome," Sam said. "Are you all right to drive after that drink?"

"It was just one drink. Anyway, that giant chimichanga soaked up all the alcohol, I'm sure." Roy lifted a hand in farewell. "Good night."

Phyllis stood up and followed him to the front door. "Is everything all right with Eve?" she asked.

"Couldn't be better," Roy told her. He paused at the door. "I assume that offer you made to let us stay here after the wedding is still good?"

"Of course it is. Are you going to—"

"We don't really know yet. We may still find a house. But if we don't, there's a good chance we'll take you up on your hospitality, Phyllis. I really appreciate it, too."

"You'll be very welcome," Phyllis said warmly. "Both of you."

Roy nodded, smiled, and again said, "Good night." He went out to get in his SUV and gradually work his way into the traffic that clogged the street.

Sam came up behind Phyllis as she stood at the door. "I'd say the evening went pretty well," he commented. "We got Eve and Roy at least talkin' on friendly terms again, and we found out he's not to blame for what happened to Miz Hallerbee. I'd call that good news all around."

Phyllis nodded. "After everything that's happened, we can use some good news."

The phone rang early the next morning, while Phyllis was still in her pajamas and bathrobe at the kitchen table, sipping a second cup of coffee. Everyone had had breakfast already except for Eve, who was a habitual later riser than the others. According to her, she had gotten up early for years in order to make it to school on time, and now that she didn't have to anymore, she was going to enjoy that extra time to sleep.

Sam and Carolyn were elsewhere in the house at the moment. Phyllis stood up and went over to answer the phone that sat at the end of the counter. She lifted the cordless phone from its base and looked at the caller ID screen. Mike's cell phone number was displayed there. Phyllis pushed the TALK button and said, "Good morning, sweetheart." Even if it was Mike's wife, Sarah, on the other end, the endearment was appropriate. A woman couldn't ask for a better daughter-in-law.

It was Mike's voice that said, "Hi, Mom. I didn't wake you, did I?"

"Oh, no, I've been up for a couple of hours. I'm going to do some baking today, so I've been thinking about that." Something about her son's voice struck Phyllis as being a little strained, so she went on, "Nothing's wrong, is it? Sarah and Bobby—"

"Sarah and Bobby are fine," Mike told her. "But I do have some bad news. I was talking to a guy I know at the Weatherford PD, and he told me that Ms. Hallerbee died about five o'clock this morning without ever regaining consciousness."

Phyllis put her free hand on the counter to brace herself. "Oh, no," she said. "You're sure?"

"Yeah, I'm afraid so. The investigation's being upgraded to homicide. I'm sorry, Mom. When I heard, though, I figured you'd want to know."

Phyllis nodded even though Mike couldn't see her. "That's right. You won't get in any trouble for telling me, will you?"

"No, they'll be issuing a statement to the press in a few minutes, so I just jumped the gun a little. It'll be public knowledge soon." Mike paused. "Are you all right?"

"Yes, I'm fine," Phyllis assured him. "It's hard because I'd hoped that Georgia would recover, but after she'd been in a coma for several days, I . . . I started to have my doubts." She took a deep breath to steady her nerves and went on, "Don't worry about me."

"Well . . . okay. Anything I can do for you?"

"No. No, I'm fine," she said again. "Thank you for letting me know."

"Yeah. I wish it had been better news."

"I do, too."

Phyllis said good-bye and replaced the phone on its base. Feeling someone watching her, she turned to see Sam standing in the doorway with a worried frown on his face. "Bad news?" he asked.

Phyllis nodded. "I'm afraid so. That was Mike on the phone. He heard from someone he knows at the police department that Georgia Hallerbee passed away this morning. She never regained consciousness."

Sam grimaced and shook his head. "Dang. I was hopin' she'd pull through. I know you were, too."

"This means a murder was committed on my front porch, Sam."

"Well, we already knew it was an attempted murder."

"And that was bad enough, but this is worse."

His eyes narrowed as he looked at her. "This is gonna make you more determined than ever to find out what happened, isn't it? It's more personal now."

"That's my front porch," Phyllis said. She shook her head and went on, "I know, I know, it doesn't really matter where the crime took place. Georgia was my friend. We weren't really what you'd call close friends, but still, I knew her for a long time and I liked her. I'm outraged that someone did this to her. It was personal to start with. That's the main reason I want find out who killed her."

"You know I don't mind givin' you a hand, if you're bound and determined to do it," he told her. "You remember what Mike told you about gettin' mixed up in an active investigation, though."

"There's no reason I can't talk to people who knew Georgia about what happened to her, is there?"

"You think that's who did it, somebody who knew her?"

"This was no random killing," Phyllis said. "The method, using that gingerbread man, may have been an impulsive thing, but whoever followed Georgia here meant to shut her up before she could talk to me. They meant to kill her."

"Which means, when you stop to think about it, that the killer was really afraid of *you*."

Phyllis's eyes widened. She hadn't thought about it that way at all.

"Not necessarily," she said as she forced her brain to think it through. "Carl Winthrop is the one she told about coming to see me, and he's been ruled out as a suspect because he was with the rest of the Jingle Bell Tour when Georgia was attacked."

"Yeah, she told Winthrop, but you don't know whether or not she told anybody else."

That was true, Phyllis thought. She couldn't rule out the possibility, or the fact that someone could have overheard Georgia talking to Carl. That was one of the things she would have to look into.

"If it's true, then I . . . I had a hand in what happened."

Sam frowned. "How in blazes do you figure that?"

"If I didn't have that stupid reputation for solving crimes—"

"If you hadn't done the things that got you that reputation, several killers would have gotten away with what they did. And more people would have died, too." Sam shook his head. "Whatever you do, Phyllis, don't go blamin' yourself, because this isn't your fault. Not one little bit of it."

She moved over to him and rested her head against his chest as he put an arm around her shoulders. "You always know what to say, don't you, Sam?" she asked softly.

"It's my rough-hewn charm."

Phyllis laughed. "Yes, you have it in abundance. Would you like some more coffee?"

"That's actually what I was lookin' for when I came in."

She poured him a cup and freshened up her own. They were sitting at the table when Carolyn and Eve came in. "That wasn't Roy on the phone earlier, was it?" Eve asked.

"No, it was Mike," Phyllis said. She looked at her friends and went on, "Georgia Hallerbee died early this morning."

"Oh, dear," Eve said.

"That's terrible," Carolyn said. "I was hoping she would make it. God rest her soul."

Phyllis nodded. "The police are going to be issuing a statement this morning. It's considered a homicide now."

"Are you going to solve it?" Eve asked as she went to the coffeemaker with a cup she took from the cabinet.

"You know Phyllis," Carolyn said. "Of course she's going to try to find the killer."

"This is going to sound terrible," Eve said, "but it's not going to interfere with the preparations for my shower and wedding, is it? You know we're supposed to pick up my dress and the dresses for the two of you in a couple of days."

Phyllis smiled and shook her head. "Don't worry, Eve. Everything will go just like we planned."

But as soon as she said the words, she remembered Sam's warning and worried that she might have just jinxed everything.

Chapter 14

After she was dressed, Phyllis took the list Laura Kearns had given her the day before and went to the computer in the living room. A few minutes of searching on the Internet gave her the locations of all the stops on the Christmas Jingle Bell Tour of Homes. She planned out the order in which she would visit them, putting numbers alongside the names and addresses.

Of course, some of the people might not be at home. In a lot of households these days, both members of a couple worked, that is, if they were lucky enough to have jobs. Phyllis suspected that most of these people probably did if they were able to afford to be part of something like the Jingle Bell Tour. All those lights and decorations weren't cheap, even if you did all the work of putting them up yourself and didn't hire someone to do it.

Sam came into the living room while Phyllis was finishing up her research and said, "I'll come with you."

"I don't think that's necessary—," she began.

"I do," he said. "You're lookin' for somebody who didn't

think twice about pickin' up that gingerbread man and bashin' Miz Hallerbee over the head with it. I don't plan on takin' any chances of the same thing happenin' to you."

Phyllis said, "I think the odds of someone else having a ceramic gingerbread man like that are pretty slim."

"You know what I mean," Sam said.

"If you have something better to do—"

"I don't."

Phyllis nodded and stood up. "Let's go, then. And Sam . . . I'm glad you're coming along. We make a pretty good team."

"Don't I know it," he said with a grin.

They took Sam's pickup. He offered to drive while Phyllis navigated. She started with the house on the list that was closest to her own house, only about four blocks away.

Despite its proximity, Phyllis didn't know the people who lived there. According to the list, their names were Dan and Holly Bachmann. Although most of the houses along their street sported some exterior decorations, it was easy to pick out the Bachmann house. It was the one where the grass on the front lawn was barely visible because of all the displays set up on it. Santa, his elves and reindeer, snowmen, and various cartoon characters competed for space with manger scenes and other religious displays. The trees and shrubs were so loaded down with lights, it looked like some of their branches might be in danger of breaking.

As Sam pulled to the curb in front of the place, Phyllis looked at it and said, "Oh, my. Our house doesn't look like that, does it?"

"Well . . . ," Sam said. "Almost. But I think these folks went a tad more overboard than we did."

"I hope so. This is just ridiculous."

"People who go on that tour want a good show."

Phyllis nodded. "They got it here; that's for sure."

Both doors of the double garage were closed, so Phyllis couldn't tell if anyone was home. She and Sam got out and went up a flagstone walk to the front porch. As they did, she couldn't help but think about what had happened on her own front porch.

As she had pointed out to Sam, though, the likelihood of finding ceramic gingerbread men on anybody else's porch was small, and there were none here. The door did have a huge wreath hung on it, however.

Phyllis pressed the doorbell button and heard loud chimes go off in the house, playing, "Hark! The Herald Angels Sing." She glanced over at Sam and said quietly, "They even have a Christmas doorbell."

"Wonder if they can change the song for other holidays," he said.

Phyllis didn't expect to be coming back here to find out, but you never knew.

There was no storm door, just the heavy, ornately carved wooden entrance door. It swung open a moment later. The woman who stood there asked, "Yes? Can I help you?"

She was in her late thirties, Phyllis estimated, based on the tiny lines around her mouth and eyes. Her body was that of a younger woman, though. It was all firm muscles and taut, sleek skin, quite a bit of which was on display at the moment because all she wore were running shoes, tight black spandex shorts, and a bright yellow sports bra. She didn't seem the least bit bothered by answering her front door in such a skimpy outfit.

Clearly she'd been working out. Her chest rose and fell

quickly, and perspiration beaded her face. Her short blond hair was tousled, as if she had just run her fingers through it.

Phyllis needed only a second to take in all of that. She said, "Mrs. Bachmann?"

"That's right," the woman answered with a nod. "If you're from some church or religious group, I'm sorry, but my husband and I aren't interested."

"No, we're not," Phyllis said. "My name is Phyllis Newsom, and this is Sam Fletcher. I live not far from here, just a few blocks over toward Main."

"Newsom, Newsom," Holly Bachmann mused, repeating the name. "I know that name from somewhere . . ." She must have remembered where, because her eyes widened slightly. "Georgia Hallerbee was attacked at your house!"

Phyllis nodded. "That's right. I was wondering if I could talk to you about her."

"Are you taking up a collection for flowers to send to the hospital? Because I'd be glad to contribute to it if you are. Just let me get my purse—"

"No, that's not it," Phyllis broke in. "Mrs. Bachmann . . . have you listened to the news this morning?"

The woman shook her head. "No. I've been working out . . ." She made a little gesture toward her outfit as if to say that should have been self-evident. "I had classical music playing. The news doesn't interest me much. My husband's the political junkie." She looked intently at Phyllis. "Why do you ask? Has something else happened?"

Phyllis didn't really like getting into it while they were standing in the door like this, but Holly Bachmann wasn't giving her much of a choice. "I hate to tell you this," she said, "but Georgia Hallerbee passed away this morning."

Phyllis liked to think she was a pretty good judge of people's reactions. Spending years in a classroom had taught her how to tell when someone was lying to her or trying to cover something up. As she looked at Holly Bachmann now, she was convinced the woman was surprised, but not overly so. A flash of sadness had appeared in Holly's eyes, too.

"I was afraid that's what you were going to say. When she didn't regain consciousness right away, I told Dan—that's my husband, Dan—that I was afraid she wouldn't make it. Such a terrible thing, just terrible."

"Did you know her well?"

"I guess so." Holly stepped back from the door. "Why don't the two of you come in? I didn't mean to be rude and leave you standing there. When I'm working out, I kind of get in a zone, and I guess my brain doesn't work too well."

She led them into the house, which was elegantly and expensively furnished, although at the moment the numerous Christmas decorations covered up a lot of it. An arched entrance to the left opened into a large parlor, where no less than six live Christmas trees were set up, each of them covered almost to the breaking point with lights and ornaments. It was like a Christmas forest, Phyllis thought. The smell of pine was thick in the air.

"Why don't you come on back here where we can talk?" Holly invited. "It's a little too woodsy in the parlor these days."

Phyllis wasn't going to argue with that. She and Sam followed Holly to a large sunroom at the back of the house, where several pieces of exercise equipment were set up. Phyllis saw a treadmill, an elliptical machine, and a weight bench with a barbell resting in its Y-shaped holders. Several large weights were slid onto each end of the barbell.

"I like to stay in shape," Holly said as she waved a hand toward the equipment. "Can I offer you something to drink? I've got water and juice." She nodded toward a small refrigerator sitting on a counter at one side of the room.

"No, thanks," Phyllis said, and Sam added, "I'm fine," the first thing he had said since they'd arrived at the Bachmann house. Phyllis glanced at him to see just how much attention he was paying to the tanned, well-toned body of their hostess. He seemed more interested at the moment in the weight bench.

"You don't mind if I keep going while we're talking?" Holly asked.

Phyllis wasn't sure what she meant by that, but she nodded and said, "Not at all."

Holly stepped up onto the elliptical machine and grasped its handles. As her arms and legs began to pump, she said, "I guess you and Georgia must have been friends."

"That's right. And you must have been, too."

"She's done our taxes for the past seven or eight years. I don't know what we'll do now. We'll have to find somebody else, I guess." Holly was able to talk while working out on the machine, and she didn't even seem breathless. She went on, "I don't mean that to sound as callous as it probably did. But we weren't close friends or anything."

"Close enough that she asked you to take part in the Christmas Jingle Bell Tour of Homes," Phyllis pointed out.

"Well, we've done that several times before. Not last year, but we were part of it the year before that."

"This was our first time," Phyllis said.

"And you didn't get to be part of it after all. That's a shame. Not as big a shame, of course, as what happened to poor Georgia." Holly continued working the machine's pedals and thrusting the handles back and forth. "Why are you here, Mrs. Newsom? If you'd like for all the people who were on the tour to go in together on a floral arrangement for the funeral, I think that would be a good idea."

"That's exactly why I'm here," Phyllis said, seizing on the excuse. "Also, I just wanted to make sure that everyone knew about what happened."

"You appointed yourself the bearer of bad news?"

"Someone has to do that job," Phyllis said.

"I suppose so. Better you than me, though." A little shudder went through Holly without slowing down her exercising. "I don't even like to think about dying. That's probably why I'm working so hard to postpone it as long as possible."

She didn't like to think about death because she was still relatively young, Phyllis thought. By the time Holly got to be the age she and Sam were, the subject wouldn't be so easy to avoid. Death was a constant companion, part of the world in which you lived once there were a lot fewer days in front of you than there were behind you.

That was one reason murder bothered her so much. Life ran its course too fast to begin with. Anything that cut it even shorter was an outrage, an injustice. The years that Georgia Hallerbee should have had left to her had been stolen from her.

"I imagine you talked to Georgia quite a bit before the tour," Phyllis said.

"Well, she stopped by one evening to talk to Dan and me, you know, to make sure we were willing to take part this year. I didn't really talk to her after that, though. She e-mailed me a few times to work out some minor details."

"Did she seem to you to be upset about anything, or worried?"

Holly shook her head. "No, not at all. She just seemed like Georgia. She was always pretty upbeat, you know."

Phyllis nodded. "Yes, she was."

Holly glanced over at her and asked, "The police haven't caught the person who attacked her, have they?"

"Not yet."

"Do you know if they have any clues?"

"They don't really confide in me, but I certainly haven't heard anything."

Holly checked something like a big wristwatch she wore on her left wrist. It probably kept track of her pulse, or the time she had spent working out, or both of those things and more. Evidently satisfied, she slowed down and gradually brought the elliptical machine to a stop. As she stepped off, she said, "Let me get you that money for the flowers. Would you prefer cash or a check?"

"Whatever you'd like," Phyllis told her. If she was going to take advantage of that ruse, she would actually have to arrange for the flowers as well.

"I'll be right back if you'd like to wait here."

Phyllis nodded. "That will be fine."

Holly left the sunroom. Phyllis went over to Sam, who was still looking at the weight bench, and said, "She certainly seems devoted to her workout regimen."

Sam nodded. "She's got nice equipment."

"I figured you probably noticed that."

"I was talkin' about this exercise gear," Sam said with a chuckle. "But she's a handsome woman, no doubt about that."

"I'd say that's putting it mildly."

"And a Christmasy name. Holly."

"What about the rest of the year?"

Sam shrugged. "Still a pretty nice name."

Holly came back a few minutes later and handed Phyllis a check for fifty dollars. "Is that enough?" she asked.

"That'll be fine," Phyllis assured her. She saw that Holly had written the notation "Hallerbee Flower Arrangement/Funeral" on the check. As she put the check in her purse, Phyllis went on, "I haven't heard yet when the funeral will be. When I find out, would you like me to let you know?"

"That would be fine, thank you." Holly looked at Sam and said, "I noticed you looking at my weight bench, Mr. Fletcher."

"Yes, ma'am," Sam said with a nod. "Professional interest, I guess you'd say. I used to be a high school coach. We had a weight room in our field house, but our equipment wasn't nearly as nice as this. What do you have on there, about one eighty?"

"One seventy-five," Holly said with a note of pride in her voice.

"Mighty impressive."

"Thank you."

"Just out of curiosity," Phyllis said, "did you and your husband do all the decorating for the tour yourselves?"

"Dan handled most of it. I probably shouldn't admit this, but he has a better eye for such things than I do. He really enjoyed playing the host when the tour came by."

"You didn't like it?"

"Actually, I wasn't here that night," Holly said. "I had an appointment. Dan and our kids took care of everything."

"It's a shame you missed it."

"Well, there are a lot worse things. What happened to Georgia is proof of that."

"That's true," Phyllis said with a sigh. It wasn't an act, either. She was still greatly disturbed by what had happened.

They said their good-byes, and Holly Bachmann showed them out. Once they were back in the pickup, driving away, Phyllis commented, "Well, we didn't learn much there."

"Oh, I wouldn't say that," Sam drawled.

Phyllis looked over at him with a slight frown. "What do you mean?"

"You said it yourself. Miz Bachmann's in mighty good shape. That weight bench was set up for a bench press. Not a lot of women can bench 175."

"I certainly couldn't. But I don't see—" Phyllis stopped suddenly. "Oh, my. You're talking about that gingerbread man."

Sam nodded. "We've said all along it'd take a pretty strong woman to lift that thing high enough to have hit Miz Hallerbee with it. From what I saw, ol' Holly back there looked like she might've been able to do the job."

"And she wasn't here Tuesday night when the Jingle Bell Tour came around. She said so herself. That's one of the things that's been bothering me. Most of the people whose houses were on the tour would have been home that night, getting ready and waiting for the tour to get there, instead of attacking Georgia on my front porch."

"You've got at least one who wasn't, and she said so herself. Question now is, what reason would she have had for doin' it? She sure didn't seem like she had anything to hide."

"In that outfit she was wearing, she wasn't hiding much at all." Phyllis nodded. "That was good work, Sam."

"Just call me Sherlock," he said with a grin. Then he shook his head and added, "Actually, don't."

Chapter 15

With Phyllis providing directions, Sam headed for the next house on their list. It was on the western edge of town, a big Victorian house on a hill overlooking Old Highway 80, which had been the main east-west thoroughfare in this part of Texas for many years.

"That's an old house," Sam said as he turned the pickup through an arched wrought-iron gate set into a stone wall that enclosed a large lawn. He started along the curving driveway that ran up the hill and went on, "I remember seein' it up there as a little kid, whenever we'd pass through Weatherford on our way to Brownwood to see relatives."

"Yes, I think it's well over a hundred years old," Phyllis agreed. "Some cattle baron built it, back in the days when there wasn't much between this hill and the square downtown. There should be a historical marker around here somewhere."

The house had three stories, with balconies along the upper two, and those balconies were festooned with lights and decorations. No cartoon characters had set up shop on the lawn at this stop on the tour, but there were a lot of more sedate decorations such as bells and candles made of lights. They weren't that impressive in the daylight, but Phyllis was sure they would be beautiful at night.

"Who lives here?" Sam asked.

"Margaret Henning. She's a widow, and quite a philanthropist. I've met her several times at school functions, but I don't know if she'll remember me."

Sam parked in the circle drive in front of the house. Well-tended flower beds bordered the drive, but at this time of year none of the plants were blooming.

The two of them got out and climbed a couple of steps to a wooden gallery porch that ran from one corner of the house to the other. Poinsettias sat in decorative pots on both sides of each step. Pretty little trees sat on each side of the door, with poinsettias decorating them. A number of rocking chairs and porch swings were on the porch. This reminded Phyllis of her own childhood, when nearly everybody had front porches and rocking chairs, where they sat out in the evening and enjoyed the fresh air. In those days people hadn't spent all their time in front of computers and fifty-inch plasma TVs. They had actually gotten out and looked at the world and talked to one another.

Not that she wanted to go back and give up all her modern conveniences, Phyllis reminded herself as she reached for an old-fashioned doorbell in an ornate brass setting. But it didn't hurt anything to try to hang on to some of the old pleasures.

The chimes attached to this doorbell rang a simple three-note summons. After almost a minute, the door opened and a stocky, middle-aged woman in an apron stood there. The expression on her face was pleasant enough but fell a little short of being a smile.

"Yes?" she said. "Can I help you?"

"We'd like to see Mrs. Henning, if she's available," Phyllis said. "I'm Mrs. Newsom, and this is Mr. Fletcher. It's about Georgia Hallerbee and the Christmas Jingle Bell Tour of Homes."

"Oh, my, yes," the woman said. "We heard the news on the radio earlier. Mrs. Henning was quite upset."

"So she knows that Ms. Hallerbee passed away this morning?"

"Yes." A faint look of suspicion came into the woman's eyes. "Why exactly are you here?"

Before Phyllis could answer, another woman's voice called from somewhere in the house, "Who is it, Sophia?"

The woman, who was probably the housekeeper and maybe the cook, turned her head and said, "Some people about Ms. Hallerbee, ma'am."

"Well, bring them in."

Sophia shrugged and held out a hand. "Won't you come in? Mrs. Henning is in the parlor."

A massive Christmas tree took up what seemed like half the parlor. The room was furnished with antiques, which suited the house's age . . . and its occupant's age as well, Phyllis thought. Margaret Henning had to be close to ninety, but her eyes were sharp and intelligent as she sat on a claw-footed divan with a Christmas quilt tucked around the lower half of her body. She had gray hair and wore a dark green dressing gown.

"Phyllis!" she said as the visitors came into the room. "It is so good to see you again."

That took Phyllis by surprise. It had been five years or more since she had seen Mrs. Henning, but the woman remembered her.

Not only that, but Mrs. Henning went on, "I was so sorry to hear about Mattie Harris. How are Carolyn and Eve?"

"They're both fine," Phyllis said. "In fact, Eve is about to get married again."

"I can't say as I'm surprised."

Phyllis went on, "I don't believe you've met my friend Sam Fletcher."

"Indeed I have not." Mrs. Henning's tone was crisp, and even though she had lived in Texas for decades, she still had her New England accent. Phyllis had heard that the late Thomas Henning, a very successful businessman who had inherited a string of farm equipment dealerships and made them even more profitable, had met his future bride while he was attending Yale as a young man. He had married Margaret there and brought her back to Texas with him. She held out a thin, somewhat bony hand to Sam and went on, "I am pleased to meet you, Mr. Fletcher."

"Call me Sam," he said as he gently shook her hand. "It's my pleasure, ma'am."

"My, you are a tall one, aren't you?"

Sam grinned. "Yes, ma'am. I used to play and coach basketball."

"I thought you must be a former teacher if you were here with Phyllis. My husband and I were quite devoted to the schools, you know, even though we did not have any children of our own."

"We always appreciated the donations you made," Phyllis

said. "There was never enough money in the budget for everything we needed."

Mrs. Henning gave a little snort. "There never is, according to those bureaucrats and bean counters who run things. People have to take up the slack when they can." She paused. "But you're here about poor Georgia. Please, sit down."

They sat in armchairs that matched the divan. Mrs. Henning went on, "If you are here to break the bad news, I've already heard. I was afraid the poor dear was not going to make it."

"We're visiting all the people who were part of the Jingle Bell Tour this year and taking up a collection for some flowers for the funeral," Phyllis explained, getting the excuse out of the way early this time.

"That is a very good idea." Mrs. Henning turned to the housekeeper, who was standing just inside the parlor. "Sophia, write these people a check for . . ." She looked at Phyllis.

"Whatever you'd like to donate will be fine," Phyllis said.

"Make it a hundred dollars."

"Fifty would be all right."

Mrs. Henning shook her head. "A hundred it is. I can afford it, my dear. And it is worth a lot more than that to express my sorrow at Georgia's passing."

Sophia left the room, and Phyllis said to Mrs. Henning, "Were you and Georgia good friends?"

"Oh, my, yes. She came by here at least once a month. She brought me flowers, little gifts, things like that, but those were just excuses, I think. She was checking on me, making sure that I was doing all right."

"Why would she do that? Just because you were friends?"

"Well, that and the fact that we were related, you know."

Phyllis shook her head. "No, I didn't know that. I don't think I ever heard her mention it."

"Well, it was by marriage, and it was a distant relation, at that. Her grandfather and my husband's father were second cousins, or something like that. So she wasn't a blood relative to me, but I still considered her part of the family, you know, out of respect for Thomas."

"I didn't know that at all," Phyllis said. "Of course, Georgia and I weren't really close. I liked her, though, and I hate to think about what happened to her."

"Especially since it happened on your front porch," Mrs. Henning said. "I keep up with the news. A dreadful thing, just dreadful. You didn't get to take part in the tour after all, did you?"

Phyllis shook her head. "No, Georgia was attacked before the tour got there, and by the time it did, the police had our entire block closed off."

"I am sure your house was decorated just lovely."

"I like what you did here," Phyllis said. "Very tasteful."

Mrs. Henning smiled. "Well, at my age, I do not care for gaudiness. The simple pleasures are best."

"I couldn't agree more," Phyllis said with a nod. "When Georgia talked to you about being part of the tour, did she seem upset or worried about anything?"

"No, not that I recall," Mrs. Henning replied with a slight frown. "Although she did say something that puzzled me."

"What was that?" Phyllis asked when the elderly woman paused and didn't go on.

"I do not want to betray any confidences . . . but at this

point, I suppose that is not really an issue, is it? Poor Georgia is gone."

Phyllis waited, sensing that this was a good moment to be patient.

"She said that she wasn't going to be involved with the tour after this year," Mrs. Henning continued. "She had been doing it for years, you know. I didn't understand why she wanted to quit, but when I asked her about it, she said she had gotten to where she did not like going into people's homes. She said that sometimes she found out things she would have just as soon not known."

Phyllis tried to keep the excitement from showing in her face or voice as she said, "Is that right?" What Mrs. Henning had just told her tied right in with what Carl Winthrop had said about something bothering Georgia. Not only that, but it also added weight to Phyllis's theory that whatever had been on Georgia's mind was connected with the Jingle Bell Tour and the homes that were part of it.

Sophia came back in then with the check, which she handed to Phyllis. Phyllis put it with the one Holly Bachmann had given her. At this rate, they were going to have enough money to get a fine arrangement of flowers for Georgia's funeral.

It would be even better, though, Phyllis thought, if she could discover the identity of Georgia's killer, too.

She was about to ask if Georgia had said anything else to Mrs. Henning when a man walked into the parlor. He stopped short and said, "Sorry, I didn't know you had company."

"No, that is quite all right, Joe," Mrs. Henning said as she lifted a hand to beckon him into the room. "These are friends.

Mrs. Newsom and Mr. Fletcher. Phyllis, Sam, this is my grand-nephew, Joe Henning."

"How do you do?" Joe Henning said as he came over and shook hands with Phyllis and Sam. At first glance he seemed like a young man, but that was only because he was the young-est person in the room. He had to be at least fifty, though, with graying brown hair and a weathered, somewhat florid face.

"Joe's come to stay with me and help me manage my af-fairs," Mrs. Henning explained. "I cannot get out and visit all the businesses like I once did, you know. And in these bad eco-nomic times, I need someone who knows something about fi-nances, of course, to keep track of things."

"You know about finances, Mr. Henning?" Phyllis asked.

Mrs. Henning said, "He should. He was a banker in Dallas for many years."

"I was an officer in a bank," Joe Henning said quietly. "Un-til I was downsized earlier this year."

Sam said, "That's tough luck."

Joe shrugged. "It left me free to come and help Aunt Mar-garet, here. You know what they say about one door closing and another door opening."

"It sounds like it worked out well for both of you," Phyllis said.

"Are you two here on business?"

Mrs. Henning said, "Goodness, no, they're just friends. They're taking up a collection for a flower arrangement at the funeral of another friend of ours."

"That Christmas tour lady?"

Phyllis said, "That's right. Did you know Georgia Haller-bee, Mr. Henning?"

Joe shook his head. "No, not really. Aunt Margaret introduced me to her once, I think, when she stopped by here to talk about that tour. I didn't have anything to do with it, though." He smiled. "That was all Aunt Margaret and Sophia."

"Were you here the night of the tour?" That seemed to Phyllis like a natural enough question.

"Nope. I'd driven out to Ranger to check on Aunt Margaret's store there, and I was late getting back."

"Then you missed all the festivities."

"Just as well," Joe said. "I never cared all that much for crowds."

"And there was certainly a crowd here that night," his aunt said. "Everyone seemed to be having a splendid time, too. Of course, at that point no one knew what had happened to poor Georgia, so they just went on with the tour as if nothing was wrong."

Laura Kearns and Carl Winthrop had known something was wrong, Phyllis thought, but the regular members of the tour hadn't, other than the fact that one of the scheduled stops had been dropped. Naturally they had gone on and enjoyed their evening.

She thought they had learned all they could here, at least for the time being, so she stood up and Sam followed suit. "We need to be going," she said.

"I expect you have some other stops to make," Mrs. Henning said.

Phyllis nodded. "That's right. Thank you for the donation, Mrs. Henning."

With a frown, Joe asked, "You didn't go overboard, did you, Aunt Margaret?"

"I gave them a hundred dollars," Mrs. Henning answered tartly. "I appreciate your concern, Joe, but I am not one of those dotty old women who hand out big chunks of their money to every Tom, Dick, and Harry who stops by."

"I know you're not," Joe said, "but you asked me to help you keep track of things, so that's what I'm trying to do."

"Of course, dear. I meant no offense."

"None taken," he assured her. He reached for his wallet and went on, "And even though I didn't really know Ms. Hallerbee, I'd be happy to contribute, too—"

"Not necessary," Mrs. Henning said. "Phyllis, dear, can you put Joe's name on the card or whatever you send with the flowers?"

"Of course," Phyllis said. "I'd be glad to."

"Well, in that case . . ." Joe shrugged again. "Thanks. And it was nice to meet you."

He shook hands with Phyllis and Sam again, then stayed in the parlor with Mrs. Henning while Sophia showed them out. Sam waited until they were in the pickup driving away before he asked, "What do you think?"

"Obviously, even if she didn't have an alibi, Margaret Henning couldn't hurt anybody. She's probably not strong enough to pick up even a little figurine of a gingerbread man, let along that big thing."

"Maybe she sent Sophia to do it."

"Sophia was here the night of the tour, remember?" Phyllis paused, then went on, "But Joe Henning wasn't."

"I figured you noticed that. He said he only met Ms. Hallerbee once, though, so what reason would he have to hurt her?"

"We only have his word for that," Phyllis pointed out. "He comes in here from out of town, moves in, starts taking care of Mrs. Henning's businesses for her . . . It would be easy enough for him to siphon off some money into his own pockets, I'll bet."

"And Miz Hallerbee's business bein' dollars and cents, she might've figured that out and threatened to tell the old lady," Sam speculated.

"It's a reasonable motive," Phyllis said with a nod. "Unfortunately we have no idea if there's any truth to it. But it's one more place to start looking."

"So we've been to two houses and got somebody at each one that we can't rule out. You know what that means."

Phyllis looked over at him. "What?"

"If this keeps up," Sam said, "you're not gonna have any shortage of suspects."

Chapter 16

No one was home at the next two houses on the list, and by that time Phyllis thought they ought to head back to the house so she could get lunch ready.

As soon as Sam pulled onto the block, Phyllis spotted the car parked at the curb in front of the house and recognized it as an unmarked police car. She and Sam went in through the garage, and as they walked up the hall toward the living room, she heard a man's voice she recognized as belonging to Detective Warren Latimer.

Carolyn was sitting in the living room with Latimer. Phyllis sensed a definite tension in the air. Carolyn wasn't that fond of the police, which was understandable since both she and her daughter had been accused of murder at one time or another. Things like that tended to put a strain on a relationship.

Detective Latimer got to his feet and nodded to Phyllis. "Good morning, Mrs. Newsom," he said. "I wish I was here on a more pleasant errand."

"You came to tell me that Georgia Hallerbee is dead," Phyllis said.

Latimer nodded. "I figured you might have heard the news by now, but I wanted to notify you officially."

Phyllis didn't say anything about Mike telling her before the police even released the information. She didn't want to get her son in any trouble. Georgia's death was public knowledge now, so Phyllis just nodded and didn't make any comment concerning how she had heard about it.

"She never regained consciousness," Latimer went on. "We were hoping she would."

"So she could tell you who attacked her."

Latimer's burly shoulders rose and fell. "Yeah, sure, that and just hoping she would recover. But it would've been all right with me if she could have told us who to look for, that's for sure."

"Maybe she did anyway, in her conversations with people before she was attacked, or in the records from her home and business."

If Latimer realized she was fishing for information, he didn't give any sign of it. Instead, he just said, "Yeah, we're looking into that. I don't suppose there's anything else *you've* thought of that you can tell us?"

"I'm afraid I told you everything I heard and saw that night, Detective, and everything Georgia said to me in the days before she was attacked."

That was true as far as it went. Of course, she had uncovered some more information since then, Phyllis thought, but Latimer hadn't asked her about that . . . exactly. She knew it was a bit childish fencing with him like this, but she did it anyway.

"Well, if you do remember anything else, I'd appreciate it if you'd give me a call. You've got my number."

Phyllis nodded to confirm that she did indeed have his number.

"I'll be going, then." Latimer nodded to Carolyn. "Mrs. Wilbarger."

"Detective," Carolyn said coolly.

Latimer nodded to Phyllis and Sam as well and went to the front door. Sam followed him, said, "So long, Detective," and closed the door after him.

"I can't stand that man," Carolyn said in the living room.

"You don't like Isabel Largo, either," Phyllis said.

"That's right, I don't. And what do they have in common?"

"They're both cops," Sam said as he came back into the room. "If anybody didn't know you, Carolyn, they might think you were Ma Barker instead of a nice, law-abidin' retired schoolteacher."

Carolyn snorted. "That's easy for you to say, Sam Fletcher," she shot back at him. "*You* haven't been arrested and unjustly accused of murder."

"Yet," Sam said with a glance and a wink at Phyllis. "Around here, there's always a chance it could happen."

"Don't be ridiculous," Phyllis said. "I'm sorry you had to deal with the detective, Carolyn."

"When I saw who it was at the door, I thought about not letting him in," Carolyn admitted. "But then I told myself it might be something important. He hadn't been here long when you got back, only about ten minutes, but I was about to call your cell phone and ask when you were going to get here." She paused, then asked, "Did you find out anything?"

"I don't know. Maybe. We talked to Margaret Henning. Her house was one of the stops on the tour."

"Margaret Henning!" Carolyn repeated. "Is she still alive?"

Sam said, "Hale and hearty and sharp as a tack, leastways as far as I could tell."

"Her grandnephew Joe was there, too," Phyllis added. "Evidently he's living with her now and helping her manage her business affairs."

Carolyn frowned in thought. "I don't believe I've ever heard of him. One of Tom Henning's shirttail relatives, I take it?"

"Something like that," Phyllis agreed. "He wasn't there at Margaret's house on the night of the tour."

Carolyn grasped what that meant right away. "So he doesn't have an alibi for the time of the attack on Georgia."

"Not really," Phyllis said. "He was supposed to be driving back from Ranger about then. But we don't know exactly when he left out there."

"Maybe we can find out," Sam suggested.

"How would we go about doing that?" Carolyn asked.

"Gimme a minute," Sam said as he went over to the computer. Phyllis had a pretty good idea what he had in mind— what she figured was the same idea that had occurred to her—but she waited to see what Sam was going to come up with. He went on, "What's the name of the business Miz Henning owns out there?"

"Henning Farm Equipment, I suppose," Phyllis said. "Just like the other stores she owns."

After a couple of minutes of searching on the Internet, Sam said, "I've got the phone number of the store. My Google-fu is powerful."

"Where in the world did you get *that*?" Carolyn asked with a frown.

"I don't really know—heard it or read it somewhere—but it stuck with me." Sam took his cell phone from his shirt pocket, opened it, and put in the number he had gotten from the computer. After a moment, someone answered, and he said in a brisker tone than his usual lazy drawl, "Hi, I need to speak to your manager if he's available, please. It's an insurance matter . . . No, son, I'm not selling insurance. I'm an investigator."

He winked at Phyllis again.

A few more moments went by, and then Sam said, "Is this the manager? Yes, sir, my name is Art Acord. I'm an insurance investigator." He named one of the giant companies everybody knew, then added, "Out of Dallas. One of our insureds was involved in an auto accident on Interstate 20 a few days ago near Thurber, and we're trying to locate witnesses. I've got a partial plate number that we think belongs to a fella named Joe Henning . . . Oh? You do know him? That's great. We haven't been able to get hold of Mr. Henning yet, but we have information that says he was at your store in Ranger on the day in question and started back to Weatherford about the right time to put him on the scene of the accident . . . No, no, he's not in any trouble at all. He wasn't involved in the accident. We just need to talk to him and get a statement from him in the event that he did witness the accident. The date was . . . let's see here . . ." Sam gave the date of the Jingle Bell Tour as if he had just found it on his paperwork. "Uh-huh . . . You happen to remember when he left? . . . No, that's too early. I don't think he would have been where the accident took place at the right time to have seen it happen. See, that's why I took a chance on calling you. Now I can cross him off my list of potential witnesses and won't have to spend any more time trying to track him down. Won't even have to bother him . . . I sure do appreciate your cooperation, partner. You have a good day now."

Sam closed the cell phone, breaking the connection, and smiled at Phyllis and Carolyn, who looked at him with an attitude that bordered on flabbergasted.

"Where in the world did you learn how to do that?" Carolyn asked.

"Movies and TV, of course."

"Who's Art Acord?" Phyllis wanted to know. "You didn't just make the name up, did you? It sounds vaguely familiar."

"He was an actor in silent Western movies way, way back when. I figured the chances of anybody under the age of fifty ever hearin' of him were pretty slim. Heck, most people under the age of eighty probably wouldn't know who he was."

"What did you find out about Joe?"

"He left Ranger between five thirty and five forty-five," Sam said. "That's as close as the fella could narrow it down."

"It takes a little over an hour to drive from here to Ranger," Phyllis mused. "Probably less if your foot's heavy and you don't get stopped by a state trooper."

"So Joe could have gotten here in time to hit Miz Hallerbee with that gingerbread man," Sam said, "although that would've been cuttin' it pretty close."

Carolyn said, "But if he was in Ranger that afternoon, how would he have known that Georgia was going to be on the front porch at that particular time?"

"Maybe she called him and told him," Sam said.

Phyllis nodded. "That's right. If she'd uncovered something fishy about how he's been handling Margaret's business, she could have called him to threaten him and told him she was coming to see me about it."

"Why would she threaten him and tip her hand?" Carolyn asked. With a decisive nod, she went on, "It's more likely she was blackmailing him."

Phyllis's eyes widened. "Blackmailing him? That doesn't sound like Georgia at all! Do you really think she would do such a thing?"

"You never know what somebody will do," Carolyn said with a shrug. "I mean, according to the police, I killed somebody a couple of years ago."

"Yes, well, *I* knew with absolutely no doubt that you hadn't done such a thing and never would. And I can't see Georgia Hallerbee as a blackmailer, either."

"Well, then, she let it slip to this Joe Henning that she suspected him, and he figured out somehow where she would be. I don't know. I'm not a detective and never claimed to be one."

"Of course, Henning's not the only suspect," Sam pointed out. "There's the Bachmann woman, too."

"Who?" Carolyn asked.

Phyllis filled her in on their visit to Dan and Holly Bachmann's house. "But we have even less reason to think she might have done it," she went on. "The only things that make her suspicious at all are the facts that she wasn't home that night, so she doesn't have an alibi—that we know of—and she looked strong enough to have picked up that gingerbread man."

"That's more than you can say for some of the folks mixed up with Miz Hallerbee," Sam pointed out. "And you said yourself this wasn't a random killin'. Whoever did it knew her."

"We still have to visit those other people whose homes

were stops on the tour," Phyllis said. "But we'll get started on that after lunch."

Those plans didn't work out, though. Just as they were about to sit down to eat the grilled pear and cheese sandwiches Phyllis had made, Eve came in, looked at Phyllis and Carolyn, and said, "Oh, good, both of you are here. I was hoping I'd find you."

"Would you like a sandwich?" Phyllis asked. "I figured you were with Roy and would probably be eating out somewhere."

"We probably would have," Eve said, "but something came up. I need you and Carolyn to come with me this afternoon, Phyllis. It's an emergency!"

Chapter 17

"The bows are all wrong," Eve said an hour later as the three of them stood in the dress shop where Eve's wedding dress and the dresses that Phyllis and Carolyn would wear as her attendants were being made.

"I had to special-order them, and they sent me the wrong thing," the owner of the shop explained. She had one of the offending bows in her hand as she gestured toward the elegant and modern two-piece stretch taffeta outfits. The bows were to be used on the attendant bouquets and they were obviously not the same shades as the formal wear. "But there's time to send these back and get the right ones."

"At this time of year?" Eve asked. "Everything is slower around Christmas. Don't you think that's cutting it awfully close?"

"I'm sure we can make it," the woman said. "But in the meantime, since all of you are here, this would be a good chance for you to try on your dresses, so I can mark them for any alterations I need to make."

"Oh, that's a good idea," Eve said. She looked at Phyllis and Carolyn. "Is that all right with the two of you?"

Phyllis nodded. "It's fine," she said . . . even though what she really wanted to do was get back to visiting the homes that had been part of the Jingle Bell Tour.

She had to admit, though, that she enjoyed seeing Eve happy and caught up in the preparations for the wedding. Now that the matter of where she and Roy would live had been, if not settled, at least smoothed over a little, Eve was starting to relax. Only slightly, though, because no woman with a wedding coming up in less than three weeks was going to be completely relaxed.

Phyllis was pleased with the dresses Eve had picked out for her and Carolyn. The two-piece dresses were actually mother-of-the-bride outfits. Neither of them would have been caught dead in one of those strapless little dresses they had for brides-maids. Their two-piece dresses had sleeves with V-necklines that didn't plunge, and pretty jeweled buttons. The trumpet skirt was slimming and created curves in all the right places. Phyllis's outfit was sapphire blue and Carolyn's was ice blue. Phyllis even thought she wouldn't mind wearing this dress again, if she had a chance and Carolyn wasn't going to wear hers. The top would also look really pretty with nice black pants.

When they were finished at the dress shop, Eve said, "I want to go by the florist to check on the flowers and let them know the bows had to be sent back."

"I'm sure they'll be fine," Carolyn said. Phyllis heard a tiny touch of impatience in her friend's voice. Carolyn had been a widow for many years, had no interest in ever getting married again, and generally didn't have a high opinion of the state of matrimony to start with. She was willing for Eve's sake to put up with all the hoopla of a wedding, but it was far from her favorite thing in the world.

"Actually, I wouldn't mind stopping at the florist, either," Phyllis said. She explained about the ruse she had adopted in talking to the people whose homes had been on the tour. "I probably ought to go ahead and see about getting the arrangement for the funeral."

"That's fine with me," Carolyn said. "Anyway, you're driving, so you can go wherever you want."

It was true, they were in Phyllis's Lincoln, but she didn't want to do anything that was going to make Carolyn too uncomfortable. A trip to a flower shop shouldn't fall into that category, she decided.

Between the time they had already spent on the dresses for the wedding and the two errands at the florist, most of the afternoon was gone by the time the three of them got back to the house. Phyllis noticed right away that Sam's pickup wasn't parked in its usual spot. She wondered where he had gone, although it certainly wasn't unusual for him to go and do things by himself. He was a grown man, after all, and she wasn't his keeper.

For some reason she couldn't fathom, though, when she looked at the empty spot at the curb, she felt a faint stirring of unease.

He had pulled off that little scam of pretending to be an insurance investigator about as well as anybody on TV could have, Sam thought. He had even been quick thinking enough to use his cell phone instead of Phyllis's landline, so no name would show up on the store's caller ID, just the number, if that much.

Since there was no telling how long Phyllis was going to be gone with Eve and Carolyn tending to those wedding problems—Sam didn't know much about that and didn't want to—he thought he might as well put the time to good use. Phyllis had the list of Jingle Bell Tour homes in her purse, but while she was studying it earlier, he had looked at it over her shoulder long enough to memorize a couple of names and addresses. He was good with such things; directions came naturally to him.

And Phyllis would be surprised when she found out he'd already talked to some of the folks. Pleasantly surprised, he hoped. If he could rule them out, that meant less work she would have to do and she could move on to investigating the others.

Of course, it was possible these people wouldn't be home, either, he thought as he pulled his pickup to a stop in front of a house that appeared to be only two or three years old. This was one of the newer residential neighborhoods in Weatherford, and the area where the developers had come in was heavily wooded, with lots of old, tall trees. Sam hated to think about all the ones that had been cut down to make room for these houses, but at least a lot of them had been spared. So there was more foliage and shade around these McMansions than usual. Sam had never been able to figure out why somebody would build a big fancy house in the middle of a bare lot, but to each his own, as the old saying went.

He got out of the pickup and went up a concrete walk. The house didn't have much of a porch, just a place to stand out of the weather while you rang the doorbell. The door, like the other places they had visited and like Phyllis's house, too, had a big, pretty wreath on it. The yard was full of decorations, and the tree trunks were wrapped with lights. Sam had spotted Santa and a sleigh on the roof.

He rang the doorbell and waited for somebody to answer. He didn't expect that Santa himself would respond to the summons, but that was what happened. When the door swung open, the big jolly fat man stood there, with gleaming black boots and belt, red suit and hat, white beard, and all.

"Yes?" a voice asked from behind the beard. "What can I do for you?"

The voice didn't sound much like Santa Claus . . . that is, unless Santa had a faint British accent and sounded a wee bit tipsy, like he'd gotten into the eggnog when Mrs. Claus wasn't looking. And Sam supposed Santa could be British. He wouldn't know, since he'd never talked to the fella before.

"You mind if I take this off?" the man asked when Sam didn't respond right away. "It kind of itches."

"No, go right ahead," Sam told him.

The man took the Santa cap off, then unhooked the plastic loops around his ears that held the fake beard on. Without the cap and beard, he had a round, florid face that was certainly Santa-like, but topped by short, curly brown hair.

"That's much better," he said. "There are so many people driving by every night to look at our Christmas decorations that my wife got it into her head I ought to stand out on the lawn dressed like Saint Nick and wave at them as they go by. A bit daft, if you ask me, but what can you do?"

"Wave and say, 'Ho, ho, ho!' I expect," Sam said.

The man grinned. "Spoken like a truly married man!" He stuck out his hand. "I'm Alan Trafford."

Sam ignored the comment about him being married. He shook hands and said, "Sam Fletcher."

"Pleased to meet you, Sam. Now, what can I do for you?"

"I'm here about that Christmas Jingle Bell Tour."

Alan Trafford's grin disappeared. "That was several days ago. You missed it, chum. Anyway, it's broad daylight."

"I know. I want to talk to you about Georgia Hallerbee."

Trafford's neutral expression turned into a suspicious frown. "No offense, but you look a little old to be a policeman. And the missus and I have already talked to a detective. Stocky fellow name of Latimer, I believe."

Sam nodded. "Yes, sir. I'm not from the police. This is about the group of homeowners on the tour gettin' together and goin' in on some flowers for Miz Hallerbee's funeral."

Phyllis had had good luck with that story, so Sam thought he might as well give it a try, too.

"Oh," Trafford said, his expression clearing somewhat. "I understand now. Come in." As he stepped back so Sam could enter the house, he went on, "You must've thought I was crazy when I opened the door dressed like Santa Claus. I thought it would be a good time to try on the suit, since my wife and kids are out shopping right now."

Sam nodded. "You look good in it."

Trafford patted his belly. "I carry around my own padding," he said, smiling again. He led Sam into a living room. "Sit down, Sam. You say you're taking up a collection?"

"That's right."

Trafford started unfastening the black buttons on the red coat. "I don't recall seeing your name on the list of homes on the tour that the newspaper printed."

"Well, that's because I don't own the house. My friend Mrs. Newsom does. We're sort of working together on this, because I live there, too. Rent a room from her," he added, so Trafford wouldn't get the wrong idea.

"I see." Trafford took the coat off and dropped it on a sofa, revealing that he wore a long-sleeved knit shirt under it. "Bloody thing's hot, although I suppose it would come in handy at the North Pole. Nobody ever takes into consideration the fact that Santa has to travel all over the world to make his deliveries, including the tropics, eh?"

"That's a good point. Maybe flyin' as high as his sleigh does, though, it stays cool."

"More than likely," Trafford said with a solemn nod, then grinned again. "Silly discussion, isn't it?" The grin pulled another vanishing act as he sighed. "But it's better than talking about something as grim as a woman being murdered. Poor Georgia."

"You knew her pretty well?"

"For several years now, anyway," Trafford said as he sat on the sofa next to the Santa coat he had tossed down. "She'd been doing Brenda's taxes for a while, and she did our joint return a couple of times since we got married."

"You and your wife, you mean?"

Trafford nodded. "That's right. I'm the stepdad. Brenda had two youngsters by her previous marriage. Love 'em like they were my own, though."

"I'm sure you do," Sam said. The man seemed to like to talk, so he was going to try to take advantage of that. With a smile, Sam went on, "I hope you don't take this the wrong way, Alan, but you're not from these parts, are you?"

"No, born and raised in London. I've been in the States for

fifteen years, though. Came over here as a young man when I got involved in international banking. I've a position with a bank in Fort Worth now, handling their international department."

"That must be pretty excitin'."

"Oh, not as much as you'd think. Money's money, wherever you go. But you didn't come here to talk about me." Trafford's eyes narrowed slightly. "And I recall now where I've heard the name Newsom before. That's the name of the woman who owns the house where Georgia was attacked, isn't it?"

Sam knew there was no point in denying it, and he wasn't surprised that Trafford had recognized the name. Phyllis hadn't been mentioned in the newspaper stories about Georgia, but her name had been on the list of participants in the Jingle Bell Tour and everyone involved with it seemed to have figured out that the attack must have taken place there. Georgia wouldn't have any other reason to be there on that block. Otherwise that Fisk woman wouldn't have showed up at the house the next day. So Sam nodded and said, "That's right. You can imagine how upset she is about the whole thing. That's why she decided to get all the other folks on the tour to chip in for a really nice bunch of flowers."

"A worthy cause," Trafford agreed. "It must be terrible to have a thing like that happen right on your doorstep."

"Yeah. We're all bothered by it."

"Of course Brenda and I would like to contribute. How much are you collecting?"

"Whatever you want to give," Sam said. "Most folks have been chippin' in fifty dollars."

"That sounds reasonable. Is cash all right?" Trafford smiled again. "I'm a banker, you know."

"Cash is fine. I'll write you out a receipt."

"That would be good. Got to document everything. Taxes, you know." Trafford reached back to his hip, then laughed. "No pockets in a Santa suit. I'll have to go fetch my wallet. Be right back."

While Trafford was gone, Sam looked around the room. It was elegantly and expensively furnished. The Traffords were doing all right for themselves. Of course, bankers usually did, Sam thought.

Trafford came back with two twenties, a ten, and a notepad and pen. He gave all of them to Sam, who tucked the money in his shirt pocket and took the pad and pen to write the receipt for the donation. As he handed it to Trafford, he commented, "You said Georgia Hallerbee wasn't doin' your taxes anymore?"

"No, I'm able to have all of that done through the bank," Trafford explained. "Starting this year, anyway." He made a face. "Hate to speak ill of the dead and all that, but poor Georgia made a botch of things last year, I'm afraid. Took me quite a while to straighten it all out, and cost me a bit more in penalties and interest than it should have, too."

"Sorry to hear that."

Trafford waved that off. "Just one of the hazards of living in a modern, very complicated world, I'm afraid."

"You got that right," Sam agreed as he stood up. "But at least we've still got Christmas."

"Yes, although it's not as simple as it once was. Witness this rigmarole." Trafford nodded toward the Santa suit.

"I'm surprised your wife didn't have you wearin' it the night of the tour."

"She hadn't thought of it yet. Anyway, it wouldn't have done her any good. I wasn't here that evening."

Sam tried not to show how interesting he found that piece of information. He said, "You had to miss the big show?"

"That's right. When it's evening here, the next business day has already begun on the other side of the world. I had to go in to the office that night and handle some negotiations with my opposite number at a Japanese bank."

"Too bad."

"Yes, I would have liked to have been here, but duty calls, you know."

"Yeah, me, too. I've got some other stops to make." Sam put out his hand. "It was mighty nice meetin' you, Alan."

"Same here, old man," Trafford said as he gripped Sam's hand. "Or perhaps I should rephrase that . . ."

Sam chuckled. "Nah, that's fine. I never deny that I'm old. I like to think that I'm dignified. Like, say, Big Ben in London."

"Definitely," Trafford agreed. "And you're rather tall like Big Ben as well."

Sam said his farewells and left the house. As he drove away, he thought about what he had learned there. Alan Trafford was no muscleman—he had fit just fine in that Santa suit without any padding, as he himself had pointed out—but his grip was firm and strong, and Sam figured he could have lifted that gingerbread man if he'd been motivated enough. Also, he hadn't been home the night of the tour, although if he had been conducting business with some Japanese banker at the time, he might have an alibi that the police could check out.

But from the sound of it, he bore a grudge against Georgia Hallerbee over the tax work she had done for him and his wife the year before. That seemed like a mighty flimsy motive for murder, Sam thought . . . but maybe it had amounted to more than that. Besides, some folks got really upset when they felt like they'd been cheated out of any money at all, even if they could well afford it.

All of that didn't make Alan Trafford a strong suspect as far as Sam was concerned, but he couldn't be ruled out just yet, either. Sam was eager to talk to Phyllis about it.

But he had another stop to make first.

Chapter 18

*T*he other address Sam had memorized took him just out of town, to a hilltop estate not far from Lake Weatherford. This house was the farthest stop out on the list, and it was where the tour had ended that night. Sam turned off the farm-to-market road between a couple of tall stone pillars that had a wrought-iron arch between them. Worked into the metal of that arch was the legend DIAMOND C RANCH. The *C* had a diamond shape around it representing the brand. In smaller letters underneath was the name COCHRAN. There was a heavy metal gate that could be closed, but right now it was open.

Sam didn't know if the place was a working ranch or not, but it had plenty of pastureland around it. The main house sat in the middle of some rolling, sparsely wooded hills. It was a single story but sprawled impressively across the top of one of those hills. A driveway that was at least a quarter of a mile long led up to it, and that driveway was lined with Christmas decorations, including Santa Claus wearing overalls, a flannel shirt, and a huge Stetson. Instead of his usual high-topped boots he

wore high-heeled cowboy boots made of what looked like liz-
ard skin. The elves and Mrs. Claus had been similarly "cow-
boyed up." Instead of a sleigh, Santa had a chuck wagon.

Sam had to grin and shake his head at the sight. It was
pretty cute, although people who weren't Texans might think it
was going a little overboard.

He saw a large metal barn and several smaller sheds and
buildings scattered behind the house. About a dozen cattle
grazed in one of the pastures to the side of the driveway. As
herds went, this one was pretty small. Sam figured the owner of
the place liked the idea of being a rancher more than he did the
actual job of raising cattle. He was willing to bet that Charles
Cochran made his living doing something else.

The yard in front of the house was enclosed by a chain-link
fence that ran on around to the back. As Sam pulled up in the
driveway beside the fence, three big dogs came loping around
the house and charged toward the fence. They were Great
Danes, and they looked big enough that they could have just
stepped over the fence if they wanted to, but they stopped on
the other side to bark thunderously at him.

Sam knew enough about dogs to be confident that he
would be all right as long as he stayed on this side of the fence.
He got out of the pickup and said, "Hello, puppies," to the
Great Danes. They responded by barking even louder. Sam
looked at the house, figuring somebody would hear the com-
motion and come out to see what was going on.

He wondered if the dogs had been penned up somewhere
on the night of the tour. They must have been, he decided;
otherwise, the people who came to look at the decorations
never would have been able to get in the house.

The front door remained closed, and he didn't see anybody

looking out the window. When the dogs settled down for a second, he called, "Anybody home?" That set them off again, of course, and still there was no response.

Sam was about to give up and assume that nobody was home when he heard the shots, three flat booms blasting out one right after the other.

Out in the wilderness, three shots like that were a signal that somebody was in trouble. This was hardly the wilderness—downtown Weatherford was ten minutes away, less than that if the lights didn't catch you—but Sam knew he couldn't just drive away without checking to make sure everything was all right. The shots sounded like they came from the other side of the barn. He started walking in that direction.

It took him a couple of minutes to get there. Before he did, another group of three shots shattered the pleasant December afternoon. This time, however, Sam was close enough to hear the laughter that followed those shots. It sure didn't sound like anybody was in trouble.

The barn doors were open, and Sam could see all the way through it because the rear doors were open, too. That was the quickest way to get where he was going. He walked through the metal building, smelling hay, manure, feed, and dirt all blending together in the distinctive aroma of barnyard.

When he stepped out the rear doors, he saw two young men, one of them sitting on the open tailgate of a pickup parked back here while the other stood a few yards away with a pistol in his hand, aiming at something down the hill. The gun was a heavy revolver with a silver sheen to it. Sam was no expert, but he judged the weapon's caliber as either .38 or .44.

The young man sitting on the tailgate said, "Chris."

The one with the gun lowered it slightly and turned his

head. He was in his early twenties, Sam guessed, tall and lean with spiky brown hair that had been tinted with blond high-lights. He wore jeans and a long-sleeved work shirt with the tails untucked. The sun was warm enough this afternoon that he had rolled up the sleeves a couple of turns. Tattoos curled over his bare forearms.

His companion was about the same age but considerably chunkier, with longish dark hair. He wore jeans, too, and a denim jacket. A couple of open cans of beer were on the tail-gate next to him, and Sam guessed that the rest of the six-pack was in the ice chest sitting in the pickup bed.

"You must be what the dogs were barking at," the young man with the gun said. He didn't sound happy about it. "Help you?"

"I hope so," Sam said. "I'm lookin' for Charles Cochran."

The young man shook his head. "He's at the hospital."

"Something wrong?"

"No." Chris managed to pack quite a sneer into two letters. "He's a doctor. That's where he works."

"So's his mom," the other young man added.

"Is she here?" Sam asked.

Chris smirked and shook his head.

"Let me guess. She's at the hospital, too, right?"

"You got it. What do you want with them? You selling something?"

"Nothing we want, I bet," the other one said with a laugh.

Sam didn't think the story about collecting for flowers for Georgia Hallerbee's funeral was going to work with these two. He had never seen them before, but he recognized them any-way. The spoiled rich kid and his sycophantic sidekick. Even in a small-town high school like the one where he had taught,

those stereotypes showed up. And they were stereotypes because they were true and everybody knew it, whether they
wanted to admit it or not.

"Were you here the other night when the Christmas Jingle
Bell Tour came out here?" Sam asked bluntly. He didn't know
if he would get an answer, but these two clearly felt so superior
to him that he just might. They wouldn't consider him any
threat.

Chris pointed the gun at the ground. Sam could see now
that they had been shooting at a target—a human silhouette—
attached to three bales of hay that had been stacked up.

"You don't look like a cop or a lawyer."

Now, why would Chris think that a cop or a lawyer would
be coming to see him about something that happened during
the tour, Sam wondered? It didn't seem likely that he would . . .
unless there had been some trouble.

"It'd be better if you just answered the question, son," he
said.

Chris bristled at that. "And what if I don't?"

Sam shrugged and said, "Then I guess I'll have to go hunt
up your daddy at the hospital and ask him about it."

For a second, as anger flashed in Chris's eyes, Sam had to
ask himself just how smart it was to be prodding a hot-tempered
young fella with a gun in his hand. He was sure glad that Phyllis
hadn't come out here with him. He wouldn't put her in danger
for anything in the world.

"Take it easy, Chris," the other kid said quietly. Obviously
he recognized the signs of possible trouble.

Chris grimaced and shook his head. "I'm not saying anything without my lawyer, dude, except that I didn't touch that
mousy little bitch, and if she says I did, she's lying."

Sam had no idea what he was talking about, but he said, "That's not the way I heard the story. Why don't you tell me your side of it? I might be able to help you."

That brought a laugh from Chris. He found the idea of him needing help from Sam amusing.

"I've got a better suggestion," he said. "Why don't you go to hell? Or at least get off my property."

"If you're in trouble—"

"Both my parents are doctors, man. Even with Medicare not paying worth a crap anymore, they still make a boatload of money. I'm not worried about what some secretary says."

"Have it your way," Sam said. "I tried."

"Go on. Get out."

Another twinge of worry went through Sam as he turned his back on Chris Cochran. Chris still had that gun.

Nothing happened, though, as Sam walked through the barn and back to his car. Before he got there, he heard more shots ring out as Chris resumed his target practice.

He wasn't sure if he had found out anything worth knowing, because he couldn't figure out what any of it meant. He had a pretty good idea who might be able to, though.

He needed to get back to the house and talk to Phyllis.

"He had a *gun*?" Phyllis asked, trying not to sound as horrified as she felt.

"Yeah. A revolver. A .38 or a .44, I think."

"I don't care what size it was," she said as she looked at Sam. "It was a gun. He could have *shot* you."

Sam shrugged. "I didn't give him any reason to."

"You antagonized him. And you were asking questions

about something he obviously didn't want to talk about. Something that could get him into trouble."

"That was the feelin' I got, yeah," Sam said with a nod. "I'm hopin' you can figure out what it was."

Phyllis shook her head. "I don't have any idea. But I had a feeling when we got back and you weren't here that something was wrong. I never dreamed, though, that you were out almost getting shot."

"Nobody almost shot me," Sam insisted. "The kid was just gettin' in some target practice."

"You said yourself that for a second you were worried he might take a shot at you."

Sam shrugged. "He didn't. That's what counts." He paused and smiled. "It's always good to hear that you were worried about me, though."

"It wasn't particularly good as far as I was concerned," Phyllis said.

In fact, worry had nagged at her so much she had come close to calling his cell phone just to make sure he was all right. But when that urge seized her, she told herself that she was being silly, that Sam was a grown man and could take care of himself, and that he had a perfect right to be out doing whatever it was he was doing. It hadn't occurred to her that he might be carrying on the investigation for her while she was busy with wedding preparations, but even if it had, that would have been all right, too.

And the things he had discovered *were* intriguing, she thought as the two of them sat in the living room talking about what had happened.

"I think I need to find out more about Alan Trafford and that Cochran boy," she went on. Sitting around arguing about whether Sam had almost gotten shot wasn't going to help any-thing. "If Trafford had a problem with Georgia over his taxes, that gives him something that at least resembles a motive."

"He may have an alibi," Sam pointed out. "He could have been on the phone with that fella in Japan at the same time Miz Hallerbee was attacked."

Phyllis nodded. "He may have been. I don't see how we can find out about that."

"Detective Latimer probably could."

"Yes, he could," Phyllis admitted, "and I plan to tell him about it."

"And when you do, he's gonna fuss at you for gettin' mixed up in the investigation."

"Probably," Phyllis said. "That's why I think it would be a good idea to find out as much as I possibly can before I talk to him about it. The more information I can give him, the less likely he is to be really upset."

Sam thought about that for a moment and nodded. "I suppose that makes sense. What about the Cochran kid?"

"The same holds true for him," Phyllis said. "I'd like to know more about what made him act the way he did before I talk to Detective Latimer about him." She thought for a moment and then added, "Luckily, I know someone I think I can ask about both of them."

Chapter 19

"I don't want to talk about it," Laura Kearns said as she looked across her desk at Phyllis. "I don't want to talk about either of those things."

Sam had gone to the Trafford house and the Cochran ranch on Friday, and the office of Georgia Hallerbee's accounting and tax preparation company had been closed over the weekend, so Phyllis had had to wait until Monday morning to pay the place a visit and talk to Laura. That was all right, because she had spent the weekend working on plans for Eve's bridal shower, which was coming up quickly. The invitations had already been sent out, but now that the RSVPs were coming in, she had a better idea of how many people were coming. She and Carolyn worked out the snacks and games. Phyllis shopped for all the things they would need.

She and Sam had also managed to visit the other homes on the Jingle Bell Tour. The excuse of collecting money for flowers for the funeral had come about by accident, but they continued it and had enough to pay for two beautiful arrangements.

Since it was the weekend, people who were working during the week were home, and although it had taken a few return visits, they had caught up with everyone else on the list . . . and crossed them off the list of possible suspects as well. All of them had been home on the night of the tour, getting ready for the visitors they expected, so none of them could have been on Phyllis's front porch, bashing Georgia over the head with that ceramic gingerbread man.

Unless someone was lying or had cleverly managed to make it appear they were home when they really weren't, and Phyllis's instincts told her that wasn't the case.

Which left them with three people connected to the tour who couldn't be accounted for at that particular time: Holly Bachmann, Joe Henning, and Alan Trafford. Holly and Trafford might have alibis that Phyllis didn't know about. Joe Henning claimed an alibi, but it was shaky.

Then there was Chris Cochran. Phyllis didn't know if he had been at his parents' home the night of the tour, but maybe Laura could tell her, she had thought.

Only now it appeared that Laura didn't want to tell her anything.

Laura had smiled and seemed friendly enough when Phyllis first came into the office. "I thought about not even coming in today, since the funeral is this afternoon," she'd said. "But I thought that doing a little work might take my mind off it for a while, and that would be a good thing. Besides, we had quite a few returns we were in the middle of preparing. I owe it to our clients to finish those up, and then I'll talk to Georgia's sister and figure out what to do from there."

"Is the sister Georgia's heir?" Phyllis had asked.

"That's right. At least I assume she is. That's what Georgia told me. Of course, I never saw her will, so I don't suppose I know for sure." Laura had sighed. "I think she'll want to sell the business. Georgia's sister, I mean. I'll have to look for another job."

"Why don't you buy it?" Phyllis had suggested. "You're certified to do this sort of work, aren't you?"

"Sure," Laura had answered with a nod. "But I don't have the kind of money I'd need to take over the business. My husband has a pretty good job as a mechanic, thank God, but even between the two of us we don't make enough to buy a business."

"Well, I'm sure things will work out," Phyllis had told her. "In the meantime, I was wondering about a couple of the families whose homes were on the tour. I visited them while I was collecting money for flowers for the funeral, and I was puzzled about a few things."

"Which families?"

"The Traffords and the Cochrans."

That was when Laura's formerly friendly and helpful attitude had started to cool off. Her eyes had narrowed and her lips had thinned as she pressed them together. She hadn't said anything, so Phyllis had continued. "I heard there was some trouble—"

That was when Laura had broken in and flatly refused to talk about it.

Phyllis wasn't going to give up that easily, though. She said, "I know there was a problem with the Traffords' tax return—"

Laura interrupted her again. "There are privacy laws, Mrs. Newsom. I can't discuss anything about Mr. and Mrs. Trafford's taxes with you."

"Not the specifics, certainly. I probably wouldn't understand them, anyway. I've never been able to make much sense out of all those forms. But if there were hard feelings involved between, say, Mr. Trafford and Georgia, that's something the police need to know about, wouldn't you say?"

"Oh, my God," Laura said, her eyes widening now. "You think Mr. Trafford is the one who killed Georgia!"

Phyllis shook her head. "I don't have any reason to think that. I was just wondering if he held some sort of grudge against Georgia because of business." She paused. "I know he thought that Georgia made a mistake that cost him quite a bit of money—"

"No." Laura was on a roll today when it came to interrupting. She looked stricken now. "Georgia didn't make the mistake. *I* did."

"You?"

Laura nodded and bit her lip for a second before saying, "It was my mistake. I overlooked a form that should have been included and wasn't. Of course, Georgia signed off on it, and the business belongs to her so she took responsibility for it, but I was really to blame for what happened." She looked across the desk at Phyllis and went on, "You don't really think that Mr. Trafford . . . that he could have . . . because of what I did . . ."

Laura's determination not to talk about the matter had vanished in an upswelling of guilt and despair. Phyllis felt bad about that, but all too often, getting to the bottom of an ugly truth involved upsetting people.

"I don't know, Laura," she said. "I'm just trying to figure out what happened."

"But . . . but isn't that the police detective's job?"

"Of course. But it was my front porch, and I can't help but take it personally. I want to do everything I can to help bring Georgia's killer to justice."

Laura managed to nod. "I understand. I feel the same way."

"So Alan Trafford *was* upset with Georgia?"

"That's right. Some of the money involved, he actually owed to the IRS to start with as taxes, but the penalties and interest they levied added up to about fourteen hundred dollars."

"That's all?" Phyllis asked, thinking about what Sam had told her about the Traffords' house and the fact that Alan Trafford worked at a bank and made quite a bit of money. "Only fourteen hundred dollars?"

"That's a lot to some people." Laura shrugged. "Not to Mr. Trafford, I guess, but he was still really upset about it, anyway. Georgia was, too. She offered to reimburse him half of the amount, but he thought she should be responsible for all of it. He was so stubborn that in the end she didn't pay him anything. He talked about suing her, but he never did."

Phyllis shook her head and said, "Wait a minute. If there was that much bad blood between them, why in the *world* would the Traffords agree to let their home be part of the Jingle Bell Tour?"

"Well, that was mostly Brenda's doing, I think. That's Mrs. Trafford. She tried to stay friendly with Georgia. I'm sure she's the one who persuaded her husband to just drop the whole thing. And to be honest, the few times I talked to Mr. Trafford since then, he seemed friendly enough, and even a little sheepish, like he'd gotten over being mad and was sorry the whole thing ever happened."

"I suppose that could be the way he felt," Phyllis said. "People do get over being mad sometimes."

But sometimes they held on to a grudge, she reminded herself, still nursing it even when those feelings were no longer apparent, until finally something just snapped . . .

Alan Trafford wasn't the only reason she was here. She went on, "What about the Cochrans? What were they angry about?"

"It wasn't the Cochrans who were angry, at least not at first," Laura said. "It was Georgia. And *that* was because of me, too."

She looked like she was about to cry now. In hopes of avoiding that, Phyllis asked quickly, "Why don't you tell me about it?"

For a moment Phyllis thought Laura wasn't going to say anything else. Then the distraught-looking young woman drew in a deep breath and started talking.

"It . . . it didn't really have anything to do with the tour. That was already all set up. Dr. and Dr. Cochran . . . My, that's awkward, isn't it, having to call them Dr. and Dr. instead of Mr. and Mrs.? . . . Anyway they had already agreed to let their home be part of the tour, and since the place wasn't right here in town, Georgia thought it would be a good idea to print up a little map to give to the people who signed up, in case they got lost trying to find it. Just as a precaution, you know. Georgia didn't want . . . didn't want anything to go wrong that night."

Emotion made Laura's voice catch. She had to stop and look down at the desk for a moment before she could go on.

"So she fixed up the map, and she wanted Dr. Cochran—Charles Cochran—to look at it and approve it before she printed a bunch of them. But she was really busy with other things that day, so she asked me to run it out there and get him to look at it. She had talked to him earlier and he said he would be there. But he wasn't. When I got there, nobody was home but his son, Chris. He told me that his father had been called in to the hospital for an emergency."

Laura stopped again and visibly struggled with what she was trying to say. Phyllis had a bad feeling about what was coming next. She had never met Chris Cochran, but Sam had told her enough about the boy that she feared the worst.

"I gave the map to Chris," Laura finally went on, "and asked him to show it to his father, who could let us know if it was all right. Then I was going to leave, but . . . he didn't want me to. He asked me to stay for a while and said his father might come back. He said that would save me another trip out there. I tried to explain to him that I wouldn't have to come back anyway, that Dr. Cochran could just call us or e-mail us to let us know, but Chris wouldn't listen. He tried to give me a beer—he'd already been drinking; I'm sure of that—and when I didn't want it, he . . . he grabbed my arm . . ."

"You don't have to go on," Phyllis said as Laura's voice trailed off miserably.

"Oh, he didn't . . . didn't rape me or anything like that. He might have . . . but I got away from him and made it to my car. He followed me out there, stumbling a little, yelling at me and calling me names. He said if I ever came out there again, he'd set those awful dogs on me. I had some bruises and my blouse was torn a little, but that was all. Still, it was enough to make me upset."

"Of course it was," Phyllis said. "You should have reported him to the police for assault. Or did you?"

"No, I came straight back here. I figured it was an unpleasant incident, but it was over and no real harm was done. I wasn't going to say anything to anybody, not even Georgia, but she was really observant. She noticed that my blouse was torn and could see that something was bothering me. She made me tell her what happened."

Phyllis had a hunch that Laura had really wanted to reveal everything to Georgia, in spite of what she said now. It was hard to make somebody say something he or she didn't want to. And Phyllis couldn't blame Laura for wanting to share her fear and anger, either.

"How did Georgia react?" Phyllis asked.

"Well, she was furious, of course. She couldn't stand to see anyone taken advantage of or threatened. She wanted to call the police, but I talked her out of that. The whole thing was . . . embarrassing, you know? I didn't want to have to go through it again with the police. Then she wanted to go right back out there and confront Chris Cochran. I talked her out of that, too. She was like, I don't know, a fire-breathing dragon or something. But after a while she calmed down, and I thought that would be the end of it." Laura took another deep breath. "But the next day she called Dr. Charles Cochran. She told him that his son had tried to . . . tried to attack me. Dr. Cochran didn't believe it. He was angry, too, only he was mad at Georgia and me. Georgia said he sounded like he thought we were trying to drum up the grounds for a lawsuit, and she said that didn't sound like a bad idea."

"All of this going on, and the Cochrans didn't drop out of the tour?"

"It was the day of the tour," Laura explained. "It was too late to change anything, and anyway, Dr. Cochran said that people could still come, since it was for a good cause. He's really a . . . a nice man. You can't blame him for taking his son's side."

Phyllis shook her head. "I suppose not, but he should have wanted to get to the truth."

"As far as he was concerned, he did. Chris denied it ever happened, and Dr. Cochran believed him."

If anybody had ever accused Mike of wrongdoing, Phyllis thought, she probably would have taken his word for it if he had said he was innocent, too. That was just what parents did.

And sometimes children took advantage of that.

Laura's story tied in with some of the things Phyllis already knew. Carl Winthrop had said that something was bothering Georgia on the day of the tour. She had refused to give him the details, and that made sense because Georgia wouldn't have wanted to embarrass Laura unnecessarily by telling Carl the whole story. She had mentioned that she wanted to talk to Phyllis before the tour started because Phyllis had solved those murders in the past.

That didn't follow, though, because there was no murder here. But maybe . . . maybe Winthrop had misinterpreted what Georgia had said. Maybe Georgia wanted to talk to Phyllis because of Phyllis's connection with law enforcement—namely, her son, Mike, who worked for the sheriff's department. The Cochran ranch was outside of Weatherford's city limits, so any crime that happened there would fall under the jurisdiction of the Parker County sheriff, Mike's boss.

It was possible, Phyllis told herself. She needed to talk to Carl Winthrop again if she wanted to be sure, though.

"Mrs. Newsom?" Laura said. "Are you all right? You . . . you look like you're a million miles away."

Phyllis summoned up a smile. "I was just thinking about what you said. When we talked before, you told me that Georgia wasn't upset about anything and there hadn't been any disputes with her clients." She tried not to make her tone sound accusatory, but Laura flushed anyway, as if she were feeling guilty again.

"The business with Mr. Trafford was months ago, and like

I said, he seemed to have gotten over it. That didn't even occur to me when you were here before. And as for the business with Chris, well, I didn't want to talk about that."

"Did you tell Detective Latimer about it?"

"I didn't want it spread all over the newspaper," Laura said miserably. "I didn't want people in town gossiping about me and looking at me."

"So you didn't tell him?"

Laura shook her head, looked down at the desk, and said in a voice just louder than a whisper, "No." With a visible effort, she raised her head and looked at Phyllis again. "Am I going to get in trouble for that?"

"I don't know. Maybe it won't have to come out."

"You don't really think what Chris did could have anything to do with what happened to Georgia, do you?"

Laura wanted desperately to be absolved from blame, Phyllis thought. But she couldn't do that. She just shook her head and said again, "I don't know."

From what Sam had told her about the violence that seemed to be lurking just under Chris Cochran's surface, she couldn't rule it out. Charles Cochran could have said something to his son about Georgia's phone call to him, and Chris could have gone out looking for her. Phyllis didn't have an answer for how Chris could have known to find Georgia at her house, but the fact that some questions still remained didn't mean the theory was wrong.

"You were with the tour that night," she went on. "Was Chris at his parents' house when you got there?"

"I couldn't tell you," Laura said. "I was with the tour earlier in the evening, but I . . . I didn't go out to the Cochran place. After what happened there a couple of days earlier, I couldn't bring myself to go back out there and maybe see . . . him . . . again."

Phyllis nodded as she thought about that. Even if Chris had been at the Cochran ranch when the tour got there, that didn't mean he was innocent. Georgia had been attacked *before* the tour started, and the Cochran house was the last stop on the evening's agenda. Chris would have had plenty of time to break that ceramic gingerbread man over Georgia's head and still get back to his parents' house well before the tour arrived there.

The next step in finding out whether that happened was talking to Carl Winthrop again and trying to pin down exactly what Georgia had said to him on the afternoon of the tour.

She could do that in just a few hours, she thought, because in all likelihood Winthrop would be at Georgia's funeral this afternoon, and so would she. Some people might think that a funeral wasn't a proper place to be investigating a murder, but it seemed appropriate to Phyllis.

What better way to mourn Georgia's passing than trying to find the brutal killer responsible for her death?

Chapter 20

The weather in recent weeks had been mostly sunny and warm, not really that common for December but certainly not unheard of in this part of Texas, either.

It was still sunny that afternoon, but a cold front had blown through at midday, after Phyllis's visit to Georgia's office, bringing with it an icy wind that whipped around the tombstones and monuments in the cemetery, rattled the bare branches of the trees, plucked at the flowers that were stacked up around the coffin as it reposed on the apparatus that would lower it into the grave, and caused the canvas cover over the gathered mourners to flutter and pop.

The church had been packed for the actual funeral. Georgia had been well known and well liked in Weatherford, both for her business and for her involvement in civic affairs. All the people whose homes had been part of the Jingle Bell Tour were there. Phyllis recognized the ones she had met, and Sam discreetly pointed out the Traffords and the Cochrans. He hadn't actually met Brenda Trafford or Charles and Helen Cochran, but he identified them on the basis of their being in attendance with Alan Trafford and Chris Cochran, respectively. Brenda was an attractive blonde, the Cochrans both middle-aged and solemn looking, as befitted their positions as doctors.

Alan Trafford appeared to be genuinely mournful over Georgia's death. Chris Cochran just looked resentful at being forced to be there and having to wear a suit. Phyllis disliked him on sight. But of course, that didn't necessarily make him a murderer.

After the funeral, not everyone who was there had come out here to the cemetery for the graveside service. In fact, less than a fourth of the mourners had made the trip, Phyllis estimated. The turnout probably would have been higher if that cold front hadn't arrived when it did. With the wind chill dropping through the thirties toward the twenties, people didn't want to stand or sit around outside in such frigid conditions.

Also, it was only a few days now until Christmas. Most people still had things to do, preparations to make. There was something particularly tragic and poignant about a funeral and burial at this time of year, but the holidays didn't stop for death.

Phyllis pressed her gloved hands together between her knees. She was sitting on one of the folding metal chairs in the last row of mourners, with Sam on her right in the row's end seat and Carolyn on her left. Eve was on the other side of Carolyn, then Roy, who was there because of Eve, not having known Georgia himself.

Laura Kearns was sitting in the front row, next to a woman who Phyllis assumed was Georgia's sister from Waco. Phyllis could see a certain family resemblance, although the woman's hair was gray and she looked several years older than Georgia. The woman's husband and a grown daughter were sitting with her, as well. A stocky man in his twenties, with short, rust-colored hair and a matching close-cropped beard, was on Laura's other side. Phyllis knew that had to be the husband Laura had mentioned. The man worked as a mechanic, she recalled.

Carl Winthrop and a thin-faced brunette who was probably his wife were in the second row. Claudia Fisk was in the same row with a skinny, bald man, most likely her husband. A few seats down from them, Holly Bachmann sat with a bespectacled man who had to be her husband, Dan. He was pale and pudgy, certainly not the workout devotee that his wife was. Margaret Henning was in that same row, accompanied by her grandnephew Joe, who looked almost as unhappy about being here as Chris Cochran had back at the church. The Cochrans hadn't come to the cemetery, and neither had the Traffords. The same was true of most of the other families whose homes had been part of the tour. Phyllis couldn't blame them for not wanting to go out in this cold.

The minister's comments were brief, probably even more so than they would have been if the weather had been nicer. After his closing prayer, the pallbearers, including Carl Winthrop, stood up and filed by the coffin to add the boutonnieres they had worn to the pile of flowers, which included the lavish arrangements paid for by the money Phyllis had collected. Then they shook hands with Georgia's sister, who remained seated with her husband and daughter.

The other mourners paid their respects as well, then began to disperse. Carolyn and Eve had come with Roy in his SUV, so the three of them were going to head back to the house. Phyllis set her sights on Carl Winthrop, and with Sam beside her lightly holding her elbow to steady her as they walked past the graves, she started toward him.

Winthrop saw her coming and leaned over to say something to his wife. She nodded and walked toward the line of cars parked along the narrow asphalt lane that ran through the cemetery. He had probably told her to go ahead and get out of the wind, Phyllis thought.

"Mrs. Newsom," he greeted her with a solemn smile. "I wish I could say it's good to see you again, but under the circumstances . . ."

Phyllis nodded. "I know what you mean." She rested a hand on Sam's arm. "This is my friend Sam Fletcher."

Winthrop put out a hand and said, "Carl Winthrop. Pleased to meet you, Sam."

"Likewise," Sam said as the two men shook hands.

"I was wondering if I could talk to you for a minute," Phyllis said. "It's about Georgia and what happened to her."

Winthrop frowned. "The police haven't found out anything new, have they? I thought they might tell you because of your previous connection to them, before they released the information to the public."

Phyllis shook her head and said, "No, I'm afraid they're keeping me out of the loop on this case. I don't know anything new."

Nothing the police had told her, anyway, she amended to herself.

"I wanted to ask you a question about that day," she went on. "If you don't mind."

"Of course not." Winthrop looked around. "Let's go over there beside that mausoleum. It'll block the wind."

The three of them walked over to the low, squarish granite building, and Winthrop's prediction proved correct. The mausoleum blocked the wind, and in the sunshine it was still cold but not nearly as bone-chilling.

"Now," Winthrop said, "what is it you want to know, Mrs. Newsom?"

"On that day . . . the day Georgia was attacked . . . you said she was coming to my house before the tour started because she wanted to talk to me about something."

Winthrop nodded. "That's right. But she didn't say what it was. Just that it was something bothering her, and she thought you might be able to help her with it because you had solved those murders in the past."

"You're sure that's what it was? It couldn't have had something to do with some other sort of crime?"

Winthrop frowned. "You mean, do I remember her exact words? Well . . . let me think. I know she said something about you being a detective . . . and having something to do with investigating crimes . . . Maybe she didn't mention murder; I'm not sure. I guess I could have come up with that on my own, since I'd read about you in the paper when those other cases happened."

"She couldn't have been talking about the fact that my son is a deputy sheriff, could she?"

Winthrop rubbed his jaw. "I'm almost certain she didn't say anything about your son. But she could have said something about you having connections with law enforcement . . ."

Phyllis waited for him to go on, but after a moment he just shrugged and shook his head.

"Sorry, that's all I can remember. I didn't have any idea at the time that it would turn out to be important. I was a little worried about Georgia, sure, because she was upset, but I didn't think it really amounted to anything."

"Of course not," Phyllis agreed.

Winthrop regarded her intently. "What's this about?" he

asked. "Have you turned up something that could have a bearing on the case, Mrs. Newsom?"

"I don't know yet. I was told something by someone . . ." Phyllis stopped and shook her head. "I can't really go into it without any proof."

"Well, if there's anything I can do to help you get that proof, you can count on me."

"Thank you." Phyllis started to turn away, then paused. "You must know the Cochrans, since their home was part of the tour."

"Doc and Doc Cochran?" Winthrop asked with a grin on his face. "Sure, I know them, and not just from the tour. They have some money with me that I manage for them."

"What about their son?"

Winthrop's grin went away and was replaced by a sour look. "I know him, too."

"He doesn't have any investments with you, does he?"

Winthrop gave a disgusted snort and said, "That would require him to actually, you know, work and make some money. He's already gotten kicked out of a couple of colleges, and as far as I know he doesn't do anything except make his folks worry. He's a professional at that." Winthrop shrugged. "He'll probably come into a pretty nice inheritance one of these days. If he hasn't changed by then, though, I'd just as soon he took his business elsewhere."

"Then it's safe to say you don't like him?"

"Yeah, it's definitely safe to say—" Winthrop stopped short and stared at Phyllis, his eyes widening. "You think that kid had something to do with what happened to Georgia?"

"I've said too much—," Phyllis began.

"No, you haven't," Winthrop cut in. "Son of a gun! I can see him doing that. He's big enough and mean enough to pick up that gingerbread man and—" He paused and drew in a deep breath. "Oh, Lord, I don't even want to think about it."

"I don't blame you. I had to see the result, and I don't think I'll ever forget it. But Chris Cochran may have an alibi."

"You couldn't prove it by me if he does," Winthrop said. "He wasn't at his parents' place the night of the tour."

"You're certain about that?"

Winthrop shrugged. "I'm sure I didn't see him, and I think I heard Charles Cochran say something to his wife about the kid not being there. He was upset about it. Seems like Chris had promised to show up for the tour." Winthrop shook his head. "I don't know why it would be important to the doctor. Maybe he was just trying to work up some Christmas spirit in the family or something. I guess parents don't ever like to give up on their kids."

"That's true," Phyllis said. "Do you have any children?"

A slightly pained look came into Winthrop's eyes. "We were never blessed that way."

"I'm sorry."

"Just tough luck, I guess. Everybody's got some, of one sort or another."

Phyllis knew that was true. No one made it through life without some misfortune. Even those people who appeared to have everything usually had some burden they were carrying, even if it wasn't obvious to anyone else.

Winthrop went on, "What you're not telling me is why the Cochran kid would want to hurt Georgia. As far as I know, she never had much to do with him. All her business was with his parents."

Phyllis shook her head. "I'm afraid I'm really not at liberty to say anything about that."

A grin tugged at Winthrop's mouth again, but this was a more savage expression. He thumped his right fist into the palm of his other hand and said, "You've figured it out! By God, I knew you would, after everything I heard and read about you, Mrs. Newsom. Are you going to go to the police and tell them to arrest Chris Cochran?"

"I don't have any proof that he did anything wrong," Phyllis said.

"Yeah, but if they bring him in for questioning, surely they can find something. He's bound to have slipped up some-where."

"Maybe. I don't know . . ."

"We can't let him get away with this."

Sam spoke up, saying, "If there's one thing you can count on, Carl, it's that whoever killed Miz Hallerbee won't get away with it."

"I hope not." Winthrop nodded and went on, "I'll trust your judgment for now, Mrs. Newsom. If there's anything I can do to help you get the proof you're looking for, don't hesitate to call on me."

"I won't," Phyllis said.

"I guess I'd better get back to the car. My wife's probably wondering what's going on. She's not in very good health. I tried to tell her she shouldn't come out in this cold wind, but she wouldn't hear of it. Georgia was her friend, too."

Winthrop shook hands with Sam again, hunched his shoulders against the wind, and hurried back to his car. Phyllis and Sam were on their way to her Lincoln when another voice sounded behind them.

"You've got your nerve, coming to the funeral in the first place and then out here to the cemetery like this."

Phyllis turned and saw Claudia Fisk standing there. Claudia was alone. Her husband was probably waiting for her in their car, Phyllis thought.

"Look, Mrs. Fisk," Phyllis began, "I'm not sure what your problem is with me—"

"I'll tell you what my problem is," Claudia broke in. "You let Georgia get killed right on your front porch, and now you have the gall to come to her funeral."

Sam said, "Now, ma'am, that's not exactly the way it was. Phyllis didn't *let* anybody get killed. She didn't have anything to do with it."

"Then what was Georgia doing there? Explain that to me, why don't you?"

"I'm sorry, Mrs. Fisk, but I don't owe you any explanations." Phyllis wasn't about to go into the whole thing about the trouble between Chris Cochran and Laura Kearns. It wasn't anybody else's business.

Except the police. She was going to have to talk to Warren Latimer again.

Claudia Fisk was red faced from more than just the wind. Sam took Phyllis's arm and steered her around the irate woman. Claudia glared at them but didn't say anything else, and Phyllis was grateful for that. She had already spent more time than she liked to think about brooding over the fact that indirectly, she actually had played a part in Georgia's death. Georgia had been killed because she was there to tell Phyllis about something, and that something appeared to be Chris Cochran's attempted rape of Georgia's assistant, Laura. Carl Winthrop hadn't been able to confirm that with his recollection of what Georgia had said that afternoon, but Winthrop hadn't ruled it out, either. And Winthrop's comment about Chris Cochran not being at his parents' house for the tour that night was one more thing to weigh on the side of Chris's guilt.

Winthrop was right about one thing: The police needed to bring Chris in for questioning. Once that happened, he might even confess. Phyllis knew the time had come to talk to Detective Latimer again.

And, speak of the devil, she thought as Sam suddenly squeezed her arm and caused her to look up. She'd had her head lowered against the icy wind, but now she saw the solid-looking figure in an overcoat leaning against the front fender of her car.

"Hello, Detective Latimer," she said.

Chapter 21

"**M**rs. Newsom," Latimer replied with a polite nod. "And Mr. Fletcher."

"How you doin', Detective?" Sam asked.

"All right, I suppose. A little chilly."

Phyllis said, "I didn't see you earlier at the funeral. Or here at the graveside service."

"I keep a low profile," Latimer said. "I need to talk to you."

"And I want to talk to you. Why don't we get in the car, so we'll be out of the wind?"

Latimer shrugged. "I was going to suggest the police station, but I don't guess there's really any need for that. The car's fine."

Phyllis took her keys from her purse and pressed the button on the little remote control that unlocked the Lincoln's doors. She and Sam climbed into the front seat, while Latimer got in the back.

Even though it helped getting out of the wind, it was still cold inside the car. "Why don't I turn on the engine so we can run the heater?" Phyllis suggested.

"That's all right with me," Latimer said, "but don't do it on my account. I'm fine."

Phyllis turned the key in the ignition. When the car started, Christmas music came from the radio speakers. Nat King Cole was singing about chestnuts roasting on an open fire. Even though that was one of Phyllis's favorite Christmas tunes, she reached over and turned the radio off. Once the heater had had a chance to warm up some, she would turn up the fan on it.

She turned a little in the seat so she could look back at Latimer. "Now, Detective, what can I do for you?"

"Well, you can start by explaining why you've been investigating Georgia Hallerbee's murder when you don't have any official standing in the case."

For a second, Phyllis thought about denying that she had done any such thing, but from the determined expression on Latimer's face, she knew it wouldn't do any good. So she said, "I just asked a few questions, Detective, and I was going to tell you what I've found out. Didn't I mention just now that I wanted to talk to you?"

"You did," Latimer admitted.

"And aren't crimes often solved by tips from civilians?"

"Yeah, but those tips don't usually come from civilians who have been going around town questioning everybody involved in the case."

"We were takin' up a collection for some flowers," Sam said. "You can see 'em right over there next to the grave with all the other flowers."

Latimer grunted. "Yeah, I know that's what the two of you told people. But just between the three of us, we all know that's not the real reason you visited everybody whose home was on that Jingle Bell Tour."

"How did you find out?" Phyllis asked.

"Because believe it or not, we question people who are connected to a homicide, too, and several of them happened to mention that you'd been to see them in the past few days. Some of them even seemed to think that you were working with the cops on the investigation."

"We never told anyone that," Phyllis declared.

"I'm sure you didn't. You're too smart for that. Which means you're smart enough to listen to a warning: Butt out."

Sam frowned and started to twist around more in the passenger seat. Phyllis knew he was about to say something angry to Latimer, so she lifted a hand and put it on his arm to stop him. She didn't want him getting into any trouble because of her.

"You've delivered your warning, Detective," she said in a voice that was almost as chilly as the wind blowing outside. "Now would you like to hear what we've found out?"

Latimer hesitated. After a moment, he said, "It wouldn't be any good as evidence."

"But it might be reasonable cause for you to dig deeper into some of the things you've been told."

"I don't guess it would hurt to listen," Latimer said. "I'm not making any promises, though."

"There were three people whose houses were on the tour who weren't at home that night."

"Meaning they don't have ready-made alibis."

Phyllis nodded. "That's right."

Before she could go on, Latimer said, "Holly Bachmann, Alan Trafford, and Joe Henning."

Phyllis's eyebrows rose in surprise.

"What, you thought we didn't ask those questions, too?" Latimer said. "That's one of the first things we did. We know about the dispute over the taxes between Trafford and Ms. Hallerbee, but you can forget about him. He was at his office in Fort Worth talking to a guy in Japan."

"You're sure about that?" Sam asked.

"Yeah." There was no doubt in Latimer's voice. "His office door was open. The security guard and the janitor both saw him a dozen times while he was there, and I talked to some Japanese banker named Nakamura, too. Trafford was thirty miles away when somebody busted that ceramic gingerbread man over Ms. Hallerbee's head."

Phyllis winced at the reminder of the brutal way Georgia had been attacked.

"As for Holly Bachmann, she's out of the picture, too," Latimer went on. "She had an after-hours appointment with her dentist. A tooth-whitening emergency."

Sam said, "I didn't know there was such a thing."

"You've seen the lady," Latimer said. "How she looks is just about the most important thing in the world to her. That was the soonest her dentist could work her in, so she was willing to miss the tour. I talked to the guy, and he backed up her story. So did the assistant who came in to help him and collect the overtime."

"What about Joe Henning?" Sam asked.

Once again Latimer acted for a moment like he wasn't going to answer, but then he said, "Henning's an interesting character. My gut tells me he's kind of sleazy, and if I was that old aunt of his, I'm not sure I'd trust him to take care of my businesses. But he's got an alibi, too."

"Not a strong one," Phyllis pointed out. "We know when he left Ranger, and he could have gotten back here to Weatherford in time to attack Georgia."

"Maybe he could have . . . if he hadn't had a flat tire out by the Brazos River and had to call AAA to come out and help him. I've got the record of the phone call, and I talked to the guy from the garage who went out there and saw the paperwork on it. Henning was twenty miles away when the attack took place."

Phyllis was impressed by the work Detective Latimer had done, but all these alibis didn't really accomplish anything except to point the finger of guilt even more at Chris Cochran.

"All right," Latimer went on. "I've been straight up with you, Mrs. Newsom. Now, what do *you* know that I don't?"

It would have been nice if she had been able to get Laura Kearns's permission to tell the police about what had happened at the Cochran ranch, but it appeared that wasn't going to be possible. Phyllis didn't want to make Laura's discomfort and embarrassment over the incident even worse, but finding out the truth about Georgia's murder came first.

"Have you talked to the Cochrans?" she asked.

"The couple who are both doctors? Yeah, sure. They were both home on the night of the tour, too. All evening, in fact, so one of them couldn't have run over to your house, attacked Ms. Hallerbee, and then made it back in time for the tour." Latimer shrugged again. "It's true that they alibi each other, and when it's a husband and wife like that, you can't ever be sure, but given their reputation in the community and the fact that they didn't have any reason to be upset with Georgia Hallerbee—"

"But they did," Phyllis broke in.

"Did what?"

"Had a reason to be upset with Georgia," she said. "You don't know about what happened with their son."

Latimer leaned forward sharply in the backseat. "With

their son?" he repeated. "Blast it, Mrs. Newsom, if you've been withholding evidence—"

"Settle down, Detective," Sam said. "Phyllis just found out about this today."

"Tell me," Latimer snapped.

"That's the main reason I said I wanted to talk to you," Phyllis pointed out, "so I could tell you about what I learned from Laura Kearns this morning."

"Laura Kearns . . . That's Ms. Hallerbee's secretary, right?"

"Assistant is more like it, but I guess you could call her a secretary. She worked closer with Georgia than anyone else. The way Laura put it, Georgia wasn't necessarily like a mother to her, but definitely like an aunt."

"Get to the point."

Sam said, "You ever hear the expression 'hold your horses,' Detective?"

"Yeah, I've heard it," Latimer said. "Sorry, Mrs. Newsom, but I don't see any point in dragging this out all day."

Phyllis nodded. "You're right, Detective. Laura Kearns told me that when she went out to the Cochran ranch the day before the tour on some business for Georgia, Chris Cochran assaulted her and tried to rape her."

"That's the son you were talking about."

"Yes. Laura didn't want to say anything about it, but when she got back to Georgia's office, Georgia saw how shaken up she was and finally convinced Laura to tell her what happened. Georgia said they should call the police, but Laura didn't want that. She couldn't talk Georgia out of telling Chris's parents about it, though. The Cochrans didn't believe her. Everyone was upset."

"This is all hearsay," Latimer pointed out. "None of it would be any good in court."

"No, but it's a reason to question Chris Cochran and find out exactly where he was on the night of the tour, isn't it? I know you talked to his parents, but did you talk to Chris?"

Latimer's silence gave Phyllis the answer to that. The young man hadn't seemed to have any connection to Georgia except through his parents, so Latimer hadn't paid much attention to him.

"How do you know he wasn't at his parents' house the night of the tour?"

"Carl Winthrop told me," Phyllis explained.

"The guy who helped set up the tour?"

"That's right."

"Ms. Hallerbee was attacked a short time before the tour started. *That's* the time that needs to be accounted for, not the whole evening. The area covered by the tour isn't so big that you couldn't get from one end of it to the other in fifteen or twenty minutes, even with holiday traffic."

"According to Carl, Chris was missing from his parents' house the whole evening. They were upset about it. They wanted him to be there."

Latimer nodded. "I'll talk to Winthrop and the Kearns woman. And I'll definitely talk to the Cochrans again, including the kid."

"So you see, Detective," Sam said, "there was nothin' for you to be upset about. Phyllis was just helpin' out, that's all."

"By questioning people with a possible connection to a homicide. That could be construed as obstruction of justice."

"Maybe so, but considerin' that she found out more than the official investigation did, it'd look sort of silly in the press to throw the book at her, wouldn't it?"

Phyllis said, "That's enough, you two," and she couldn't help but sound like she was talking to a couple of rowdy eighth graders pushing each other in the school hallway.

"All right, forget it," Latimer said. "We'll just let it go. And," he added grudgingly, "thanks for the tip."

Phyllis started to ask him if he would let her know what he found out when he talked to Chris Cochran and the young man's parents, but she decided that might be pushing things a bit too far. Instead she said, "I hope this helps you clear everything up, Detective."

Latimer grunted.

Phyllis went on, "And I'd appreciate it if you'd be as considerate as possible with Laura. She's still very upset and embarrassed about the whole thing."

"Why?" Latimer asked. "From the sound of it, she didn't do anything wrong, except for not calling the cops on the kid when it happened. If she had . . ."

The detective's voice trailed off as Phyllis nodded. "Exactly," Phyllis said. "If Laura had reported what Chris did, or at least let Georgia report it, then Georgia might still be alive today. Laura blames herself for what happened."

"Yeah, well, she shouldn't. She's not the one who got hotheaded and broke a ceramic gingerbread man over a woman's head." Latimer frowned. "How did the Cochran kid know he could find her at your house?"

Phyllis shook her head. "I don't know. But maybe he can tell you."

"He'll tell me," Latimer said. "Whatever he did, he'll tell me." He reached for the door handle. "I hate to get back out in that cold wind."

"I can drive you to your car," Phyllis offered.

"Nah, it's just right over there," Latimer said, pointing. He gave the two of them a curt nod. "So long."

He got out and slammed the door closed behind him. The car had warmed up nicely, but even the few seconds the door had been open had let quite a bit of chilly air into the vehicle.

Sam said, "I don't think you've won the detective over yet, but at least he had enough good sense to listen to what you had to say."

"That's certainly better than being arrested for obstruction of justice, isn't it?" Phyllis said with a smile.

Sam snorted. "Like that's ever gonna happen."

Chapter 22

*P*hyllis didn't expect to hear anything from Detective Latimer, and she didn't the rest of that day. She probably wouldn't know what had happened until she read in the paper or heard on the news about an arrest being made in Georgia's murder.

She wasn't completely convinced of Chris Cochran's guilt, but everything certainly pointed in his direction. She wasn't sure what he had hoped to gain by killing Georgia. Maybe his thoughts hadn't even been that rational. When he heard that Georgia had been talking to his parents about what he did to Laura, maybe he had been so upset that he tracked her down and attacked her out of sheer rage and spite. That fit with what she knew of Chris's personality.

The next morning, Phyllis discovered that she wasn't the first one up, like she usually was. Carolyn had beaten her to it this morning, and as Phyllis came into the kitchen and found her friend sitting there with the newspaper spread open before her, she instantly knew why Carolyn had risen early.

She had a pretty good idea, as well, what Carolyn had

found in the paper. "Congratulations," Carolyn said, and although there was a slight grudging sound to her voice, Phyllis could tell that her friend was being sincere, too. Carolyn was genuinely happy with what she'd read . . . although a slightly different outcome probably would have made her even happier.

"Really?" Phyllis asked. With everything that had been going on, she had forgotten all about the newspaper's Christmas cookie contest. She and Carolyn had delivered their recipes and sample cookies to the newspaper office more than a week earlier, and Phyllis hadn't really thought about them since then.

Carolyn turned the paper around so that Phyllis could see her photo and a photo of the plate of cookies she submitted. She saw her name printed there along with the winning recipe.

"Oh, my," she said. A warm feeling went through her as she thought about how people would be trying the recipe and baking their own cookies. She hoped most of them enjoyed those cookies. Of course, some wouldn't, no matter how good the recipe was. You couldn't please everybody.

"It's a well-deserved win," Carolyn said.

"What about your gingerbread-boy cookies?"

Carolyn shrugged. "Not even an honorable mention."

"Oh. I'm sorry. I thought they were really good."

"They probably weren't sweet enough," Carolyn said. "You know people and their sweet tooths. Teeth. Whatever."

"Well, I liked them."

"Liked what?" Sam asked as he strolled into the kitchen, still in pajamas and bathrobe like the two women.

"Carolyn's gingerbread-boy cookies," Phyllis said.

"Yeah, they were mighty good," Sam agreed. He noticed

the newspaper on the table. "Dang, is it time for the contest results already?"

"It's almost Christmas," Carolyn said. "If they had waited much longer to publish the list of winners, it would have been too late."

Sam reached for the paper. "Lemme see . . . Well, what do you know!" He put his arm around Phyllis's shoulders and squeezed. "Congratulations!"

Phyllis started to shake her head and say that she didn't deserve it, but she stopped herself. She had never been one for false modesty. So she smiled instead and said, "Thank you."

"What about those gingerbread-boy cookies, though? Where'd they come in?" Sam started to frown as he scanned the list of runners-up and honorable mentions.

Carolyn said, "I'm afraid my recipe didn't make the cut this year."

"Well, that's just not right," Sam insisted. "Those cookies were mighty good."

"You don't have to say that, Sam."

"I'm not just sayin' it. I wouldn't do that. They *were* good. I probably ate a dozen of 'em, if you remember right."

Carolyn shrugged. "You *did* seem to like them."

"Darn right I did. There's a reason why there's an old sayin' about how there's no accountin' for taste. Some people just don't know what's good."

Carolyn pointed at the picture of Phyllis's German chocolate cookies. "They knew Phyllis's cookies were good."

"Well, I . . . uh . . ."

Phyllis smiled and patted him on the back. "Don't worry, Sam. I know what you meant."

"So I can stop tryin' to dig myself outta that hole I'm in?"

"You're not in a hole. You're just fine."

"I'm glad to hear it." Sam looked around. "Coffee brewin' yet?"

"I'll get it started," Phyllis said.

"Let me," he offered. "You sit down and look at the paper."

Phyllis took him up on that offer. She sat down at the table to read what the local food editor had written about the winning cookies. The praise was a little extravagant, she thought, but she was honest enough to admit that she liked seeing all those kind words about her work.

Eve came into the kitchen, yawning, and said, "Why are we all gathered around the paper this morning?"

"Phyllis's cookies won the contest," Carolyn explained.

"Oh, congratulations, my dear! You'll have to bake some of them for the shower."

Phyllis nodded and said, "I was just thinking the same thing." Christmas Eve and Eve's bridal shower were only a couple of days away now.

"I think I'll try a variation on those gingerbread-boy cookies," Carolyn mused. "Maybe I'll cut them in hearts and use a cream cheese icing on them." She paused. "You know, Eve, some people might say that it's unseemly to be having a bridal shower at your age."

"People can say whatever they want," Eve replied. "I make no secret of how old I am or that I've been married before. But if Roy and I are going to set up housekeeping together, there are a lot of things we need. I haven't had a house of my own for quite a while, you know." She sighed. "And I still don't. It looks like we're going to have to take you up on that offer to live here after we get back from our honeymoon, Phyllis."

"You'll both be very welcome, and you know that," Phyllis told her.

"No luck on findin' a house, eh?" Sam asked as he switched on the coffeemaker, which he had finished preparing to brew.

"No, and at this late date, I don't think we will have time to find one until after the wedding," Eve told him. "There are other things to take care of right now that are more important, like the dresses and the flowers and the cake."

"Which I assume you want Phyllis and me to bake?" Carolyn said.

Eve nodded. "That's right. I hate to ask it of you; you're both doing so much already—"

"It's all right," Phyllis said. "We'll put our heads together and think about it, and after Christmas we can have a tasting to see what you like best."

"That sounds like a wonderful idea," Eve agreed. "Thank you, Phyllis, and you, too, Carolyn. I don't know what in the world I'd do without you."

"Hey, don't forget me," Sam put in with a grin. "I'm the best man."

Eve patted his arm. "Of course you are, dear, and you have the most important job of all."

"What's that?"

"Keeping Roy from getting cold feet and leaving me at the altar!"

"Not much chance of *that* happenin'," Sam said.

Phyllis thought it might be a good idea to distract Carolyn from the outcome of the Christmas cookie contest, so later that morning they sat down together to talk about the cake for Eve's wedding.

"I don't know why she didn't just get one done professionally," Carolyn said.

"Maybe she thought that wouldn't be personal enough."

Carolyn lowered her voice. "Or she thought it would be too expensive. No matter what she says, Eve would still like for everybody to believe that she's thirty-nine!"

Phyllis smiled as she caught the reference to Jack Benny, famous for his terrible violin playing, his refusal to admit his own age, and his thriftiness. Actually, downright cheapness was the personality he had adopted for radio, movies, and TV.

"Eve's nothing like Jack Benny," Phyllis said.

"Maybe not, but she doesn't believe in being extravagant. She didn't offer to *pay* you for the cake, did she?"

"Well . . . no."

Carolyn nodded. "I rest my case."

"Regardless of why she asked us, we agreed to handle this for her, and we want to do a good job."

"Absolutely," Carolyn agreed without hesitation. "We want everybody who comes to this wedding to be talking about the cake for a long time."

"Wouldn't it be better if they were talking about how radiant Eve was and what a lovely couple she and Roy made?"

"No," Carolyn said. "They need to talk about the cake."

Phyllis had to laugh. "We'd better come up with a good one, then."

"Cake is cake. It's all in the decorations. Have you ever decorated a wedding cake?"

"A few," Phyllis said.

"So have I. Here's what we should do . . ."

The idea was to keep the cake as simple as possible so few things could go wrong. After considering different cake fillings and decorations, they decided the best was a layered white cake with smooth white icing. The layers would be wrapped with snowflake silver see-through ribbon with a smaller blue satin ribbon behind it to show through. A bow would go on, too, with the cake topper, and plastic snowflakes would be placed on the top and second layer, leaving the bottom layer plain, but sitting artfully on some tulle. They could put more snowflakes on the table around the cake.

After they had talked about it, Phyllis didn't think it would hurt to get a head start on the process, and Carolyn needed some ingredients for the icing for the new version of the gingerbread-heart cookies she was going to bake for the shower, so they agreed to go to the store that afternoon. The idea of venturing out into the crowds of shoppers three days before Christmas was rather daunting, but it would only be worse the next two days. They would go to one of the smaller grocery stores, Phyllis decided, instead of Walmart.

The roads were full of cars, and even at the smaller store the check-out lines were long anyway, so Phyllis was a little tired and stressed that afternoon as she and Carolyn left the grocery store. Phyllis was pushing the cart full of plastic bags that held their purchases. The cold wind of the day before had died down, thankfully, so while the air was still chilly and their breath fogged a little in front of their faces, the weather wasn't too uncomfortable.

"Oh, good grief," Carolyn said as they approached Phyllis's Lincoln. "Would you look at that?"

Phyllis slowed the grocery store cart and stared in dismay at the right rear tire on her car. It was as flat as it could be. Flatter than a flitter, as Phyllis's mother would have said.

"You must have picked up a nail somewhere," Carolyn went on. "We're going to have to change that tire."

Phyllis knew she was right. That didn't stop her from glancing around to see if there was some man nearby who might be kind enough to offer to help them. Unfortunately, nobody was paying any attention to them. They were all too intent on their own errands.

"Or maybe you should call Sam," Carolyn suggested.

"We can do this," Phyllis said. "It's plenty cool enough out here that the refrigerated things we bought will be fine for a while. Come on."

It wasn't like she had never changed a tire before, she told herself. She had, on numerous occasions. But the last of those occasions had been quite a while in the past.

She parked the buggy next to the car and opened the trunk. The carpeted bottom in there lifted up, and the spare and jack were underneath it. Phyllis found the catch and lifted it. Something about the spare didn't look right to her, however, so she leaned into the trunk, rested her hand on the tire, and pushed. The rubber gave softly under her fingers.

"Oh, no," she said. "The spare is flat, too."

"Don't you check it?" Carolyn asked.

Phyllis looked at her. "When was the last time you checked the spare tire in *your* car?"

"All right, all right, you made your point. So you're going to call Sam now?"

"I guess I have to. He can take the spare and get it aired up, then bring it back to us."

Phyllis got out her cell phone and thumbed in the speed-dial number for the house. It rang several times before the answering machine picked up. "Sam, are you there?" she asked.

"Sam?" She sighed. "I'll try your cell, but if you get this and I haven't spoken to you, call me, please."

She broke the connection, then called Sam's cell phone. The call immediately went to voice mail.

"He's got his phone turned off for some reason," Phyllis said in exasperation.

Carolyn was starting to look annoyed. "All right, we'll have to hunt up somebody who's willing to help us."

"Wait a minute," Phyllis said. "I'll call AAA. I've been a member for years, but I hardly ever call them. You know how it is. Our generation was brought up to handle our own problems."

"You're handling it," Carolyn pointed out. "Call them."

Phyllis opened her purse. "Let me find the card . . ."

A few minutes later, she was connected with a dispatcher who promised to send someone to help them as soon as possible. "This is a busy time of year for us, too, because there are so many folks on the road," the man told her. "So it may be a little while. Shouldn't be more than half an hour, though, since you're right here in town. If it's that long."

Phyllis glanced at the groceries in the cart. "I hope it's not," she told the dispatcher.

"Is there someplace warm nearby where you can wait?" the man asked.

"Yes. Don't worry about that. Just get someone here as soon as you can."

"Will do, ma'am."

Phyllis hung up and nodded toward the store as she said to Carolyn, "You might as well go on back inside where it's warm. It's going to be a little while before somebody can get here."

"No, I'll wait here with you," Carolyn said in a tone that

proclaimed she wasn't going to argue about it. "Do you think these groceries are going to be all right?"

"We didn't get anything frozen, and it's almost as cool out here as it would be in a refrigerator, so I think they'll be fine as long as we keep them out of the sun. They'll stay cooler out here than they would in the car."

"Should we get in?"

"I don't see why not. We can keep an eye on the groceries from in there."

"That's a good idea," Carolyn said. "People these days will steal anything."

Phyllis unlocked the doors and they got in the car. The sky was partly cloudy today, with enough sunshine to warm the inside of a closed vehicle. It was a little cool in the Lincoln, but not uncomfortable.

As always whenever someone had car trouble, the time spent waiting for help to arrive seemed interminable. Minutes dragged by, and Phyllis kept checking the time on her phone.

It rang suddenly, surprising her. She saw that it was Sam calling and flipped the phone open.

"Hello, Sam."

"I got your message," he said with a note of worry in his voice. "What's wrong?"

"It's the craziest thing. I've got a flat tire, and when Carolyn and I went to change it, we found that the spare was flat, too."

"Where are you?" Sam asked. "I'm on my way."

"No, no," she said quickly. "There's no need for you to do that. I've called AAA, and they're sending someone."

"Lord knows how long *that'll* take. If you're on the side of the road—"

"We're not," Phyllis told him. "We're in the parking lot at

the grocery store. The tire went flat while we were inside. So it's fine, Sam. We're perfectly safe, and—" She saw a tow truck turning into the parking lot. "And the person they sent out is coming right now. So you don't have to come and help us."

"You're sure?" He didn't sound convinced.

The truck pulled up a couple of parking spaces away. STRICKLAND'S GARAGE was painted on the door.

"I'm positive," Phyllis said. It was possible that the truck *hadn't* been sent out by AAA, that the driver just intended to go into the store and buy some groceries, but the likelihood of that seemed pretty remote.

"All right, if you're sure," Sam said. "But call me right away if you need me."

"I will, don't worry."

They said good-bye and hung up, and Phyllis opened her door and got out of the car as a man in a grease-stained baseball cap, a denim jacket, and jeans stepped down from the cab of the tow truck. He nodded to Phyllis and asked, "You called AAA about a flat tire, ma'am?"

"That's right," Phyllis began, "and the spare—"

She stopped short as she recognized the driver of the truck.

He was the man who had been with Laura Kearns at Georgia's funeral the day before.

Chapter 23

"I know you," Phyllis said. "You're Laura's husband, aren't you?"

The man looked surprised, but he nodded and said, "Yes, ma'am, I am, if you're talking about Laura Kearns. My name's Rusty, or that's what they call me, anyway." Recognition dawned in his eyes. "You were at the funeral yesterday."

"That's right. I'm Phyllis Newsom."

Rusty Kearns nodded again. "Yes, ma'am. I know who you are now."

He didn't sound quite as friendly this time. Maybe that was because he realized it was her front porch where Georgia had been attacked, and the whole situation had caused a lot of stress and grief for his wife. None of that was really Phyllis's fault, though.

Kearns went on, "I can change that tire for you, if you'd like."

"I'm afraid the spare is flat, too."

"Has it been in the trunk for a while?"

Phyllis nodded. "Yes. I don't really remember the last time it was used."

"Probably nothing wrong with it, then," he said. "It just needs some air. I've got a compressor on the truck. I'll air it up and take a look at it, and if it's okay I can go ahead and put it on the car. You will want to get your regular tire replaced as soon as you can, though."

"I'll do that," Phyllis said.

Kearns got to work, taking the spare tire out of the trunk, rolling it over to his truck, and pulling down a hose attached to some sort of apparatus that Phyllis assumed was the air compressor. The machine made a loud racket as it pumped air into the tire. After a couple of minutes, Kearns unhooked the hose and rolled the tire slowly back and forth on the pavement, leaning down to study the rubber as he did so. When he had checked out the whole tire, he nodded in satisfaction and replaced the cap on the valve stem.

"It ought to be fine," he said. "It just went down while it was sitting. They'll do that."

He used a hydraulic jack from his truck to raise the rear end of the Lincoln, rather than using the jack that was in the trunk. With swift, practiced ease, he removed the flat tire from the wheel and put the spare in its place, then tightly dogged down the nuts.

"You're good to go, Mrs. Newsom," he announced as he straightened from his task.

"Thank you so much," Phyllis told him. "Do you do a lot of this kind of work?"

"Answering stranded-motorist calls for AAA, you mean?" Kearns smiled as he put the flat tire in the Lincoln's trunk and closed the lid. "Yeah, we handle a lot of 'em, and I'm always the guy they send out."

"So you're on call all the time, like a doctor?"

Kearns got a rag from the back of the truck and started wiping grease and road dirt from his hands. "I wouldn't compare myself to a doctor, but yeah, I can get called out pretty much any time of the day or night. My boss doesn't believe in hiring a lot of extra workers when he can get by without it, you know what I mean?"

"How does Laura feel about that?"

Kearns made a face. "She puts up with it, whether she likes it or not, just like I do. This day and age, with money as tight as it is, what choice does anybody have?"

"That's certainly true. It would be nice if she could afford to take over Georgia's business."

"Yeah, since she spends nearly all her time there anyway," he said. He shook his head and went on, "But there's no chance of that. We could never afford to have our own business."

"It's a shame, though."

"Yeah." Kearns tossed the rag back into the truck. "Is there anything else I can do for you, Mrs. Newsom?"

"No. Like you said, I think we're good to go."

"All right. I need to get to my next call, but before I go, I've got some paperwork you'll need to sign so we can bill AAA."

He filled out one of a stack of forms on a clipboard, checking his watch to make a note of the time, then handed the clipboard and pen to Phyllis and pointed out where she was supposed to sign. When she had done that, he tore off a carbon copy and handed it to her.

"There you go. Thanks."

"Thank you, Mr. Kearns." Phyllis held out a ten-dollar bill she had taken from her purse. She didn't know if she was supposed to tip him, but she wasn't going to take a chance.

Kearns hesitated before taking the bill, but only for a second. "Thanks," he said again.

"Say hello to Laura for me," Phyllis called after him as he climbed into the truck.

Kearns nodded but didn't say whether he would pass that sentiment along.

When Phyllis got in the car after putting the groceries in the backseat, Carolyn commented, "You spent a lot of time talking to that mechanic."

"Didn't you recognize him?"

Carolyn frowned. "No. Should I have?"

"That was Laura Kearns's husband."

"You're talking about the woman who worked for Georgia Hallerbee?"

"That's right," Phyllis said with a nod.

"So you were just being polite because you know his wife?"

"Yes."

But in truth, it was more than that, Phyllis realized. Something Rusty Kearns had said had set her mind to working as she remembered something else she had heard. The wheels of her brain were turning now, turning like the wheels of a car with fully inflated tires. She wasn't sure what the thoughts whirling through her head added up to, if anything, but she was certain about one thing.

She was going to have to find out.

Sam must have heard the garage door going up, because he was waiting in the open doorway to the kitchen when Phyllis pulled in. "Let me give you a hand with the groceries," he said as he came into the garage while Phyllis and Carolyn were getting out of the car. "I'm sorry I didn't hear the phone when you called."

"That's all right," Phyllis said, then asked, "What were you doing?" before she realized that maybe it was none of her business.

Sam reached into the backseat to snag several of the bags. "I was takin' a nap," he said with an embarrassed look on his face.

"Well, goodness, there's nothing wrong with that," Phyllis told him.

"Yeah, but I'm a grown man, not a toddler."

"You're an old man," Carolyn said bluntly. "I'm not surprised you get cranky when you get sleepy in the afternoon. Old men are *always* cranky."

"That's not true," Phyllis said.

Carolyn made a scoffing sound. "It is in my experience."

"Anyhow," Sam said as the three of them carried the grocery bags into the kitchen and set them on the counter, "I didn't hear the phone because I was poundin' my ear when you called the first time. I'd turned off my cell phone, too. I won't let that happen again."

"Nonsense," Phyllis said. "Take a nap anytime you want to." She paused. "It's actually sort of cute."

Sam rolled his eyes and said, "I'll get the rest of the groceries."

When he had gone back out to the garage, Carolyn leaned closer to Phyllis and asked quietly, "Did you know he takes naps?"

"No. It's none of my business." Her look and tone of voice made it clear that she didn't think it was any of Carolyn's business, either.

"*If* that's actually what he was doing," Carolyn went on.

"Why would he lie about something like that?"

"I'm sure I don't know, but with most men, you'd be doing good to take everything they tell you with a grain of salt."

Phyllis didn't believe that, but she knew better than to argue with Carolyn on the subject of men. It was a waste of time.

Anyway, she had a lot more important things on her mind right now. Her information had sent Detective Latimer probing deeper into the whereabouts of Chris Cochran on the night of Georgia's murder, but she didn't feel quite as strongly now that Chris was guilty. The question of how he would have known where to find Georgia had continued to nag at Phyllis, and now another theory had begun to form in her head, one that didn't involve Chris at all.

The idea was still vague and she needed more information to fill in some of the missing pieces, but she felt like she was on to something.

She needed to talk to Sam about it. That always helped her get her thoughts in order.

He brought in the rest of the groceries. "Need my help puttin' these up?"

"No, that's all right, we know where everything goes," Phyllis told him. She saw the relief in his eyes. He didn't mind helping carry things, but he just wasn't wired to remember where everything went in a kitchen and pantry.

Sam went out to the living room while Phyllis and Carolyn put the groceries away, except for the things Carolyn would need for the new batch of gingerbread cookies. Phyllis said, "While you're doing that, I'm going to go see if I can find a good wedding cake recipe on the Internet."

She was really going to talk to Sam, though. She found him

in the recliner where he usually sat, looking through the newspaper.

"I need to talk to you for a few minutes," Phyllis said, and he looked up immediately as if he sensed how serious she was.

"If this is about that nap—"

"No, it's not. I really don't care how many naps you take, Sam. I'm not your mother."

"Well, that's true."

"This is about Joe Henning and Rusty Kearns."

"Joe and Rusty?" Sam looked confused. "What? Who's Rusty?"

"Laura Kearns's husband."

"Oh, yeah." He nodded. "Stocky guy, short beard. Mechanic, right?"

"That's right," Phyllis said. "He works for a garage that handles most of the roadside assistance calls around here for AAA. And Rusty is the one who's nearly always sent out on those calls."

Sam set the newspaper aside and sat up in the recliner, a frown on his face as he obviously thought about what Phyllis had just told him.

"Wait a minute," he said. "Joe Henning had a flat tire out on the interstate by the Brazos on the evening of the Jingle Bell Tour."

Phyllis nodded. "That's what Detective Latimer told us."

"So his alibi for the time of the attack on Miz Hallerbee was the fact that he called AAA and they sent somebody out to help him."

"Exactly."

"That somebody more than likely bein' this fella Rusty Kearns."

"More than likely," Phyllis agreed. "But the only proof of that would be the dispatcher's log, Rusty's testimony, and the form he filled out for Joe to sign so the garage could bill AAA."

"Now, hold on," Sam said. "I'm gettin' confused. The dispatcher's log proves that Henning called."

"Yes, but it doesn't prove *where* he called from. When you call AAA, you just give them directions to wherever you are when you need their help."

Sam let out a low whistle. "So he could've been anywhere and just *said* he was out on the highway, twenty miles from here."

"That's the way it looks to me."

"But if that's true . . ."

Sam didn't finish the sentence, but Phyllis could see in his eyes that he understood.

"But if that's true," she said, "then he had to be working with Rusty Kearns and everything was set up ahead of time. Rusty could fill out the paperwork and Joe Henning could sign it whether or not any of the other really happened."

"But the only reason to do that would be to create an alibi for Henning."

"Which he wouldn't need," Phyllis said, "unless he was planning to murder Georgia Hallerbee."

Chapter 24

*T*hey sat there in silence for a long moment. Phyllis could tell that Sam was considering everything she had just told him, turning the pieces over in his mind to see if they fit together, and, if so, whether they formed the same picture she saw.

Finally, he nodded slowly and said, "It could've worked that way, all right. They would have had to be in it together from the start. But I got a couple of questions, and the first one is . . . why?"

"Why murder Georgia? The only reason I can think of is the first one that occurred to us. Joe has been stealing from his great-aunt, Georgia found out about it and was going to tell me, and Joe had to kill her to keep her from doing that."

"But how did Henning find out that Georgia was gonna spill the beans to you?"

This was the part Phyllis really didn't like. She drew a deep breath and hesitated, but no amount of hesitation would change the answer.

"He knew because Laura Kearns told him."

Sam gave her an intent look. "The little gal who worked for Miz Hallerbee. The one who's married to that fella Rusty."

"That's right. She was right there in the office with Georgia. They worked together all the time. It makes sense that if Georgia uncovered Joe Henning doing something wrong, then Laura would know about it, too. That's when she saw her chance."

"To cash in," Sam guessed.

"Yes. She and Rusty are struggling, financially. When Georgia found out about Joe's wrongdoing, Laura realized she could blackmail him with that knowledge."

"But not if Georgia went to the law, or even to you, about it, because you'd call the cops for sure."

Phyllis nodded. "Yes, I would have, or at least I would have told Georgia she was right to do so. On the day of the tour, when Laura overheard Georgia telling Carl Winthrop that she was upset about something and coming to talk to me about it, Laura knew what it had to be. Maybe she and her husband and Henning were already planning to kill Georgia, or maybe they had to scramble to put the plan together right then, but either way, they figured out a way to give Joe Henning an alibi so he could hustle back here to Weatherford and shut Georgia up permanently."

"Henning didn't know about those ceramic gingerbread men on the front porch," Sam pointed out.

"He didn't have to," Phyllis replied with a shake of her head. "That really was spur of the moment. Henning probably planned to strangle her or something like that. But he saw the gingerbread men, grabbed one of them, and used it instead. That could have been a terrible mistake, though, because after that crash he couldn't hang around to make sure Georgia was dead. He had to hope that he had killed her then and there. As it turned out, he hadn't, and those days that she lingered in a coma must have been torture for him."

"No worse than what the son of a . . . what the varmint deserved."

Phyllis nodded. "True. And, of course, in the end Georgia died without regaining consciousness and without revealing his secret. That left Henning in the clear . . . except for the fact that now he wasn't just an embezzler; he was a murderer, as well."

"Doesn't look like he thought that through too well," Sam said.

"No, because now Laura and her husband have even more of a hold over him. He'll have to keep stealing from Margaret so he can pay them off. In time he'll bleed her dry, and Laura and Rusty will do the same thing to him."

"Wait a minute," Sam said. "They can't do that. They helped with the murder. If they give Henning to the law, they'll be confessin' to their own part in it, too."

"They didn't actually kill Georgia, and they weren't even here when she was attacked, so the charges against them would be less than the ones against Henning. Besides, they're both pretty bitter about money. They may figure that this is the only real chance to get rich they'll ever get, so they're willing to run the risk that Henning will pay rather than dare them to go to the police."

Sam nodded again. "You're probably right about that. And all the rest of it fits together, as far as I can see. Which brings me to that second question I mentioned a while ago."

"And that is?"

"How are you gonna prove any of this?"

"I don't know. I can't just go and ask Laura or Joe Henning about it. And since it's just a theory, without any evidence to back it up, I can't very well go to Detective Latimer with it. Besides, he's already looking at Chris Cochran as the killer. He probably wouldn't appreciate having a whole new theory dumped in his lap."

"Of course, he only considers Cochran a suspect because of the things you dug up about him," Sam pointed out.

Phyllis sighed and nodded. "I know. Which means I'll be responsible if he's innocent and winds up being arrested for killing Georgia. Don't think I haven't thought of that."

"I wouldn't be feelin' too bad about what might happen to that young fella," Sam told her. "Even if he winds up havin' to spend a few hours in jail, it won't hurt him any. Might even do him some good, although I doubt it. But his daddy'll bail him out in a hurry; you can count on that."

"I suppose so. I think I'll go see Margaret in the morning. Maybe she can tell me if Joe has been acting any different lately."

"I'll come with you," Sam said.

"I don't know if that's necessary—"

"Henning's liable to be there. If there's a chance he's a murderer, I'm not lettin' you go in by yourself."

"I'm not going to charge in like a SWAT team and try to arrest him or anything like that," Phyllis pointed out.

"No, but I'd still feel better if you weren't by yourself."

Phyllis nodded. To tell the truth, she would feel better about it, too.

"Today?" Eve asked the next morning. She and Carolyn were sitting in the living room. Phyllis had gotten her coat from the hall closet and was putting it on. "You're going out running around today? But the shower is tomorrow."

"I know," Phyllis said. "Don't worry—everything will be ready."

"It's only a little more than twenty-four hours away."

That was a bit of an exaggeration, since the shower was scheduled to start at two o'clock on Christmas Eve afternoon, and it was now ten o'clock in the morning on the day before Christmas Eve, but Phyllis understood her friend's concern. Eve wanted everything to be perfect. Given her history, there was no way of being sure about such things, but at her age there was at least a reasonable expectation that this would be her final marriage.

"Carolyn will be here working on the preparations," Phyllis assured her. "Anyway, there's not really that much to do. A few decorations to put up, some snacks and punch to get ready—that's all. We can handle it tomorrow morning without any trouble."

"What about entertainment?" Eve asked. "Have you arranged for entertainment?"

"You don't have male strippers at bridal showers," Carolyn said. "Those are for bachelorette parties, and then only when the bride and her friends are degenerates. Anyway, we're long past such things."

"Speak for yourself," Eve said. "What about games?"

"We're not going to play any silly games, either," Carolyn said. "Again, those are for—"

"Degenerates, I know. You don't expect everyone to just sit around and do nothing, do you? That would be boring."

"I prefer to think of it more as dignified," Carolyn said.

Phyllis slipped out of the living room while she could, leaving Eve and Carolyn to wrangle over the details of the bridal shower. She and Carolyn had talked about games earlier but weren't able to find any that they felt their guests would really want to do. She buttoned her jacket as she went down the hall to the kitchen. Sam was waiting there.

"Ready to go?" he asked her.

"Yes, I suppose so. Although I feel a little bad about abandoning Eve today."

Sam smiled. "She and Carolyn are goin' 'round and 'round about the shower, eh?"

"They'll work it out," Phyllis said.

She hoped that was true.

They took Sam's pickup, since Phyllis hadn't had a chance to get that flat tire repaired or replaced, and she didn't like driving too much on the spare. She didn't really trust it since it had already gone flat, too. Maybe she would look into replacing it as well, she thought, but that would have to wait until after Christmas. She just didn't have the time to mess with it now.

Sam drove to the big old house on the hill on the western edge of town. As they pulled up in the circle drive, Phyllis saw a car that was somehow vaguely familiar parked in front of the house.

"Who's that belong to?" Sam asked as he brought the pickup to a stop behind the other vehicle.

"I don't know, but I think I've seen it before."

"Do we go ahead and go in?"

She nodded. "Yes, I want to talk to Margaret. If she has another visitor, we'll just have to wait."

They went up the steps to the porch and Sam rang the bell. A moment later, the housekeeper Sophia opened the door. She smiled and said, "Oh, hello, Mrs. Newsom. Are you here to see Mrs. Henning?"

"That's right," Phyllis said.

"She's in a business meeting at the moment, but if you and your friend would like to wait . . ."

"That would be fine, thank you."

Sophia ushered them in and indicated that they should go into the formal living room across the hall from the parlor. A beautiful old set of folding doors had been closed across the entrance to the parlor, so Phyllis couldn't see who was in there with Margaret, but she heard the faint murmur of voices.

"Can I get you some coffee or something else to drink?" Sophia asked as she indicated that the visitors should have a seat.

Phyllis and Sam sank onto a heavily upholstered divan. Phyllis shook her head and said, "No, thank you," while Sam added, "No, thanks, I'm fine."

"It shouldn't be much longer," Sophia said as she backed out of the living room.

When the housekeeper was gone, Sam looked around the room, which was furnished with spindly legged antiques and decorated with a multitude of fragile-looking Christmas figurines and knickknacks for the tour, and said, "I feel like that ol' bull in the china shop you hear about. I don't want to move because I'm afraid these gawky arms and legs of mine will knock something over and bust it."

"You'll be fine," Phyllis told him.

"Who do you reckon is in there with the old lady?"

"I don't know. Sophia said it was a business meeting, though."

"Then Joe's liable to be part of it."

Phyllis nodded. "Yes. I thought about that. I was hoping we could talk to Margaret without him being around."

"Yeah, it's gonna be hard to ask her if he might be a murderer with him standin' right there."

Phyllis lifted a finger to her lips to shush him. She heard footsteps approaching the other side of the folding doors across the hallway.

Those doors opened up, and the bulky figure of Joe Henning appeared. He stopped where he was as he looked across the hall into the living room and saw Phyllis and Sam sitting there. His hesitation was only momentary, though, before he smiled at them and nodded a greeting. Then he stepped aside and held out a hand to usher the other visitor to the front door.

Laura Kearns looked just as surprised as Henning when she stepped into the hall and saw Phyllis and Sam.

She smiled, too, though, and said, "Why, hello, Mrs. Newsom. I didn't expect to run into you here."

"I didn't expect to see you, either, Laura." Phyllis understood now why the car outside in the driveway had looked familiar to her. She had seen it a couple of times in the parking lot of the shopping center when she visited Georgia's office. Obviously it was Laura's car.

Phyllis stood up and went on, "I guess you must be delivering some of the paperwork you and Georgia took care of for Mrs. Henning."

"It's better than that," Laura said. "It's just . . . it's the most wonderful thing in the world."

From inside the parlor, Margaret Henning called, "Phyllis, is that you? Come in, dear, come in."

Laura started to duck toward the front door. "I really have to be going—"

"Wait, Laura," Margaret said. "Why don't you come back in? I'm sure Phyllis will be interested in hearing the good news, since she and Georgia were friends. She'll be glad to know that Georgia's business is going to be in such good hands."

"Well . . . all right," Laura said, although she looked like she would have just as soon been somewhere else.

The four of them went into the parlor, where Margaret Henning sat on the sofa with a different Christmas quilt spread over her legs this time. Margaret smiled up at Sam and said, "Hello, Mr. Fletcher. It's good to see you again, too."

"Likewise, ma'am," Sam said as he took the hand she held up to him and squeezed it gently in both of his.

"What's this about Georgia's business?" Phyllis asked.

"Laura's going to be taking it over," Margaret said. "She's the absolute best choice, don't you think? She worked with Georgia for several years, she knows all the clients, and she can keep things going almost the same as they were before." The old woman sighed. "Although no one can really replace Georgia, of course."

"I'd never try to," Laura said. "I just want to do my best to continue all the good work she did."

Anger threatened to boil up inside Phyllis. She was convinced that this young woman had played a large part in Georgia's death, and now it looked like she was going to profit from it even more than Phyllis had thought.

"I thought you told me you couldn't afford to buy the business," Phyllis said to Laura.

"I couldn't . . . until Mrs. Henning made the wonderfully generous offer to loan me the money."

"It's a business decision, dear," Margaret said. "Purely a business decision."

Laura smiled down at her. "You can say that all you want, but I still think it's incredibly kind of you." She looked at Joe. "And kind of you, too, Mr. Henning."

As if explaining to Phyllis and Sam, Joe said, "Aunt Margaret was upset that she was going to have to find somebody else to take care of her bookkeeping and taxes. She said she didn't like starting over on anything at her age. So all I did was say that maybe we could figure out a way for Mrs. Kearns here to keep handling things."

"And that made perfect sense to me," Margaret said. "So now it's all arranged. Georgia's sister has agreed to sell the business to Laura, and I'll handle the financing. Or rather, Joe will. He's so good at such things."

"I just try to help out where I can, Aunt Margaret."

Phyllis glanced at Sam. She could tell by the grim set of his mouth that he wasn't happy about this development, either. Phyllis had to take a deep breath to force down the outrage she felt and keep a smile on her face. The whole thing fit together perfectly. Laura was getting the business after all, as payment for the help she and her husband had given Joe Henning in getting rid of Georgia before she could tell anyone what he'd been doing.

But it would be only partial payment, Phyllis thought. Chances were, Laura would continue blackmailing Henning as long as she could get away with it.

"Now, Phyllis, what was it that you and Mr. Fletcher wanted?" Margaret asked, breaking into Phyllis's angry musings.

"Oh, we were just out running some errands, and I suggested that we stop to wish you a Merry Christmas," Phyllis said. With Laura and Joe here, she couldn't very well ask some of the questions she'd intended to ask.

Anyway, she had learned enough now that surely Detective Latimer would see that her new theory was much stronger as far as motive went than the one involving Chris Cochran, and it didn't have nearly as many holes in it, either. Joe Henning and Laura and Rusty Kearns wouldn't get away with what they had done, Phyllis vowed to herself. She would keep pushing and prodding until the truth came out.

But at this point, that was probably going to have to wait until after Eve's shower and Christmas.

Laura wasn't going anywhere, though. She owned a business now. And Joe Henning couldn't afford to leave town. He had to stay here so he could continue siphoning money away from his great-aunt's wealth.

"Why, thank you," Margaret said. "Merry Christmas to you, too, dear, and you, Mr. Fletcher."

"Thanks, ma'am," Sam said. "I hope Santa's good to you this year."

Margaret laughed almost like a little girl. "Oh, I'm sure he will be. I've been good all year."

Phyllis could think of three people who hadn't been, she told herself as somehow she managed to keep smiling at everyone in the room. All Joe, Laura, and Rusty had coming in their stockings were lumps of coal.

And maybe three sets of handcuffs, Phyllis added grimly.

Chapter 25

"Well, that was awkward," Sam said as he drove away from the Henning house a few minutes later. "I never have been real good at makin' small talk with killers."

"Neither have I," Phyllis said. "I'm worried about Margaret, Sam. What if Joe decides that it would be a lot quicker and easier just to get rid of her and inherit all her money."

"Well, for one thing, we don't know that he'd inherit everything," Sam pointed out. "We haven't seen the old lady's will. For all we know, she could leave everything she owns to some foundation for homeless cats or some such."

Phyllis nodded. "That's true. And even if Joe *does* inherit everything under the terms of the will, he's smart enough to know that if anything happened to Margaret, he would be the primary suspect."

"Unless he made it look like an accident or natural causes."

That was the problem, Phyllis thought. There was no way of knowing what Joe Henning was capable of. Was he smart enough, cunning enough, to come up with a way of killing his great-aunt without making it look like murder?

"Let's go to the police station, Sam," she said. "I want to talk to Detective Latimer now."

"I don't blame you," he said as he sent the pickup down a residential street, cutting through to South Main without having to deal with the traffic around Weatherford's courthouse square.

Another side street took them to Santa Fe Drive, where the police station was located. Phyllis had been here more times in the past couple of years than she had ever thought she would be. Sam found a parking place, and they went inside to the reception area.

"I need to speak to Detective Latimer if he's here," Phyllis told the uniformed officer behind the counter. She had never seen him before.

"What's your name, ma'am?"

"Phyllis Newsom."

Something in the way the young officer's eyes lit up told her that he had heard of her, even though she didn't know him. "Just a minute," he told her as he picked up a phone and pushed one of the buttons on its base. "I'll see if he's available. Why don't you and the gentleman have a seat?"

Phyllis nodded and went with Sam over to one of the chrome-and-plastic chairs along the wall, which were only borderline comfortable. She heard the officer talking in low tones into the phone but couldn't make out the words. When he hung up, he looked over at Phyllis and Sam and said, "Detective Latimer will be out in a few minutes."

"Thank you," Phyllis said.

The officer turned back to the computer on the counter

and hit a few keys on the keyboard, but his eyes kept straying over to Phyllis and Sam. He smiled, clearly a little embarrassed that she had caught him looking at her. A few more moments went by; then the young man gave in to his obvious curiosity and said, "Excuse me, ma'am, but . . . uh . . . you *are* the lady who . . . well, who solved those other murders, aren't you?"

"I helped the police figure out a few things," Phyllis acknowledged. She didn't believe in false modesty, but she didn't think it would be a good idea for her to start bragging about the murders she had solved, especially when she was sitting in the police station at the moment.

The young officer grinned. "That's not the way I heard it. I heard you've caught more than one killer."

"I just try to get to the truth," Phyllis said.

"Yeah, well, I wouldn't want to have you after me if I'd committed a crime, especially if I'd killed somebody."

"I'm sure a nice young man like you would never do anything like that," Phyllis told him. At the same time, Warren Latimer pushed through a swinging door and stepped into the lobby.

"Do anything like what?" he asked. "Garvey?"

"Uh . . . murder somebody, Detective."

"I should hope not," Latimer said. He walked over to Phyllis and Sam, both of whom stood up. "What can I do for you, Mrs. Newsom?"

"I was hoping I could talk to you about the Georgia Hallerbee case," Phyllis said.

Latimer's face hardened. "That's what I was afraid you'd say. That's an active, ongoing investigation, Mrs. Newsom. I'm afraid I can't discuss it with you."

"I wouldn't be here bothering you if I didn't think I'd found out something important, Detective. You wanted me to cooperate and turn over any information I had to you, didn't you?"

"That's what I said," Latimer replied with a curt nod.

"Well, then, I think this is important." Phyllis took a deep breath. "I believe I was wrong about what we discussed after Georgia's funeral."

Latimer was already frowning. The creases in his forehead deepened as his bushy brows drew down even more. He didn't say anything for a moment as he considered what Phyllis had just told him.

Then he nodded and said, "Come on back to my office, both of you."

He led them down a hallway to a large office with several desks in it. Phyllis saw Isabel Largo working at one of them. The woman looked up and gave her a nod and a faint smile. Phyllis wondered if Detective Largo was glad that she wasn't handling the Hallerbee case.

Latimer motioned Phyllis and Sam into chairs in front of his desk. "All right, what's all this about?" he asked.

Phyllis didn't answer. Instead she asked a question of her own. "Have you questioned Chris Cochran?"

Latimer frowned. "I can't tell you that."

"But you haven't arrested him and charged him with murder. You would have announced that if you had."

"Mrs. Newsom, I don't want to be rude," Latimer said with a sigh. "But it's two days until Christmas. I have a family, and things I'd like to do. Please, if you have any new information, just tell me."

Phyllis reined in her temper. She could tell that Sam was angry at Latimer because of the detective's tone, as well.

"I think that Joe Henning killed Georgia," she said.

"That's not information. That's an opinion. And an opinion without any basis in fact, because Henning wasn't even in Weatherford when Ms. Hallerbee was attacked."

"Based on the fact that he called AAA about a flat tire?"

Latimer spread his hands. "Well, yeah."

"You can call AAA from anywhere and say that you're somewhere you're really not."

"I talked to the dispatcher who handled the call and the driver who went out to help Henning."

"I never said he didn't make the call," Phyllis pointed out, "and what if the driver lied?"

"Why would he do that?"

"Because he and his wife were blackmailing Joe Henning and had to help him kill Georgia in order to protect him, so he could keep stealing money and profit for all of them."

Latimer leaned forward, interest finally sparking in his eyes. "What? This is the first I've heard about any blackmail."

Phyllis took a deep breath. "You understand, this is a theory. I don't have any way of proving any of it. But I'm sure you can find the proof, Detective, if you know where to look."

"Why don't you tell me?" Latimer suggested.

Phyllis did, launching into the idea she had worked out. Latimer clasped his hands together on the desk and listened intently. Phyllis detailed everything, right up to and including the visit she and Sam had paid to the Henning house that morning, where they had seen the fruits of the plot hatched by Joe Henning and the Kearnses.

"I'm sure Joe put the idea of loaning Laura the money to buy the business into his great-aunt's head," she concluded.

"Maybe he came up with it himself, but I have a feeling Laura probably demanded that he do it. The loan is just one more part of Joe's payoff to his blackmailers."

Latimer nodded slowly as he looked across the desk at them. "Is that all?" he asked.

"That's all," Phyllis said. "Like I told you, you'll have to dig into Margaret's finances and Joe's activities, and if you do, I'm sure you'll find the proof you need."

"Well, I might do that . . . if there was any reason to."

Phyllis knew she probably looked confused. She certainly felt confused by Latimer's reaction as he leaned back in his chair and grinned.

"What do you mean?" she asked. "I just explained how Joe could have killed Georgia with the help of Laura Kearns and her husband."

"And it all ties together very neatly," Latimer admitted. "There's only one thing that keeps me from believing that any of it ever happened."

"What's that?" Phyllis asked coldly. She was angry at Latimer for his attitude, but she also had a sinking feeling. He wouldn't sound so confident unless he knew something she didn't.

"Joe Henning couldn't have killed Georgia Hallerbee. He was twenty miles away when she was attacked, getting a flat tire changed on his car."

"But I told you—"

"Getting a flat tire changed on his car by Jimmy Strickland, the owner of the garage. Rusty Kearns didn't answer that trouble call because he was already handling another one on the highway between here and Mineral Wells."

For a moment, Phyllis was so stunned that all she could do

was stare across the desk at Latimer's grinning face. She felt Sam looking at her, but she didn't turn her head to meet his gaze. When she could speak again, she asked, "Are you sure?"

Latimer nodded. "I interviewed Strickland twice. He's a Baptist deacon, has owned his business here in town for forty years, and doesn't have any connection at all with Ms. Hallerbee or anybody else involved with this case, other than the fact that Rusty Kearns works for him. At least, I couldn't dig up any connection, and I promise you, I did plenty of digging. I shouldn't admit this, but I don't like Joe Henning very much. It wouldn't have bothered me to shoot holes in his alibi. There just aren't any."

And if Joe's alibi was sound, there was no reason to think that he was involved in any sort of plot with Laura and her husband, Phyllis realized. She could see the whole carefully constructed theory collapsing in her mind once the foundation of Joe Henning's guilt was removed.

"Then . . . then the only real suspect is Chris Cochran," Phyllis managed to say.

"Whose only real alibi is that squirrelly friend of his, who's not what I'd call a reliable witness." Latimer made a face. "I shouldn't have said that much."

"But you did," Phyllis said. "Obviously you've checked into his whereabouts on the night Georgia was attacked."

Latimer hesitated, then said, "Look, if I tell you what we've found out, will you promise me you'll let it alone from now on?"

"Of course," Phyllis said.

"The Cochran kid and his friend Nelson Blake claim they went to a strip joint on the west side of Fort Worth on the night of the Jingle Bell Tour. But they didn't pay for anything with credit cards. They said they used cash." Latimer rolled his eyes.

"Big surprise there, right? Anyway, I talked to the dancers and the bartenders who work at the place and showed them pictures of both Cochran and Blake. Some of them said they thought the guys *might* have been in there that night, but they couldn't be sure. The lighting in a place like that isn't the best, and it's not like there are clocks all over so people can keep track of the time, either. Even if Cochran was there later, there's no reason to think he wasn't on your front porch earlier that evening, busting that ceramic gingerbread man over Ms. Hallerbee's head."

A little shudder went through Phyllis. She wondered if she would ever get used to the idea that someone had been murdered on the very doorstep of her home.

Sam spoke up for the first time, pointing out, "We still don't know how the kid would've known to look for Miz Hallerbee at Phyllis's place."

"No, but if he's guilty—and my gut says he is—sooner or later he'll tell us."

Phyllis couldn't stop thinking about that shattered gingerbread man . . . the way the shards and the larger pieces were scattered around Georgia's limp, bloody form as she lay sprawled on the porch . . . and something stirred in the back of her brain as that horrific picture filled her mind's eye. Whatever it was, though, it was also elusive, because it slipped away before she even had a chance to grasp it.

"Do you have Chris Cochran in custody?" she asked.

Latimer looked stubborn. "I've already said all I'm gonna say."

"Does he still deny that he attacked Laura Kearns?"

"What'd I just tell you, Mrs. Newsom?"

Phyllis knew she wasn't going to get anything else out of the detective. She nodded and said, "All right."

"That was a good job of putting together a theory," Latimer told her. She couldn't help but hear the slight note of condescension in his voice. "For a second there, you almost had me convinced that Joe Henning was guilty, even though I knew he couldn't be. The problem is, you didn't have all the facts available to you when you put that theory together."

"No, I suppose I didn't," Phyllis admitted. "That's because I'm not a police detective."

Latimer nodded. "Right." He moved some papers around on his desk, a sure sign that the conversation was over. "Is there anything else I can do for you?"

"No," Phyllis said. "No, that's all. I'll leave you to your work now."

Latimer got to his feet as Phyllis and Sam stood. "Thanks for trying to help. I'll show you out—"

"That's all right," Phyllis said, her voice dull with defeat. "I know the way."

Chapter 26

"That smug, insufferable son of a gun," Sam said once they were back in his pickup. Phyllis could tell how angry he was by the way his hands clenched so tightly on the steering wheel for a moment. "Actin' like you're some ditzy old lady playin' detective—"

"Maybe I am," Phyllis said.

"You know that's not true. You've solved murders and helped catch killers before. You're the only one who's come up with any real ideas in this case."

"One of those ideas has just been proven completely wrong," Phyllis pointed out, "and the other one is still pretty weak."

Sam looked over at her. "But what if you weren't wrong? What if there was some way Joe Henning managed to kill Ms. Hallerbee anyway, despite that alibi of his?"

"You mean some impossibly complicated plan that no one could ever pull off in real life?" Phyllis smiled and shook her head. "No, Sam, I don't think that's what we're looking at here. As we've known all along, this was a crime of passion. Using one of the gingerbread men as a murder weapon proves that. It wasn't all intricately planned out ahead of time."

"Yeah, but wouldn't it be nice to shove the real solution right down that smug so-and-so's throat?"

"I don't care about that. I just want Georgia's killer caught. Maybe Chris Cochran is guilty, despite the questions. We'll have to wait and see."

"You're givin' up?" Sam sounded like he couldn't believe it.

"I don't see what else I can do. I've considered everything I know about the crime. I've turned it all over in my head again and again. I can't come up with anything else."

Sam sighed. "And I guess you know more about it than anybody else. You were closer to it than anybody except Miz Hallerbee."

"And whoever attacked her," Phyllis said. "The killer knows what happened, too." She brightened. "Well, at least now I can concentrate all my energy on Eve's shower tomorrow and her wedding next week."

Sam started the pickup. "Yeah," he said, not sounding all that enthusiastic.

"Cheer up," Phyllis told him. "It won't be that bad. You and Roy don't have to attend the shower. We're all old-fashioned enough to believe that the groom doesn't have to be there, so you and Roy can go do something else for those two hours. And the wedding will be fine. You've been a best man before, haven't you?"

"I have," Sam said with a nod. "As long as I don't lose the ring, I suppose it'll all be okay."

"Of course it will," Phyllis said.

She wished she could say the same about the way she felt right now.

. . .

"Where have you been?" Eve asked frantically when they came into the house a short time later.

"You knew we were going to be gone for a little while," Phyllis said. "It's not even noon yet."

"Yes, but this is an emergency. Roy's gone!"

"Gone?" Phyllis repeated. "What do you mean, gone?"

"He's run out on me! He's leaving me at the altar!"

"The wedding's still a week off," Sam pointed out. "He can't be leavin' you at the altar, because you're not there yet."

Phyllis winced. As upset as Eve was, this wasn't the time to be taking things literally. Eve was a little wild-eyed as she turned toward Sam, so Phyllis moved quickly to insinuate herself between them.

"I take it he's not answering your phone calls," she said.

"That's right," Eve said. "He was supposed to call me this morning. He told me he would. So when he didn't, I called him, only he didn't answer. I tried calling the motel and having them ring his room. No answer! I tried his cell phone, and it goes straight to voice mail. He's ignoring me. For all I know, he's already left town and is headed back to Houston!"

"Roy doesn't strike me as the type to do something like that," Phyllis argued. "He's too much of a gentleman. If he was going to call off the wedding—"

Eve's nostrils flared and her eyes widened even more. Phyllis hurried on, "If he was going to leave for any reason, he would tell you. I'm sure of it. There has to be an explanation."

"There does? Well, what is it?"

"I . . . don't know." Phyllis looked helplessly at Sam. "You're his friend. Has he said anything to you?"

"Well, it's not like we've been bosom buddies for years," Sam said. "But no, he hasn't mentioned anything about bein' worried or upset or havin' cold feet. He seemed fine the last time I saw him. Seemed like he was anxious to be married to you, Eve."

"Then why has he disappeared?"

Carolyn had been standing in the background during this conversation, her arms folded across her chest and a disapproving look on her face. Now she spoke up, saying, "I'm sorry, Phyllis. I knew she was going to pounce on you the moment you came in. I tried to convince her that she's worried about nothing, but she won't listen to me."

"What do you care?" Eve shot back at her. "You don't care if you *never* get married again!"

"That's right," Carolyn said calmly. "I don't. In fact, I don't intend to and can't think of any circumstances where I would want to."

"Not everybody feels the same way you do!"

"Let's all just settle down," Phyllis suggested. "Eve, I know you're upset. But think about it. Roy's been unaccounted for, for a few hours—that's all. That's nothing to get upset about, and it's certainly no reason to think that he's going to call off the wedding."

"Then maybe something happened to him," Eve said without missing a beat. "He's not a young man. He . . . he could have had a heart attack or a stroke. That would explain why he didn't call me and why he's not answering the phone."

Phyllis didn't like to think about it, but she had to admit that Eve might be right about that. None of them were young anymore. The odds of one of them just keeling over dead one of these days were getting better all the time. And she didn't really know anything about Roy's medical condition, she reminded herself. He appeared to be healthy, but he could have high blood pressure or a weak heart or any number of things that wouldn't be apparent just looking at him.

She turned to Sam. "Do you think you could drive out to the motel and check on him? I hate to ask you, but . . ."

He was already smiling and nodding as her voice trailed off. "Sure, I don't mind."

"I'm coming with you," Eve declared. "Let me get my coat."

"I don't think that would be a good idea," Phyllis said.

Eve faced her. "Why not? Because Roy might be lying there dead on the floor of his room? Or because I'd see that he's gone and abandoned me?"

"Because you're upset, and when it turns out that everything is fine, you don't want Roy to know how worried you were."

"Won't he know that anyway, what with Sam going out there to check up on him?"

Sam said, "I won't tell him that's why I'm there. I'll come up with some other excuse for comin' to see him. I can say that I wanted to find out what we're doin' tomorrow afternoon while you ladies are havin' the shower. I was gonna suggest bowlin'."

"That's a good idea," Phyllis said.

"I have 'em every now and then."

Eve took a deep breath. "All right. Fine. Use that story. But as soon as you find out what's going on, you let me know, Sam Fletcher."

"Sure," Sam said as he nodded. "But I'll be discreet about it."

Phyllis followed him into the kitchen as he turned around to leave again. She put a hand on his arm and squeezed. "Thank you, Sam," she said quietly.

"You don't really think there's gonna be a problem, do you?" he asked, equally quietly.

"I hope not. Eve's so worked up about everything, I'm afraid if anything goes wrong she'll have a nervous breakdown."

"Can't have that. Keep your cell phone handy. I'll call you when I know anything."

Sam liked Eve; he really did. When he had first moved into the house, she had gone after him so blatantly that he sometimes wondered if the whole thing was an act. She had the whole predatory, man-hungry older-woman bit down so pat, he caught himself thinking that she was just playing a part, doing what was expected of her since she had been married several times before. He sometimes even toyed with the notion of responding to her not-so-subtle advances, just to see if she would turn tail and run.

He had decided that wouldn't be a good idea, because she might not. And he had realized right from the start that the only woman in the house who really interested him that way was Phyllis.

But Eve had turned into a good pal, and he didn't want to see her get hurt. If Roy had been leading her on for some reason . . . well, he was old-fashioned enough that he might have to do something about it, Sam thought.

Maybe it wouldn't come to that. He hoped not. And as he pulled into the motel parking lot, he spotted Roy's SUV, so at least Roy hadn't hightailed it out of town.

Sam parked the pickup and walked over to the room. Roy responded almost instantly to his knock, opening the door and smiling. "Hi, Sam," he said. "What are you doing here?"

As far as Sam could tell, Roy was fine, dressed in slacks and an open-throated shirt and looking as fit as a fiddle. He stepped back and motioned for Sam to come in. As Sam entered the room, he said, "I just dropped by to see if you knew what you wanted to do tomorrow afternoon while the shower's goin' on. I tried to call your cell phone but didn't get an answer."

"That's because the stupid battery in it has gone bad," Roy answered without hesitation. "I've been out looking for a replacement, but I haven't been able to find one for this particular model. If I order one online, do you think Phyllis would mind if I had it shipped to her house?"

"I can't think of any reason why she would," Sam replied honestly. He was relieved that he hadn't had to pump Roy for answers about what was going on. Roy had volunteered everything he needed to know, and the story was more than reasonable; it was completely plausible. The only thing that hadn't been explained in those few brief sentences was why he had failed to call Eve this morning like he had promised.

"Good," Roy said. "I'll have it shipped overnight, although it probably won't actually get here tomorrow. Not on Christmas Eve! But it ought to be here the day after Christmas, or maybe Monday at the latest."

"Sure," Sam said. "I guess you can live without a phone for that long."

Roy smiled again. "I suppose, although it's hard, once you get used to all these modern conveniences." He paused, then glanced at the bedside clock and said abruptly, "Oh, shoot! It's after twelve o'clock."

"Yeah," Sam said. "What about it?"

"I promised Eve I'd call her this morning." Roy banged the ball of his hand lightly against his forehead. "I thought about it earlier, but then that phone battery was bad, so I figured I'd run out and get one, but then I couldn't find the right one, and I forgot all about Eve!" He gave Sam a worried look. "She's mad at me, isn't she?"

"I don't really know," Sam said. That wasn't a complete falsehood. Eve had been mad, all right, but she had been worried, too, even a little scared that something had happened to her fiancé, and Sam wasn't sure which emotion was dominant.

"I'll call her in a minute and apologize," Roy said. "Now, what was it you wanted?"

"I just thought I'd ask you how you feel about bowlin'."

"I love it. You want to roll a few games tomorrow afternoon while the ladies are having their shower?"

Sam nodded. "Fine with me. I'll come by here and get you sometime between one thirty and two, all right?"

"That'll work." Roy clapped a hand on Sam's shoulder. "Thanks, Sam. It's been good having a friend here, as well as the lady I'm going to marry."

"You're sure welcome," Sam told him as he left the motel room. They exchanged waves, and Sam went back to his pickup.

He thumbed the speed dial for Phyllis's cell on his own phone as he pulled away. When she answered, he said, "There's nothing to worry about. Roy's fine, and he's not gonna leave Eve at the altar."

"I know," Phyllis said. "He just called. She's talking to him now."

Sam chuckled. "I'll bet she was pretty mad."

"The atmosphere sounded a little chilly at first, but I think it's warming up now."

"That's good to hear," Sam said. "I reckon everything's full speed ahead from here on out."

Chapter 27

Phyllis was standing at the living room window that evening, watching the traffic stream past the house, the cars full of onlookers taking in the sight of all those Christmas lights and decorations. She was a little surprised when one of the vehicles turned into the driveway instead of cruising on by.

But she recognized it in the glow from the lights as Mike's SUV. She smiled as she watched her son and daughter-in-law get out. Sarah opened the back door and unstrapped Bobby from his seat, then held his hand and led him up to the front porch. Mike was already there, about to ring the bell when Phyllis opened the door before he could push the button.

"Hi," he said with a smile as Phyllis opened the storm door to let them in. "It's like rush hour in Dallas out there."

"Yes, a lot of people want to look at the Christmas lights," Phyllis said.

"Bobby did, too," Sarah explained as she knelt to unbutton her son's coat. "We've been driving around town looking at them. Mike told him that you had the best lights, though, so we saved your place for last."

"Hi, Gran'mama," Bobby said as Phyllis picked him up and he wrapped his arms around her neck.

"Hi, yourself." She hugged him and looked over his shoulder at Mike and Sarah. "Is his ear infection still all cleared up?" she asked, referring to the ailment that had kept him from visiting his other grandparents in California a month earlier. The infection had persisted for longer than any of them had expected.

"He's fine," Mike said. "Good as new."

"I'm glad." Phyllis smiled at the little boy. "Are you coming over here for Christmas dinner?"

Bobby nodded emphatically, wearing a big grin of anticipation on his face.

"Where is everybody?" Mike asked.

"Eve's out with her fiancé, Roy. And Sam and Carolyn are both up in their rooms, I think."

From the stairs, Sam said, "No, I'm right here. Hello, Mike. Good to see you again."

Sam came down the stairs, shook hands with Mike, and hugged Sarah. He shook hands with Bobby, too, both of them looking solemn about it.

"You can stay and visit for a while, can't you?" Phyllis asked.

"Sure," Mike replied. "Anyway, I'm not sure I could get back out on the street right now, what with all that traffic."

"It's been like that every night."

"I guess even though the Jingle Bell Tour never got here, enough people read about the lights and decorations that they want to see for themselves."

"I suppose so," Phyllis said. "Would you like some hot cranberry apple cider?"

"Not the hard stuff, I hope," Mike said with a smile.

Phyllis sighed and shook her head, secretly pleased by the teasing.

Carolyn must have heard the voices, because she came downstairs, too, and helped Phyllis with warming up the cider left over from the Jingle Bell Tour night. Carolyn had poured it in an empty water jug and put it in the refrigerator.

Having the rest of her family here made a pleasant evening even nicer, and Phyllis was able to forget all about Georgia Hallerbee's murder for a while.

But when everyone had finished the cider, Mike helped her carry the empty cups back into the kitchen, and as Phyllis put them in the sink, he leaned a hip against the counter and asked, "Have you heard any more about the Hallerbee case?"

Phyllis hesitated. It was bad enough that her theory had fallen apart and Detective Latimer had all but made fun of her as a meddling old woman.

She knew Mike wouldn't do that, though, so she said, "I thought for a while that I was on to something, but as it turns out, I was wrong."

"Tell me about it," he suggested.

She did so. He listened intently, nodding every now and then. When she finished, he said, "Mom, that all makes perfect sense. It could have happened that way."

"But it didn't."

He shrugged. "Maybe not. It was good thinking, anyway."

"And I suppose I need to keep my brain active," she said with a trace of bitterness creeping into her voice. "Maybe it'll help keep the Alzheimer's at bay."

"You shouldn't feel like that. You couldn't know that this guy Henning had a real alibi. All you had to go by was what people told you. That's all any investigator has, when there's no physical evidence, or at least not any that pays off."

"I suppose so. They must not have been able to get any fingerprints off the remains of that ceramic gingerbread man, or else there would have been an arrest by now. I'm guessing that either the killer wore gloves, or else he used the Mrs. Claus costume to keep his prints off the ceramic surface."

"Yeah. I've been keeping my ear to the ground, but I haven't heard much. I think Latimer will keep pushing on that Cochran kid, but in the end, there may not be enough to charge him. Right now, the case against him is pretty circumstantial."

Phyllis nodded. "I wanted to believe he was guilty, but now I'm not so sure."

"Who's left? Everybody else is accounted for, right?"

"I think so," Phyllis said. Her brain ran through the list of everyone connected with the case and where they had been on the night of the Jingle Bell Tour. Something bothered her, a familiar feeling of unease, but she couldn't isolate it. She tried to grasp it as she rinsed out the cups and put them in the dishwasher, but again the missing piece slipped away from her.

It wasn't the only piece that was missing, she thought. She still didn't have enough to put the picture together and make sense of it.

And she wasn't going to find it tonight, so she might as well relax and enjoy the rest of the evening with her family, she told herself. With everyone's busy schedules these days, people didn't get together like they once did. They wound up seeing a lot more of the people they worked with than they did their own families. They had to grab moments whenever they could.

With that in mind, she took Mike's arm and led him back toward the living room. "Do you think everybody would think I was terribly old-fashioned if I suggested we sing some Christmas carols?"

The smile that spread across his face warmed her heart. "I think it's exactly the sort of suggestion we all need right now."

The morning of Christmas Eve dawned cold, cloudy, and blustery. Phyllis worried that Eve would take the weather as some sort of omen. It wasn't supposed to rain or snow, though. It just wasn't as pleasant as it had been.

The night before, as they were all sitting around the living room singing Christmas carols—and none of that "Grandma Got Run Over by a Reindeer" nonsense; she had warned Sam before they even started—Phyllis had succeeded in forgetting completely about Georgia's murder for a while.

The memories had come flooding back, however, when she stepped out onto the front porch to wave good night to Mike, Sarah, and Bobby, and they still plagued her this morning as she fixed breakfast. She had prepared the dough for buttermilk refrigerated biscuits the night before. She took the dough out of the refrigerator, rolled it out, and cut them with a biscuit cutter, being careful to push down without twisting. Twisting would make the biscuits turn out tough.

While the biscuits were baking, Phyllis made some good old-fashioned sausage gravy to pour over them when they were done. She browned the sausage in an iron skillet, drained the grease, and stirred in a little olive oil and a little salt and pepper. Adding milk and flour thickened it into gravy. These were tasks she had performed hundreds of times before, and she thought they might distract her . . . but it didn't work. She knew she wouldn't be able to rest properly until Georgia's killer was caught. Someone had come onto Phyllis's porch . . . almost into her house . . . and committed unspeakable violence. Justice had to be done.

So she knew what she had to do. It was time to start over. She couldn't shake the feeling that somewhere along the way she had overlooked something vital, seen or heard something that would give her the answer even though she hadn't noticed it at the time.

Joe Henning was out as a suspect, at least for now. So were the other people whose homes had been part of the tour, except for a few. Those were the ones she would start with, Phyllis decided.

Of course, Eve wasn't going to be happy about this, she realized. Eve would feel like Phyllis was abandoning her on the day of the shower. But she would be back in plenty of time. She just wanted to pay a few quick calls during the morning. The shower wouldn't start until two o'clock . . .

"You're going to do what?" Eve reacted with predictable surprise and dismay when Phyllis said at the breakfast table that there were a few things she needed to check on that morning.

"I won't be gone long," Phyllis promised. "Most of the snacks are already prepared, and Carolyn can get the rest of the cookies in the oven and make the punch. Is that all right, Carolyn?"

"You mean while you go out and play detective?" Carolyn asked. "That's what you're going to do, isn't it?"

"I just need to talk to a couple of people. It won't take long."

Eve and Carolyn both turned to Sam. Eve said, "Sam, can't you talk some sense into her?"

Sam held up both hands, palms out. "My job's to keep Roy entertained this afternoon," he said. "Other than that, I'm stayin' out of it, ladies."

Carolyn said, "Actually, I don't mind doing the work. There's really not much left to do at all. But you shouldn't let these things consume you like this, Phyllis."

"It was on my front porch," Phyllis said. "Someone came across my yard, up my steps, and onto my front porch to kill one of my friends."

Eve said, "I'm sorry about that, but Georgia will be just as dead after Christmas. After New Year's and the wedding, for that matter. And maybe by then the police will have caught whoever killed her."

They wouldn't, Phyllis thought. She wasn't sure how she knew that, but she did. It was true that she didn't have all the information she needed to solve the case, but maybe the police didn't, either. She was haunted by the idea that maybe there was one fact out there, just one, that would make everything else fall into place.

"I'm sorry, Eve," she said. "I'll be back before lunch, and everything will be fine."

Eve looked like she wanted to frame some angry retort, but with a visible effort she controlled her temper. She looked at Sam again and said, "Will you at least go with her, so we can be sure that nothing happens to her?"

"Now, that I can do," he replied with a smile and a nod.

Phyllis hadn't asked him to come along, but she would be glad for his company. They worked well together.

When she was dressed after breakfast, Phyllis avoided the

living room, where Eve and Carolyn were talking about the shower, and went to the kitchen to wait for Sam. He came in a few moments later wearing jeans and a denim jacket.

"We're takin' my pickup again?" he asked.

"If that's all right."

"Sure," he said. As they went out through the garage, he continued, "It doesn't feel much like Christmas Eve, does it?"

"That's because we've had this hanging over our heads the whole time," Phyllis said. "Last night was the first time since the night of the tour that I really felt like I had the Christmas spirit . . . and even then, it didn't last."

"Where are we goin'?" Sam asked as they got into the pickup.

"The Bachmann house. I want to talk to Holly Bachmann again, if she's home. Who in the world has a tooth-whitening emergency?"

A dubious frown appeared on Sam's face as he pointed the pickup toward the street where the Bachmanns lived, only a few blocks away. "I'm pretty sure Detective Latimer said he talked to the lady's dentist. She was where she said she was."

Phyllis sighed. "I know. I'm grasping at straws, aren't I?" Suddenly she felt ridiculous. She was neglecting her friends and her other responsibilities in order to chase after some elusive hunch. Was it just vanity? Was she starting to believe the things people said about her, to the extent that her pride was wounded because she hadn't been able to solve this murder? Surely she wasn't that shallow . . . as shallow as a woman who would have to go and get her teeth whitened on the night when a whole tour full of people were coming to her home.

"Turn around, Sam," she said with a sigh. "This is crazy. Let's just go home and let the police do their job."

Sam looked over at her and frowned again. "That doesn't sound like you, Phyllis."

"Maybe not. But maybe I don't like what I'm becoming."

"You're still who you always were," Sam said, his voice firm with conviction. "I don't know what else is eatin' you all of a sudden, but you haven't done anything wrong." He brought the pickup to a halt at the curb. "Anyway, we're here."

It was true. They were parked in front of the Bachmann house. On this gloomy morning, the multitude of decorations didn't look nearly as festive and cheerful as they had the last time Phyllis and Sam had been here.

"We might as well go talk to the lady, since we're here," Sam went on.

"You're right," Phyllis said. "But this is the end of it. I have more important things to do."

"We'll see."

The man Phyllis had seen with Holly Bachmann at Georgia's funeral answered the door. He smiled at Phyllis and Sam but obviously didn't have any idea who they were. "Can I help you?" he asked.

"Mr. Bachmann?" Phyllis asked.

"That's right. I'm Dan Bachmann."

"My name is Phyllis Newsom, and this is Sam Fletcher. We were here and spoke with your wife a few days ago—"

"Holly's not here," Bachmann interrupted. "What's this about?"

"We collected some money for a flower arrangement for Georgia Hallerbee's funeral," Phyllis explained.

Bachmann's slightly suspicious expression cleared. "Oh, sure," he said. "I thought you looked a little familiar. You were at the funeral, weren't you?"

"That's right."

"Well, come on in, out of the wind," Bachmann said as he stepped back and held the door open. "Holly's gone to get her hair done. She paid you our part on the flowers, right? It wasn't like a pledge or anything like that?"

Phyllis smiled as she and Sam went into the house and Dan Bachmann closed the door. "No, we're not here to collect any more money," she said. "But we were thinking about putting together some sort of memorial for Georgia, something that would tie in with next year's Jingle Bell Tour."

She had come up with that off the top of her head, but Bachmann nodded eagerly and said, "I think that's a great idea. Georgia worked on putting those tours together for a long time. There must be something we can do that would honor her. Come on in and sit down. Would you like some coffee or something else to drink?"

"No, that's fine, thank you, and we really can't stay," Phyllis said. "We'll start putting together the details later. Right now we're just checking with everyone to find out who wants to be involved when the time comes."

"Well, count us in, for sure. We thought the world of Georgia."

"Is that so?"

Bachmann nodded. "Yeah. That's why Holly wanted to look her best on the night of the tour." He smiled. "Although, let's face it, you've met her, so you know that Holly's the sort of woman who always wants to look her best. I don't know how I got so lucky as to land somebody like her."

Something nibbled at the edges of Phyllis's brain, some instinct that told her not to leave just yet. Instead she said, "She was at the dentist on the night of the tour, wasn't she?"

"Yeah." Bachmann shook his head ruefully. "Boy, nothing worked out right that night, did it? All Holly could think about was looking good for the people who showed up on the tour, and then she wasn't even here for it because Georgia never got a chance to rearrange the order of the stops."

"What's that?" Phyllis asked. "Georgia was going to rearrange the tour?"

Bachmann nodded. "Yeah. Our house was before yours, and she was going to ask you if she could switch them around since we live so close together. That would have given Holly time to get back from the dentist's office. But then . . . well, you know what happened to Georgia. She didn't get a chance to even speak to you about it, did she?"

"No," Phyllis said. "She didn't. That's why she was coming to my house before the tour?"

"That's right. I heard Holly talking to her on the phone. Georgia said she would stop by your place to see if you were ready and wouldn't mind swapping places with us. But as it turned out, the tour never even got to your house, did it?"

Phyllis's pulse thundered in her head as the implications of what Dan Bachmann had just told her soaked in. "No," she managed to say. "The tour never got to my house."

And with that, she knew what she had overlooked before. The missing piece slipped into place.

Sam looked at her intently as he put a hand on her arm. "I think we'd better be goin' now," he said to Bachmann. He held out his other hand and shook with the man. "We'll be back around to talk to you later on."

"Don't forget, we want to be part of whatever you do to honor Georgia," Bachmann said.

"We won't forget," Sam promised.

Phyllis was grateful for his strong hand on her arm as they left the house. By the time they got back in the pickup, she was breathing a little harder than usual as her thoughts raced.

"I've seen that look before," Sam said as he reached for the key. "You're gonna honor Georgia Hallerbee by catchin' the lowlife who killed her, aren't you?"

"Yes," Phyllis said, "I am."

And this time she knew it was the truth.

Chapter 28

"*D*rive to Georgia's office," Phyllis told Sam as she took her cell phone out of her purse. She didn't dial 911 but punched in the regular police number instead. That wasn't a number that most people had memorized, but she had called it enough over the past few years that it was stuck in her head.

"You think Laura Kearns will be there?" Sam asked. "It's Christmas Eve, after all. Place could be closed."

"We'll find out." The operator at the police station answered, and Phyllis asked to be connected to Detective Warren Latimer. When she was told he wasn't there, she said, "Can you give him a message? This is Phyllis Newsom. I need for him to meet me at Georgia Hallerbee's office. It's very important . . . Thank you."

As she hung up, Sam asked, "You think Latimer will really show up?"

"I hope so. If nothing else he'll want to yell at me for getting mixed up in the case again and tell me to butt out."

Sam grinned. "He's about to learn better, isn't he?"

"We'll see," Phyllis said. Even though she was confident in this new theory, more so than she had been in either of the others, a small, nagging doubt remained.

Some of that doubt vanished when they pulled into the shopping center parking lot and she recognized two of the cars parked in front of Georgia's office, even though the CLOSED sign was up on the door. One of the vehicles belonged to Laura Kearns. The other was the car Carl Winthrop had gotten into at the cemetery, after Georgia's graveside service.

"He's here," Phyllis said.

"Who?"

"Carl Winthrop. He killed Georgia."

Sam frowned as he guided the pickup into a parking space in the lot's back row. "How could he? He was with the tour that night."

"Who told us Winthrop was there the whole time?" Phyllis asked. She provided her own answer. "Laura Kearns."

"But if she lied—"

"Then she was part of it, just like I thought before."

"But her husband didn't go out on that AAA call . . . Wait a minute. This doesn't have anything to do with that, does it?"

Phyllis shook her head. "Joe Henning's connection to the case, the fact that he had a flat tire, the fact that the garage Rusty Kearns works for handles emergency calls for AAA, Margaret's generosity in giving Laura that business loan . . . All of those things were coincidences that just muddled things. The key—one of the keys—to the case is that Carl Winthrop told me Georgia was upset and wanted to see me about some sort of crime, because of my reputation for solving them."

"While Dan Bachmann said she just wanted to switch around the order of the tour."

Phyllis nodded. "So if Bachmann is telling the truth, and as far as I can see he wouldn't have any reason to lie about that, then Winthrop had to be lying to me about why Georgia was coming to the house."

"What about the Cochran kid?" Sam wanted to know. "I thought we figured that was why Miz Hallerbee wanted to talk to you."

"They led us into thinking that," Phyllis said with a note of grim anger in her voice. "They manipulated me into believing that's what the case was all about, and look what happened. Chris Cochran is really the only suspect the police have right now. They're not even considering Winthrop and Laura. They *used* me to make the police believe that Chris is guilty."

Sam frowned in thought. "You mean the reason the kid claims he never attacked Laura is because it never happened?"

Phyllis nodded. "That's right. Again, we had only Laura's word for it. Georgia couldn't confirm or deny any of it because she's dead."

"But if you're right and Winthrop and the Kearns woman are in it together," Sam said, "they were trying to frame Chris for the murder, or at least throw enough suspicion on him that the cops wouldn't go after anybody else. How did they know he wouldn't have an ironclad alibi for that night?"

"I don't know yet," Phyllis admitted.

"I'm not tryin' to throw cold water on your idea," Sam said. "Not after what happened before. But why would they want to kill Miz Hallerbee in the first place?"

Phyllis shook her head. "I don't know that, either. But here's the thing that's been bothering me for several days now, the thing I knew was wrong but could never quite figure out. It all comes back to the gingerbread man."

Sam stared at her.

"I know, that makes it sound like I'm crazy," Phyllis said. "But when we were at the cemetery, Carl Winthrop mentioned the killer using the gingerbread man as a weapon. *That wasn't in the newspaper stories.* The police held back that detail."

"And the cops closed off the whole block and didn't let anybody near the house until after everything was cleaned up," Sam mused. "Nobody knew about the gingerbread man except the folks in the house, the cops, and . . ."

"And the killer," Phyllis finished for him. "When Dan Bachmann told us the real reason Georgia showed up at the house before the tour started, and I asked myself whether it was him or Winthrop who lied—because one of them had to be lying—I remembered what Winthrop said at the cemetery. I didn't put it together then, but now it seems clear."

Sam shook his head. "What if other people with the tour saw Winthrop at the same time Miz Hallerbee was bein' attacked?"

Phyllis thought back to everything she had heard and read about the Jingle Bell Tour. She called up an image of the list Laura Kearns had given her. That list had been arranged in the running order of the tour stops.

"The tour began fairly close to our house," she said. "And remember, Georgia was attacked *before* the tour started. People would have just been showing up and getting ready then. Laura was probably the only one who said that Winthrop was there the whole time. Nobody else would have noticed whether or not he was gone for ten minutes or so . . . but that would have been long enough for him to intercept Georgia and smash that gingerbread man over her head."

Sam nodded slowly. "Maybe. It sounds like it could be true."

"But so did the case against Joe Henning and the Kearnses, I know," Phyllis said. "But this theory has Winthrop's slipup at the cemetery on its side."

"Yeah, I heard him say that, too," Sam mused. "And you're right, there was nothing in the paper about the killer usin' the gingerbread man to kill Miz Hallerbee. That ought to be enough to convict him right there."

"I was hoping Detective Latimer would be here by now so we could tell him about it. Winthrop and Laura are both here. He could confront them about it, maybe break down Winthrop's alibi."

"What about Laura's alibi?"

Phyllis shook her head. "She couldn't have picked up that gingerbread man like that. Winthrop is big enough and strong enough that he could."

"Yeah, you're right about that."

"She's part of it, though. There's no doubt about that." Phyllis leaned forward in the seat. "Wait a minute. I see somebody moving around in there."

Two figures came up to the door, inside the office. Laura Kearns was first. She twisted the lock and pushed the door open. Carl Winthrop came up behind her and stepped past her to leave. He paused, though, and leaned back into the office to give Laura a kiss. One of her arms went around the back of his neck and held him there for a moment.

"Well, I reckon maybe we're lookin' at a motive," Sam said.

"I think so, too. Winthrop and Laura are having an affair. Georgia found out about it and threatened to tell Rusty Kearns or Winthrop's wife or maybe both of them."

"You think somebody would commit murder over something like that, this day and age?"

"People have before . . . Oh, no."

Winthrop had broken the kiss and turned around, and his gaze went across the parking lot and focused like a laser on the pickup as he looked through the windshield at Phyllis and Sam.

"He saw us," Sam said.

"Yes. But what's he going to do about it?"

Winthrop said something to Laura, then started across the parking lot toward the pickup.

Sam reached for his door handle. "Stay in here. Lock the doors. Call the cops again."

"I'll do no such thing," Phyllis said. She had her door open and was stepping out of the car before Sam could stop her. As she stepped out of the pickup, she reached down into her open purse and thumbed 911 on her phone. She left the door open a few inches and rested one hand on it.

"Hello, Carl," she said with a smile.

"Mrs. Newsom," he greeted her. A suspicious frown creased his forehead. "What are you doing here?"

"I just came by to wish Laura a Merry Christmas," Phyllis said. Laura had followed Winthrop and came up alongside him now. Phyllis smiled at her and went on, "Hello, dear."

"I don't know what you think you just saw," Laura said, "but it wasn't what it looked like, I swear."

Phyllis tried to put a puzzled look on her face. "I don't know what you're talking about, Laura."

"Carl just gave me a hug to comfort me because of all I've been through, and to congratulate me on taking over the business. That's all it was, I—"

"Stop it," Carl said, his voice hardening. "She knows. We knew she'd try to figure it out. Hell, we counted on it. She finally realized what I said wrong at the cemetery. I didn't catch myself quick enough when I slipped up." He angled his head toward the office. "Tell your friend Sam to get out of the truck. We're going back inside."

"Carl," Laura began, "we can't—"

Winthrop was still smiling, but his eyes were cold and dead. "Come on, Mrs. Newsom," he said as he came a step closer to Phyllis.

"You can't kill us," Phyllis warned him. "You'd never get away with it."

"I never said anything about killing anybody. We'll work this out—"

Phyllis knew better, though. She had seen what happened when rage boiled up in Carl Winthrop. She had seen the bloody evidence of it on her own front porch. If he got her and Sam inside the office, where no one could see, then anything was liable to happen.

"No," she said. "We won't work anything out."

And with that she shoved the pickup door at Winthrop, smashing it into him as hard as she could.

The impact drove Winthrop back a couple of steps. His face contorted with fury as he caught himself. By that time, Sam was out of the pickup and moving fast, circling the front of the vehicle to get between Winthrop and Phyllis. Winthrop swung a punch that Sam ducked. Sam grabbed him, struggling to pin Winthrop's arms to his sides. Winthrop was younger, heavier, and stronger, though, and shrugged out of Sam's grip.

With a screech of tires, an unmarked police car with lights flashing roared into the parking lot and skidded to a stop. Warren Latimer was out of the car almost before it stopped moving. He tackled Winthrop from behind, driving him to the pavement. Winthrop yelled in surprise and pain as he landed face-first. That stunned him long enough for Latimer to yank his arms behind him and secure them with a plastic restraint around his wrists. Then Latimer pinned Winthrop to the ground with a knee in the small of his back and looked up at Phyllis.

"You see what happens when you keep sticking your nose into things?" he demanded.

"I'll tell you what happens," Sam said. He pointed at Winthrop, who had stopped struggling. "You catch a killer—that's what."

Chapter 29

Chief Ralph Whitmire sat in on the interview at the police station as Latimer took Phyllis and Sam through everything that had happened. Phyllis could tell that the chief wasn't happy, but he didn't say anything and let Latimer ask the questions. Phyllis explained how she had figured out that Carl Winthrop had killed Georgia. When she had finished explaining her reasoning, she said, "I don't know exactly why they decided that Georgia had to die, but I'm sure it had something to do with the fact that they've been having an affair. I don't know how they came up with the idea of framing Chris Cochran for the murder, either."

"You let us worry about that—," Latimer began, but Chief Whitmire spoke up, interrupting him.

"Laura Kearns has given us a full statement, Mrs. Newsom. She was pretty quick to turn on Winthrop and try to save herself. The affair was part of it. Ms. Hallerbee was going to tell Rusty Kearns about it, along with Winthrop's wife. It had more to do with the fact that Winthrop had been stealing from some of his money-management clients, though, and Ms. Hallerbee discovered that as well. She threatened to ruin Winthrop all the way around."

Phyllis shook her head. "That sounds almost . . . vindictive."

"Oh, it was, I suppose," Whitmire said with a nod. "Georgia Hallerbee was mad to start with because Winthrop dropped *her* and took up with Laura Kearns instead."

Phyllis's eyes widened. "You mean Georgia and Winthrop . . . ?"

"Yeah. That's what Laura Kearns said, anyway. Sorry if you would have rather not known that."

Phyllis shook her head. She had said all along that the murder had been a crime of passion, and in a way she'd been right. The feelings left over between ex-lovers had contributed to it. And at one point she had speculated that there might be more than friendship between Georgia and Winthrop, she reminded herself.

"How about the Cochran kid?" Sam asked. He sat with his right ankle cocked on his left knee. "How did they know he wouldn't be at his folks' house on the night of the Jingle Bell Tour?"

"According to Laura, they decided a couple of days earlier to get rid of Ms. Hallerbee. Winthrop was at the hospital, talking to Dr. Charles Cochran. Winthrop handled some of his money, too. Chris Cochran happened to be there, and Winthrop overheard him talking on his cell phone to that friend of his, Nelson Blake. They were making plans to hit that strip club in Fort Worth on the night of the tour. Chris thought it was funny because he knew his parents wanted him to be home that night. Winthrop realized then that Chris wouldn't have an alibi, and he came up with the idea of killing Georgia that night and setting things up so it looked like Chris would have a motive. Laura took some papers out to the Cochran ranch and dropped them off, but nothing else happened. Laura concocted the story about Chris trying to rape her."

"By waiting, they were taking a chance that Georgia wouldn't go ahead and reveal the affair and Winthrop's embezzling," Phyllis said.

Whitmire shook his head. "No, Georgia had told them that she wouldn't say anything until after the tour was over. She wanted Winthrop to break it off with Laura and come back to her. She thought the embezzlement business was the lever she needed to make it happen." The chief paused. "It was a gamble, and it got her killed instead."

Latimer didn't look happy. "No offense, Chief," he said, "but all this is going to come out at the trials. I'm not sure it's a good idea to be telling these civilians all about it."

"If these civilians hadn't pushed Winthrop into panicking, and if Mrs. Newsom hadn't put that 911 call through so we could hear what was going on, Winthrop and Kearns would have lawyered up and we probably wouldn't have been able to shake their stories enough to convict them. Now we've got a pretty good shot at it, thanks to Mrs. Newsom and Mr. Fletcher, and I'm confident we can trust them not to compromise our case." Whitmire gave Phyllis a hard stare. "But really, this needs to stop. One of these days, your luck's going to run out, and I don't want that to happen. Neither does anybody else who knows you."

"I called Detective Latimer before we went to Georgia's office," Phyllis pointed out. "I wouldn't have confronted Winthrop if he hadn't spotted us. Even then, I tried to make him think I didn't suspect him so we could get away from there."

"Well, the best way to protect yourself from murderers is to stop trying to catch them. Consider that a friendly warning."

Judging by the glare Latimer was giving them, he was warning her, too, Phyllis thought . . . but it wasn't as friendly as the one Chief Whitmire had just issued.

"Do you need us for anything else?" she asked.

Whitmire glanced at Latimer, who shook his head and said, "We'll get your statements typed up and you can come by and sign them later." He sighed. "Just don't get into any more trouble between now and then, okay?"

"I'm going to a bridal shower," Phyllis said. "How could I possibly get into any trouble there?"

Recipes

German Chocolate Cookies

Topping
1 cup white sugar
1 cup evaporated milk
½ cup butter
3 egg yolks, beaten
1 teaspoon vanilla extract
1½ cups flaked coconut
1½ cups chopped pecans
3 squares German sweet chocolate bar, grated

Cookie
1 (18.25-ounce) package German chocolate cake mix
¼ cup all-purpose flour
⅓ cup butter, melted

Instructions

For the topping, in a heavy 2-quart saucepan, combine the sugar, milk, butter, and egg yolks. Blend well. Cook over medium heat for 10 to 13 minutes or until thickened and bubbly, stirring frequently. Stir in the vanilla, coconut, and pecans. Remove from the heat, and cool to room temperature. Reserve 1 cup of the topping mixture.

Preheat the oven to 350°F. Grease cookie sheets or mini muffin pans.

Stir the grated German chocolate into the reseved topping, and set aside.

For the cookies, in a large bowl, combine the cake mix, flour, melted butter, and remaining topping mixture. Stir by hand until thoroughly moistened. Shape the dough into 1-inch balls. Place the balls 2 inches apart on an ungreased cookie sheet or place them in mini muffin pans. Using your thumb, make an indention in the center of each ball. Fill each indention with ½ teaspoon of the reserved topping.

Bake for 12 to 14 minutes. Allow the cookies to cool on the baking sheet or in the mini muffin pan for 5 minutes before removing to a wire rack to cool completely.

Makes about 50 cookies

Dark Delicious Chocolate Cashew Cookies

½ cup butter, at room temperature
½ cup cashew butter
½ cup granulated sugar
1 egg
1 teaspoon vanilla extract
1½ cups all-purpose flour
1 cup salted cashews, chopped into large pieces
1 cup (6 ounces) semisweet chocolate morsels
1 teaspoon vegetable shortening

Instructions

Preheat the oven to 350°F.

In a large bowl, beat the butter and cashew butter until creamy. Add the sugar gradually, beating well. Beat in the egg and vanilla. Add the flour and mix by hand until well blended.

Drop the dough by tablespoonfuls about 2 inches apart on an ungreased cookie sheet. I prefer to use parchment paper on the pans. Flatten each ball of dough lightly with fingers or the bottom of a floured glass. Press chopped nuts generously onto the tops of the cookies.

Bake for 14 to 16 minutes or until cookies are lightly browned.

Let cool about 1 minute, and then remove from the cookie sheet to a cooling rack. Let cool completely.

If you used parchment paper, you can now use it to hold the cookies as you top them with chocolate. Wax paper works great for this, too.

Place the chocolate morsels and vegetable shortening in the top half of a double boiler. Over simmering water, melt the chocolate and vegetable shortening. Stir gently until combined. Spoon the chocolate over the cookies. Let set.

Makes about 2 dozen cookies

Gingerbread Boys

Cookie

1 (3.5-ounce) package cook-and-serve butterscotch pudding mix

½ cup butter

½ cup packed brown sugar

1 egg

1 cup all-purpose flour

½ cup oat flour°

½ teaspoon baking soda

1 teaspoon ground ginger

1½ teaspoons ground cinnamon

Vanilla Icing

2 cups powdered sugar

1½ tablespoons softened butter

½ teaspoon vanilla extract

¼ teaspoon salt

3 to 4 tablespoons milk

Instructions

For the cookies, in a medium bowl, cream together the dry butterscotch pudding mix, butter, and brown sugar until smooth. Stir in the egg. In a separate bowl, combine the all-purpose flour, oat flour, baking soda, ginger, and cinnamon; stir into the pudding mixture. Cover, and chill dough until firm, about 1 hour.

°Oat flour can be made by processing or blending oats until they become the texture of flour. To make ½ cup of oat flour, put a mounded

½ cup of oats in a blender or food processor and blend until the oats look like flour.

Preheat the oven to 350°F. Grease baking sheets. On a floured board, roll the dough out to about ⅛-inch thickness, and cut into man shapes using a cookie cutter. Place cookies 2 inches apart on the prepared baking sheets.

Bake for 10 to 12 minutes or until cookies are golden at the edges. Cool on wire racks.

For the icing, in a medium bowl, cream together the powdered sugar, butter, vanilla, salt, and milk. Stir until smooth and well blended. Adjust for spreading or piping consistency by adding more milk or powdered sugar. If you don't have pastry bag, use a heavy-duty, quart-sized, resealable bag. Fill the bag half-full with icing and push the mixture toward one corner. Fold the other corner over and remove the excess air. Twist the bag right above the top of the icing to seal it in so it can't work its way out of the bag. Snip off a tiny bit from the corner. You're now ready to pipe your icing.

I call these cookies Gingerbread Boys because they're mild gingerbread cookies that kids like.

Makes 2½ dozen cookies

Cream Cheese Frosting

1 (8-ounce) package cream cheese, softened
1 tablespoon softened butter
2 cups confectioners' sugar
½ teaspoon vanilla extract

Instructions

Beat the cream cheese and butter with an electric mixer in a bowl until smooth. Add the confectioners' sugar and the vanilla extract. Beat until no lumps remain. Spread the frosting on the cooled cookies, and allow to dry completely before storing. You can also frost one cookie and top it with another to make a sandwich.

Chocolate Mint Coffee Spoons

1 cup (6 ounces) mint chocolate chips
24 sturdy plastic spoons
2 or 3 crushed candy canes

Instructions

Cover cookie sheets with waxed paper or parchment paper.

Melt the mint chocolate chips in the microwave or a double boiler. If using the microwave, place the chocolate chips in a heatproof cup. A small, deep cup gives the best results. Microwave the mint chocolate chips at 50 percent power for 1 minute. Remove and stir; then continue microwaving at 50 percent power, stirring every 30 seconds, until the chocolate is melted and smooth. Do *not* overheat the chocolate.

Dip a spoon far enough into the chocolate to coat the bowl of the spoon. Remove excess chocolate by tapping the tip of the spoon gently against the side of the cup. If the chocolate thickens, return it to the microwave for 30 seconds at 50 percent power, and stir gently.

Place the dipped spoon on a waxed-paper-covered cooking sheet, and sprinkle with crushed candy canes. Repeat with the remaining spoons.

Cool thoroughly before wrapping individually with plastic wrap. Add a festive ribbon to keep the wrap on.

Winter Cranberry Cider

1 (12-ounce) can frozen cranberry juice
1 (6-ounce) can frozen lemonade
1 (12-ounce) can apple juice concentrate
9 cups water
5 (3-inch) sticks cinnamon
6 whole cloves
1 teaspoon ground nutmeg
½ cup sugar
2 lemons, thinly sliced

Instructions

Thaw the undiluted juices. Combine the juices with the water, cinnamon, cloves, nutmeg, and sugar in a large pot and bring to a boil. Cover the pot and reduce heat. Simmer 15 minutes. Serve warm with thin slices of lemon.

Makes 20 to 24 servings

Grilled Cheese and Pear Sandwiches

8 slices white bread
3 tablespoons butter
2 cups grated Gouda cheese°
2 pears, thinly sliced

Instructions

Preheat skillet over medium heat. Lightly butter one side of a slice of bread. Place bread butter side down in the skillet and spread with ⅛ cup grated cheese. Add a layer of sliced pears on top of the cheese, then another ⅛ cup grated cheese. Butter a second slice of bread on one side and place it butter side up on top of the sandwich. Grill until lightly browned. Carefully flip the sandwich over, and continue grilling until the cheese is melted. Repeat with the remaining 6 slices of bread, butter, grated cheese, and pears.

°You can also use thinly sliced cheese. Place 1 slice on the bread, followed by the pears, and then a second slice, followed by the second slice of bread.

Makes 4 sandwiches

Refrigerator Buttermilk Biscuits

4 cups all-purpose flour
1 teaspoon salt
2 tablespoons baking powder
2 tablespoons white sugar
⅓ cup butter or margarine
⅓ cup shortening
2 cups buttermilk

Instructions

In a large bowl sift together the flour, salt, baking powder, and sugar. Cut in the butter and shortening until the mixture has a fine crumb texture. Add the buttermilk and stir with a fork. Stop stirring when the mixture forms a soft dough.

Turn the dough out onto a floured surface. Form a ball and knead it about 25 times. The dough should be smooth and elastic. Wrap the dough tightly in plastic wrap and refrigerate overnight, or for at least 8 hours.

Preheat the oven to 425°F.

Working on a floured surface, roll or pat the dough out to 1-inch thickness. Cut with a 2-inch biscuit cutter, or the floured rim of a glass. Always press straight down and up with the cutter. Twisting will keep the biscuits from rising nicely. Gather up the pieces left and make a ball; roll the ball out and repeat the cutting process. Don't work the dough too much at this point. Place the cut biscuits about 1 inch apart on an ungreased baking sheet (light-colored pans work best), and allow to rest for 10 minutes.

Bake until lightly brown, 12 to 15 minutes. Serve warm.

Makes 12 biscuits

Old-Fashioned Sausage Gravy

1 pound ground sausage
¼ cup water
¼ cup extra-virgin olive oil
¼ cup all-purpose flour
2 cups milk
Salt and black pepper

Instructions

Crumble and brown the sausage in a large skillet over medium heat until completely cooked. Add the water and stir. Drain the sausage grease and water, leaving the meat in the skillet. Add the olive oil, and heat until sizzling. Stir in the flour until dissolved. Cook the sausage, oil, and flour mixture for at least 1 minute. Gradually stir in the milk. Cook the gravy until thick and bubbly. Season with salt and pepper to taste. Serve hot over biscuits.

You can skip adding the water and olive oil and leave in the sausage grease if you want, but I prefer the healthier olive oil.

Makes 4 servings

Slow-Bake Gingerbread Ornaments

16 ounces applesauce
1 cup cinnamon
2 tablespoons allspice

Instructions

Preheat the oven to 150°F.

Combine the applesauce, cinnamon, and allspice, mixing well. Roll the dough out on waxed paper. Cut out ornaments with appropriately shaped cookie cutters. Poke a hole in the top of each ornament using a straw, knife, chopstick, pencil, or similar object.

Bake for 90 minutes. Turn the ornaments over. Bake for an additional 90 minutes. Allow the ornaments to cool and continue drying for 1 to 3 hours after baking.

Since these are ornaments, not cookies, you can use glue to decorate them with Red Hots, buttons, sequins, yarn, ribbon, beads, or pretty much anything.

Makes 12 to 15 great-smelling ornaments

Author's Note

While the Christmas Jingle Bell Tour of Homes is a product of my imagination, there is an actual Christmas light tour in Weatherford, Texas. Sponsored by the Parker County Heritage Society, the Annual Candlelight Tour of Homes has showcased turn-of-the-century homes and the Chandor Gardens. All of the participants graciously open their beautiful homes and gardens with holiday decorations and give the historic background of each site.

Photo by James Reasoner

Livia J. Washburn has been a professional writer for more than twenty years. She received the Private Eye Writers of America Award and the American Mystery Award for her first mystery, *Wild Night*, written under the name L. J. Washburn, and was nominated for a Spur Award by the Western Writers of America for a novel written with her husband, James Reasoner. She lives with her husband in a small Texas town, where she is constantly experimenting with new recipes. Her two grown daughters are both teachers in her hometown, and she is very proud of them. Visit her Web site at www.liviajwashburn.com.